GADARENE

A NOVEL

MICHELE FRIEDMAN

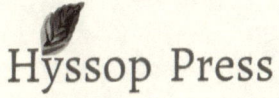

Hyssop Press

For Daniel and Llewyn

For while we have our eyes on the future, history has its eyes on us.

—AMANDA GORMAN, *The Hill We Climb*

NOW

Amelia roamed, indiscernible except for the white spots on her fawn skin shawl. Her hair, a tangled strawberry mess, framed her face. Her legs, bare in the springtime cold, moved easily through the overgrown trail. They were skeletal, her knees knobby freckled things.

But if she moved quietly, I was quieter. If she felt me, she didn't acknowledge my shadow, trailing behind her as she foraged. With a small spade, she dug for the carrot-like root of Queen Ann's lace and snipped unfurled fiddleheads. Her wicker basket slowly filled.

Within the old-growth forest in which we walked, she appeared sprite-like, unreal in her ethereal beauty. A crown of flowers and brambles adorned her head, which I had watched her weave, dexterous fingers bending the flora to her will. I imagined delicate, trembling wings folded beneath her sweater. If only I had a camera, the photos would prove what Elsie Wright could not.

She consulted with a frayed book, sometimes reading and rereading before she decided on which plants to gather. It was nestled in her waistband when it wasn't held between dirt-covered hands. The book, Henderson's Field Guide to Wild Plants, was idolized and its interpreter, a high priestess.

Amelia's sanity had clung to that book through the dark days of winter when the snow piled heavy on the roof of our shack. The margins were heavily marked with notations and incoherent scribbles. Amelia was certain it would keep us from starvation and botulism, a death that lurked in dented cans. I promised her I'd fill a whole bookcase dedicated to the delicate art of feeding oneself.

The fall we first arrived in these mountains had taught us nothing, and winter had yielded only death. The rough shacks we constructed allowed the freezing wind to whistle through cracks, finding cradles and the sick. We burned the dead, not being able to dig through the frost before they started to stink. Others disappeared in the night; their bones discovered days later, picked apart and scattered by coyotes.

When the ground thawed, we abandoned our pitiful refugee camp to flee deeper into the mountains to start again. Turning our heads upwards, we climbed to where the snow had not yet melted beneath the pines.

We planted our first seedlings, twisted clumsy snares, and heaved logs into the trees for deadfalls. The daffodils and tulips unfurled their elegant petals, and we worked beneath the warming sun, our backs becoming strong.

It was wrong, I knew, to watch Amelia so. Her feet began catching on roots and rocks, dragged down with the intuitive enmity of my presence. I wanted the anonymity of the forest to swallow me, to fade away. But I couldn't. It felt like I was being drawn behind her as if by a trolling line.

I had intended to set traps today, unused snare wire still clutched stupidly in my hand. Following the crisscrossing tracks of a loping rabbit that morning, I came across a wild green glade set close to the edge of a ridge. The land beyond stretched on and on, with towns that had once bustled, now quiet. The encroaching forest was waging a slow, deliberate battle against modernity to reclaim what had been stolen long ago.

But instead of rabbits, I found Amelia. Engrossed in Henderson's, she was flipping through its worn and weather-stained pages. It was rather unlucky that she didn't notice me emerging from the brush. I could have feigned normalcy, focusing on the task at hand while only entertaining the thought of circling back for an unguarded glimpse. A thought, harmless unless acted upon.

You're becoming unhinged. A whispered phrase that kept repeating itself in my mind. A triggered alarm warning of madness as it spread. It started yesterday when I had left a small bouquet of clover on Amelia's pillow. She told me to stop, please. My face burning, I mumbled sorry, picking up the flowers and shredding them before her. She watched this act, arms crossed, refusing to feel anything.

A light mist had been falling all day, drops of water pitter-pattering from the canopy high above to run in rivulets down the mountain. My shoes grew increasingly muddy as I left tell-tale footprints on the trail. I felt like a leech, a soul-sucker, peering from the cover of darkness.

Straightening suddenly from where she knelt in the dirt, Amelia looked around, eyes roving for the niggling threat. I drew behind a great beech tree, holding my breath, sure that she had caught me. Ants ran up and down its bark, as frantic as I felt.

She gathered the cuttings into her wicker basket and shouldered the air rifle from where it leaned against a tree. Its black metal was unnatural amongst the green of spring. With a last penetrating look, she left the clearing.

I followed.

She had become wily and vicious; made so by the Panic and the unendurable winter we had just experienced. Amelia reminded me of a fox, a sleek, sly creature. And if she was a fox, I was a bat hoping for the day I'd fly too close and she'd pull my wings off, ever so slowly. How I would love her full attention in that moment, how I loved her.

The day grew darker, the rain beginning to fall heavier from dense gray clouds. Finally, with her basket nearly overflowing, she packed away her trowel. Standing, she brushed aside fly-away strands of hair and started off in the direction of home. It was then that I felt free, the imaginary line that held me snapping with such force that I stumbled.

Spanning a heartbeat, Amelia fired the air rifle. The familiar sound of the safety clicking sent me sprawling for cover, landing in twisting mountain laurel. The bullet buried itself in the side of a pine I had been standing near a moment before with a sharp thud. My breaths came in shallow gasps, shame flushing my face.

The underbrush crackled as she stepped off the trail, coming close to where I hid, a coward I was. There was a pause, time that caught on the fabric of the world before she spooked, fleeing for home. I raised my head in time to watch her disappear down the trail, surefooted once again.

I waited, listening intently before standing, brushing bracken and the mountain laurel's sticky pink flowers from my clothes. When all was quiet, save for the warblers and robins, I ran. My feet pounded the packed earth of the trail and I threw my arms up to save my face from whip-like branches.

Creeping brambles snagged on my clothes, thorny fingers lacerating my skin. Tossing aside the snare wire, I nearly flew, body singing on adrenaline.

Choosing lesser-traveled paths, I hoped to avoid Amelia in her mad dash for safety. If I was seen, she'd know it had been me following her. I would explain, palms turned in peace as she seethed. I needed to make it home before she did to alibi myself.

A stitch pierced my side, pain that made me gasp but I dared not stop. The trail catapulted out onto a rocky crag, scree sliding beneath my shifting feet.

The Great Meadow lay below, an expanse of scrub brush, honeysuckle, and blueberry bushes a half-mile wide. A dense copse lay at its end. At its very heart, an ancient oak cocooned a hidden tree house behind its gnarled branches. Hexagonal shaped, the house was rustic and homey, an embodiment of fantastical living.

Heath was the first to imagine it. With a pencil in hand, he sketched out a structure that would be raised amongst the trees. Rambling and random, it would be full of storerooms, bedrooms, and workshops.

From the mountains, we walked down into the silent town and raided for materials. We painstakingly pried windows loose from empty houses to carry them home for miles on our backs.

When the first hint of a structure was erected, some twenty feet off the ground, we laid across it, sighing with pleasure and the kind of exhaustion you only experience when working on something you completely enjoy. Our fingers blistered, our nails blackened from where we missed with the hammer, we ate fresh brook trout and thumped each other happily on the back.

After much coaxing, Amelia climbed the rope ladder and stepped onto the platform with shaky knees and splayed hands, terrified of the fall. "It calls my name," she said.

The main room of the tree house was a thing to behold with knotted pine shelves built into the walls and windows that looked out upon the forest. I built a fireplace in the southeast corner with river stones and clay harvested from the stream. I imagined the dancing light it would throw across Amelia's cheek-bones as we sat wrapped in furs together, in love. A weaver finch I was, wooing with promises of a brighter, safer future. And just like the weaver finch, the choice was always hers to make.

We had just started construction on the second floor, the beams appearing crown-like. A faint knocking could be heard, hammer-on beam. To those who didn't know, it might be mistaken for a red-headed woodpecker on the hunt for grubs. But they would be wrong, that is, if they were alive at all.

The structure abutted a sheer cliff. Water from the nearby stream cascaded weightlessly over the edge until thundering and churning on the rocks below. If by chance, you happened upon the stream and decided to follow it, the deep pools beyond the waterfall would call to you in a siren song of fish and freshwater. You would dream eagerly of your first bath in weeks and a full belly.

The cliff was treacherously steep, and we hoped you would slip on your way down and break your neck. Only realizing as you somersaulted through the air that an elaborate tree house rose camouflaged above you. We'd wave as your body washed away, as Joanna waved to McLeach, apathetic to your plight.

I started across the Great Meadow, breathing heavily from panic and exhaustion. Wishing for binoculars, I squinted to the trailhead I guessed she'd come from, far down to the south side, where dark firs stood straight and ominous. The clouds were breaking up above, weak sunshine sending tendrils of steam from the ground.

A pheasant took off not too far from my stamping feet, wings beating hard as it flew skyward. I reached instinctively for my bow, slung across my back. I caught sight of Amelia too late, crouched low with the air rifle aimed at my head. I jerked to a stop, knowing perhaps my death had finally arrived. Instead, she pulled the barrel upward, shooting the bird mid-flight. In a burst of feathers, it fell back to the ground, lifeless.

I waited as she sauntered to the bird, gun upside down and balanced on her shoulder. Her cheeks were flushed from the flight, her hair bedraggled and tangled with bracken.

"Amelia..." I said, breathless from running.

She traipsed through the honeysuckle to retrieve the pheasant. Its iridescent blue feathers were speckled with blood, a round hole in its chest where the bullet had entered.

"Grab the basket. I'm tired of carrying it," she said, walking towards home.

THEN

Light streamed in from original factory windows onto reclaimed wooden tables that functioned as desks. Open concept plans were meant to encourage collaboration but instead fomented social anxiety and microaggressions between co-workers.

I worked for an apartment rental start-up that promised to alleviate the tortuous process of securing a place to live in New York City. I sat next to Thom. He was an earnest ladder-climber, spending too much money on an expensive wardrobe that he then didn't dry clean. He carried the stench of old money trying to make a go of it until he could settle comfortably into his family's philanthropy efforts.

I hated him for several reasons. First, he radiated a caffeinated, manic glee at all hours of the workday that was hard to stomach at all hours of said workday. Second, he kept multiple framed photos of himself and his friends, their tanned arms slung over each other effortlessly on a sailboat, in an upscale bar, in a basketball arena.

I discreetly stole one, throwing it in the dumpster on my way home, but he replaced it within a few days. New frame, same smiling chiclet teeth and coiffed hair.

"Have you seen the latest projection scenario for that hemorrhagic fever?" he asked the moment I arrived at work, sweaty and irritated from the morning commute.

"I thought that was mostly overseas." I turned my computer on, sifting through emails and not making eye contact, trying to discourage conversation.

"Well, the CDC is projecting there could potentially be millions of people catching this thing."

I made a non-committal noise.

"Look," he said, turning his computer monitor towards me, gesturing to a line graph.

"So, by next fall, we'll all be dead?" I asked.

"No, this line is just cases. That line represents deaths."

I studied the graph closer. "Okay, so they're saying it's not that deadly then."

"Exactly, they're saying it isn't deadly, but hemorrhagic fever liquefies your insides. I think they're just trying to buy time and avoid mass panic. There's already nothing stocked at the grocery stores. Can you imagine a bunch of morons causing a run on whatever is left?"

The exotic fruits had been the first to go once news of a mysterious fever began spreading. Signs were affixed to empty produce bins at grocery stores. OUT OF STOCK DUE TO HEALTH AND SAFETY REGULATIONS. That's okay, we said, we'll eat U.S. of A. peaches, apricots, and avocados!

No one realized the outsized foreign produce plug that kept the grocery stores filled. Shipping containers packed with bananas, corn, and soybeans from Brazil, Mexico, and Italy rotted on the wrong side of the ports, caught up in the red tape of paranoia and suspicion that foreign produce could spread the virus because of "uncleanliness" in their processing. People took to lining up at dawn at the grocery stores to squabble over a bag of Idaho potatoes and New York apples. Otherwise, the produce section remained hauntingly empty.

And we were quickly reminded of the California drought. When Colorado turned the water pipes off to save itself, the California farmland dried to dust and blew away. Teenagers made it a game on social media to see whose windowsill accumulated dust the fastest.

The government could not justify the farm subsidies when there was no farm left to subsidize. It all imploded with the slow-moving majesty of an elephant poisoned at the watering hole, the deflated carcass feeding the debtor vultures and carpetbaggers.

The American Farm Bureau Federation kept a suicide counter on their webpage of all the liquidated farmers that had stepped off the milk bucket.

Next to go were the processed foods that were bulk manufactured in China, which the vegans and Food Network chefs all lauded as a 1960s back-to-the-earth revival. It was all well and good until the new parents frantically reminded us that baby formula was also mainly produced in China, and their precious infants were all starving. Breast milk drives were organized, and milk banks reinflated those chubby rolls, but now the La Leche League was furiously protesting over the nearsightedness of it all.

"Isn't there always some plague threatening to wipe us off the face of the earth? The CDC comes to the rescue, and their budgets are expanded nicely the following year," I said.

Thom shook his head knowingly. "I already bought surgical gloves. They're reporting that it can be spread through body fluids. You grab the subway pole with a hangnail, BAM! You'll be throwing up your guts in no time."

"Maybe it'll save the mountain lions," I said, getting up for coffee.

It was a Friday which was usually the busiest day of the week for apartment showings. Curiously, several clients canceled due to illness. In one of the only showings I did have, the man poured sweat the entire time and complained of a stomach bug.

***

Saturday rose hot and humid, the kind of day that leaves your creases sticky with sweat no matter how recent your last shower was. My roommate and I had been lolling about in our apartment, a day without end. It was a tiny thing with old wooden floors and a half stove. Our view was of brick walls and a side alley filled with dumpsters and slime. We signed the exorbitant lease because it was Astoria and a haven it seemed, filled with young people and their dogs.

An advisory had been issued earlier that morning by the city's mayor, an inadequate sniveler, to remain indoors. There were mass protests taking place near Wall Street. Resentment and anger had been growing regarding the student loan bubble.

Kids, whose parents could no longer afford to pay their entire tuition due to the meteoric rise of prices, took student loans from predatory banks, from the government themselves. They agreed to ridiculous terms, such as not being able to consolidate loans, the inability to refinance, or a lightening of the load with bankruptcy. The promise of jobs, of having a career that you have been dreaming about for your whole life, made dealing with the devil a little easier.

So, come graduation day, millions found that there were no jobs to be had, having disappeared over two decades of political swindling. Many returned home, taking jobs far below their educational skills if they could find any at all.

I had been relatively lucky, my parents told me, to find a decent job that would cover the cost of a six-hundred-dollar loan payment coupled with rent. And it was okay, according to the bank that held my loan note, that I merely subsisted, eking out a living while paying their non-negotiable interest rates. We were the ones responsible, they said, for taking the money in the first place at seventeen years old.

Tent cities had sprung up amongst the maze of Lower Manhattan, where the streets were still made of cobblestones. I read once that much of the water piping down there was nearly as old as the streets themselves, giant rusting behemoths where monsters multiplied.

Thousands of people were there from across the country to protest. They languished, having little access to basic human necessities. The talking heads were dubbing it a disaster, worse even than the Occupy Wall Street movement. I could see what they meant, but that didn't stop an ember of pride to glow within my chest.

Entrances to banks were overrun with kids, refusing the suits that tried to push past them. One squabble ended with a banker getting clocked in the head with a rock. After that, the bankers understood the situation and retreated to their Hamptons summer shares to lick their wounds and plot.

And whether by coincidence or devious actions, a rumor of sickness continued to grow. Hemorrhagic fever, the television said, was brought accidentally through air travel from plague-like conditions in Mongolia. The newscasters, with just a slight hint of maliciousness, said the disease flourished in unsanitary places, like in fact, the slum that had sprung up in their beloved streets.

Later that evening, a sweet breeze swept through the apartment as the sun went down bringing with it a city smell of garbage and dreams. My roommate and I were becoming antsy, having eaten all the freezer-burnt sherbet and the last vestiges of pickles found on the back shelf of the fridge.

With the advisory hanging over our heads, we left for the dive bar a few blocks away, my roommate believing this to be the luckiest place for discounted drinks. "I slept with the bartender. Don't you remember?" he laughed.

On the way there, a Black man jogged past, wearing a fluorescent vest with "JOGGER DO NOT HARM" written on the back. From the lapel, the red light of a small camera blinked, live streaming. Those who were filled with hate and wished to do harm could now be held accountable with facial recognition software. Those with pointy hats hidden in their closets banged their drums about big brother and invasions of privacy.

The bar was a filthy place, seemingly held together by layers upon layers of grime. Once called Heaven's Gate, the bar had gone through a series of changes, somehow lighting upon pop art in its current reimagining. Giant cartoons had been painted on the walls, characters with skin-tight clothing and eyes the size of saucers. Instead of the usual bar fare, the menu featured odd interpretations of Hawaiian dishes, priced as if anyone had money.

Upon seeing my roommate, the bartender frowned and insisted that we leave. But he schmoozed, and glasses full of beer were plopped down in front of us. I rubbed away the lipstick smudges from the last person who drank from it and pushed a few dollars to the bartender.

With the place nearly empty, it wasn't long before my roommate was behind the bar, pouring shots of cheap whiskey. Heads buzzing, my roommate persuaded the bartender to abandon her shift with drunken kisses and promises of adventure, leaving a sullen man-child of a bartender behind to see the night out alone in a pop art bar that held no interest to anyone.

So we left, bouncing from bar to bar, looking for something, anything. When we didn't find it, we all agreed that downtown would be magical, closer to the epicenter of righteousness and passion felt by the protesters.

We hopped the turnstiles, catching the N train just as the doors closed. Two drag queens sitting across from us eyed us warily until the bartender admired one of their particularly outrageous wigs. At that, they relaxed, but only until they had to be on guard all over again because of the rise of unprovoked violence against the queer community.

My roommate puked, narrowly missing the bartender's lap as we careened through the belly of the city. It ran in rivers, rolling chunks of pickles and whiskey. The doors opened, and a group of waiters, their bow ties eschew, hopped expertly over the mess.

My roommate didn't look good, so suddenly, as if he'd been shrink-wrapped in a sheen of sweat.

Mildly disgusted, the bartender asked if he was alright, but he waved her off, twirling his fingers playfully in her hair and threatening to wipe his face on her dress until she screeched. We stepped off the train downtown, the air on the platform hot enough to boil your insides. Climbing out of the crumbling station, we fell into a bar called Max Frog that had large, clear windows showing the fun it held within. It was dim inside, the only light coming from a string of bulbs hung crazily across the ceiling. The space was packed, wall-to-wall, dripping bodies with colorful clothes and ironic facial hair. Some people were wearing hospital masks. If it was an attempt at cleverness or real fear, I wasn't sure.

I shoved my way to the bar, leaning across the wooden counter, my last ten bucks clutched in my hand. With the bartender pointedly ignoring me, I nicked two bottles of beer and slid them slyly into my pocket. A girl watched me from where she sat on a stool, her gaze a spotlight of smoky eye shadow. A face of angles, she had full lips and a pointed nose. I turned to go, concerned by her acute attention.

She followed me into the crowd. I tried avoiding her, wondering if she'd confront me about the theft. Instead, she slipped her hand into my pocket and took one of the stolen beers. Opening the cap with a lighter, she took a long drink, watching for my reaction.

I smiled, wondering what it all meant, complacent now in our shared crime. Her dress was a plunging, pretty thing, her face full of mischief. I tried telling her so, but she shook her head, cupping her ear.

"Outside?" she mouthed.

I nodded and through the crowd we fought, leaving our stolen beers by the door. Darkness had made the air no less stifling hot, the air so humid it felt like breathing water. Two bouncers stood stoically on either side of the entrance, eyes roving for suspicious behavior or underage kids, ready to spit out facts detailed on fake licenses.

The girl sat on the curb, face turned up to mine, waiting for me to join. "The music's too loud in there," she said.

I sat down, laughing at her sour expression. I reached to touch her shoulder tentatively, to trail my fingers over the freckles that dotted her skin. It curved ever so slightly, the spaghetti strap of her dress jumping the gap between shoulder and collarbone. It was fascinating and beautiful in a way that caught me off-guard, that such a trivial thing could stir such feelings.

She lit a cigarette and offered to share; pink lip gloss stuck to the filter. I shook my head no. She was comfortable in silence, a rarity in a world where people often babbled nonsense when faced with such a moment. With a last inhale, she flicked the butt into the street and took my hand, leading me back inside.

We kissed in the bathroom, the walls covered in graffiti, from love notes to existential blather. Lifting her onto the lip of the sink, I wound my fingers through her strawberry-colored hair, loose and long down her back.

From the other side of the bathroom door, my roommate pounded to get in, then puked again. I shouldered the door open, my mouth agape at the unidentifiable gunk that pooled on the floor.

Abruptly, the lights were flicked on, the crowd collectively gasping and looking about, faces showing confusion and apprehension.

A booming voice came on overhead, "New York City has issued a mandatory curfew, effective immediately. Anyone not home within the hour will face persecution." There was a pause, "Unofficially, quarantine efforts have commenced on the tent city, and reports are they're sweeping the surrounding area, which encompasses Max Frog."

The air went dead, and two hundred people started stampeding towards the door. I hauled my roommate up from the floor and grabbed the girl, her lips pursed with worry.

"Bridget!" she screamed across the bar. A girl with corkscrew curls fought her way to us, and we rode the wave of people outside.

We wandered the hot streets, avoiding scuttling rats and cockroaches so big you could hear their feet tick on the concrete. It was impossible to catch a cab, and we watched helplessly as they zoomed by, filled to capacity with the intoxicated. It was a disparaging have-not situation, jealous of those lucky enough to hail at the right moment. I threw my empty beer bottle, green glass bursting on the pavement.

The subway entrances were jammed with people pushing, crying, and fighting to get on the trains. Faint booms could be heard over the noise and then the scream of sirens. Smoke curlicued above iconic towers, thick and black against the night sky.

Giving up, we decided to regroup in a bakery. The brightness shining from its pink, frilly curtains drew us in like flies to a carcass. We ran our dirty fingers over the gleaming glass cases, salivating over delicate cakes and doughnuts. We chose a corner table, and I propped my roommate on a chair, thoroughly passed out, his skin ashy and dull. A terrifying thought popped into my head that he could be sick with this unnamed fever. I tried pushing it away just as fast, worried the girls would see it floating above my head, comic strip-like.

Paying with crumpled cash from her purse, the girl ordered a chocolate cupcake. Walking back to the table, she wiped away crumbs with an impatient hand before sitting down. She pulled her phone out and tip-tapped on the screen, the backlight showing a fine smattering of freckles across her face. Bridget, biting her pinky nail nervously, read over her shoulder.

"We've got to leave," the girl said finally. "The National Guard is rounding up all protesters for mandatory inspection. If you have a body temperature over 99 degrees, you'll be quarantined for up to 48 hours."

I gestured helplessly to my roommate, who was slumped over with noxious alcohol fumes rolling off him. The bakery clerk, a balding, mid-50ish man, who had been listening to our conversation intently, snapped on the darkened television that hung suspended in a forgotten corner. He flipped through the channels, trying to find coverage, but only slop shows were playing about cops or doctors or vampires.

Suddenly, there was a great commotion outside as though an exodus was upon us. I twitched the curtain aside. Dozens of people, protesters by the look of them, were streaming past like a multicolored river flooding around cars, hydrants, and post office boxes. Their faces were masks of exhaustion and terror.

The bakery clerk abandoned his post to open the door, leaning out anxiously. His knuckles were white where he gripped the door frame.

"Close the door!" the freckled girl commanded, "whether you're staying or going."

He ignored her, eyes darting back and forth at the chaos outside. "Hey," he called to a passing protester, who darted around his reaching hand. "What's happening? Please!"

"Quarantine," a man yelled, a filthy hiking pack bouncing wildly as he ran.

Our phones all made a horrible screeching sound collectively. There was a scramble to see what was going on, hands rummaging in pockets and pocketbooks. A message glowed: STAY IN PLACE. THIS

IS AN ORDER FROM THE FEDERAL GOVERN-
MENT OF THE UNITED STATES.

"I've got to get home," the clerk said, distressed, and with that, he was gone. The door closed behind him with a soft jingle.

A blinding flash lit up the street, a bang following a half-second later. I fell out of my seat, my hands over my ears. Some people on the street had also fallen, and others were yelling. I dragged my roommate away from the window and around the counter. He murmured angrily. Somewhere close, Bridget screamed.

Soldiers marched into view in full combat gear, gas masks covering their faces. Armored trucks rolled behind. A popping sound filled the air as soldiers fired rubber bullets into the crowd.

The clerk crumpled to the street, bleeding from his temple. He squirmed on the ground in pain. Soldiers flanked him on either side, swooping down like camouflaged buzzards. They hauled him upright and threw him into the dark recesses of one of the trucks.

The freckled girl stood upright from a crouching position beneath a table, and walked resolutely to the door, sliding the deadbolt into place.

Our cell phones stopped working before long, jammed from the millions all trying to call each other at once. An impromptu announcement cut through the television's programming. The blue sky behind the orange-toned President had a water stain and was peeling at the seams. Apparently, he didn't have enough time to reach his best bunker.

We stayed there that night, falling asleep in uncomfortable wooden chairs, the morning light showing smeared makeup and five o'clock shadows. My roommate became feverish and unresponsive, the skin on his face sagging as if he was an old man. Bridget followed soon after, temperature spiking as she shook with cold. Even then we dared not leave, hearing the ricochet of bullets and watching the sick stumble by and the violent creep, maleficent intent obvious in their movements.

We ate stale pastries and mopped sweaty brows, longing to escape the confectionery prison and get our friends the help they needed. The power failed by noon, and panic set in. Riot mobs were seen from the bakery's windows. Huddling in the back room, squeezed between commercial ovens and utility sinks, I grasped for her hand as the city raged and sickness spread.

"What's your name?" I whispered.

"Amelia," she answered, and every cell of my body was filled with her name forever.

NOW

"Heath!" shouted Amelia, holding the pheasant like a newly won wrestling belt beneath the eaves of our exalted oak tree.

"I saw," Heath said, looking down from the unfinished second floor of the tree house. "We're eating good tonight."

"What did you get?" Mabel asked from where she hung alongside the tree house on a scaffolding system. Engrossed for weeks now, she was painting the tree house a swirling brownish-green color in mimicry of the forest. The pocket of her New Paltz University sweatshirt was heavy with brushes and acrylics.

"Dinner," Amelia said tersely.

The look of cheeriness vanished from Mabel's face, replaced by mild bewilderment. She turned back to her pallet, swirling the brush in a large glob of paint.

She was afflicted with vitiligo, but I thought it made her look all the more interesting, with light splashes of missing color across her face and body. It was like she had yet to be completely painted in.

Amelia peeled off her shawl, draping it over a foldable chair. With nimble, confident fingers, she began plucking the pheasant. Downy feathers floated around her head.

I dropped her foraging basket near the fire pit, made of stones and clay. Pots and pans hung from metal hooks inserted into the joints between stones. A fire was always burning, whether it was dying embers or a roaring cooking fire. We stoked it only during dawn or dusk hours to keep the smoke from rising visibly above the treetops.

"Amelia..." I started, not knowing if I should apologize.

"I could have killed you."

"I know, I'm sorry," I said miserably. "Fuck off, Atticus."

I swung up the rope ladder to the tree house, heaving the heavy mahogany door open. We stole it from an ostentatious house and sawed it down circular, like a manhole. It was big enough only for one person at a time to enter and exit, a fire hazard, sure, but also an attack deterrent. A solid wooden bar slid across the top at night, pioneer-style.

The first floor felt cramped with five hammocks hanging from the ceiling. Our clothes and tools and anything that couldn't get wet were strewn about on tables, shelves, and the floor.

One wall was entirely dedicated to seedlings. Lily encouraged the tiny green sprouts to grow from biodegradable starter pots. From curly bean sprouts to mini tomato trellises, she was determined to start a garden and spent most of her time in a high field that she plowed herself. She counted the days until the dangerous late mountain frosts were over and the tiny shoots could fend for themselves.

I set my bow down on the kitchen island, constructed from driftwood pulled from the lake. The surface was polished to a mirror shine. A porcelain sink sat empty; a blue jug of water was positioned above to give the illusion of indoor plumbing. The cabinets, yet unstained, held food and cooking supplies. Top Ramen, basmati rice in bags, sugar in Tupperware. Drying herbs hung from racks and propagated wild carrots in plastic water bottles crowded the windowsills.

I climbed the stairs, slabs of wood ascending around the tree to the second level. They were slick and muddy from the construction site above. Heath worked alone beneath the filtered light of the tarp that protected the lower level from rain and bugs. Despite the chill air, he wore no shirt.

"What happened between you and Amelia?" Heath asked, not looking up from where he swung the hammer. His accent was Baltimorean drawl, cultivated in the row houses of his city. Working summer construction jobs during his youth, he had now become a master builder, at least in the opinion of our group of five.

"What do you mean?" I asked.

I thumped my knuckles on a beam, admiring Heath's work. Here was where the landing would be, there the bedrooms, arranged circinate around the tree trunk. Heath's original plans included three bedrooms, not four, until Amelia asked him to reconfigure the dimensions. I reached out to touch her arm at that moment, confused, but she stalked off. Heath winked at me in kindness, taking his pencil from behind his ear and adjusting the design.

"Amelia came running from the forest as if being chased. I called out to her, but maybe she couldn't hear me." He paused, wiping his brow. A leather work belt held up his shorts, steel toe boots on his feet. "Then when she took a knee to sight the pheasant, you came running just as fast. I was afraid she'd shoot you by mistake."

I stepped to the very edge of the platform, looking out over the mountains. The vista extended for miles at this height, from dense woods and rocky outcrops to bottomless lakes hidden within valley folds.

He waited for me to answer, hammer quiet.

"How are we on building supplies? Are we running low on anything?" I asked.

"I was thinking we can finish with what we've got." Heath nodded towards the last of our planks piled on the ground below. "Then we'll have to cut more trees."

There was a forester's cabin, perched upon a precipice not too far from the park's entrance. Heath and I systematically pilfered it, stripping it to its stone foundation. It turned out to be a wasted effort, the wood falling apart in our hands, damaged by termites and rot. At camp that night, Lily looked at us funny after hearing what happened. "Just cut a tree down, no? Instead of hauling unusable wood up the mountain, send it down the stream, and we can make a log jam at the bend before the meadow." Mabel grumbled about the benefits of upcycling, which we aggressively ignored after Lily's epiphany.

I nodded, "Shouldn't be a problem. There's even a felled fir that we never sent down."

"Thinking about it, we're running low on nails," he said, spitting over the side.

"I can make a run into town, hit the hardware store."

Heath grunted a non-committal noise. "What about garages or sheds that are closer?"

"Most of those were cleared out last fall to build the shacks."

He frowned, "What a fool's fucking errand that was."

A beat of silence passed. "We'll figure it out later. Let's talk after dinner." I clunked back down the stairs, wondering if I should stay hidden from Amelia.

"Att!" Amelia called. I shimmied down the rope ladder, squaring my shoulders for a possible argument.

"Here, can you finish?" she asked, handing me the half-plucked bird. I took it from her, its body still warm, scaly feet limp and reptilian.

Amelia unloaded her basket and then busied herself with stoking the fire, hunched over the embers to protect the tinder from the wind. She took the cast iron skillet from its hook, setting it on the metal grate above the coals. She cut the mushrooms and a few of the leeks she had gathered in quick, efficient slices, tossing them in the skillet where they sizzled.

Once the bird was naked aside from a few awkward pinfeathers, I washed it in the stream, blood streaming ribbon-like from its wound. I set it on a flat rock and lopped its head off, then removed the guts, throwing them into the water. I handed it back to Amelia, avoiding eye contact. She carved it expertly, laying each piece into the stir-fry.

These were not our real lives, living in the woods, cheeks carved from nearly endless toil with little to show for it. The Panic had stolen those lives, a pandemic of unimaginative proportions. Sometimes, we liked to imagine what was happening elsewhere. Could it be that we accidentally strayed into a quar-

antined area, going north instead of south as initially directed? Was the rest of America alive? Was
Europe pestilence-free? Mozambique?

These were dreams, fairy tales, so we didn't feel
so entirely alone. We'd turn on the hand crank radio,
ears lowered and fingers turning the knob gingerly,
searching, ever searching, for a transmission. It was
foolish.

Lily hiked into the clearing as the sun was setting,
dirt up to her elbows. The knees of her jeans were
muddy and worn. She washed in the stream, using
the makeshift shower we had constructed with hose
and plywood, sputtering from the cold.

"Smells good, Amelia," Lily called, her hair whiter
than a unicorn's flank, seen above the wooden walls
of the shower. "What'd you get?" The pipes squeaked
as she turned the water off, stepping around the corner wrapped in a towel.

"Bird," Amelia answered, adding a pinch of salt to
the boiling pot of soup. "I've got it frying, but we'll
have to add something to the soup, it's thin."

"How about some frog legs, Heath?" Lily shouted, climbing the rope ladder, one rung at a time,
hanging on to her towel.

"What are you demanding?" he joked, leaning
over the side of the tree house to look at her.

"Frogs!" she laughed, disappearing into the darkness of the round door.

The meat crackled pleasantly as the stars winked above us, the night quiet and serene. Heath and I walked along the stream, catching frogs in nets. He cleaned them swiftly, their skinless legs disturbingly humanoid. Amelia added them to the pot with the rest of the diced leeks and wild carrots. We hovered, mouths salivating.

When the edges of the pheasant were blackened and the frogs tender enough, Amelia removed everything from the fire. We ate from a hodge-podge collection of plates and bowls, some delicate china, others that IKEA crap found in every cabinet from here to California. It was utterly delicious, my stomach greedy for a cooked meal of meat and fresh vegetables.

Bats flew low, darting and dancing, eating bugs by the hundreds. Amelia put the kettle on when we finished eating, and Lily took the plates down to the stream to rinse.

"I was thinking," Amelia said, "That we should look into canning. We don't have a proper refrigeration system, and if we learned anything from this past winter, it's preparation." She looked around as if daring anyone to disagree.

I groaned inwardly, conjuring up the mephitic stench of canned asparagus.

"What would you need for something like that?" Heath asked.

"Ah, large pot, mason jars I'd imagine," she said, not looking up from where she ground baked dandelion rootstock into a survivalist's coffee-like drink. She added it to the kettle, and an earthy smell filled the camp. "I'm not a hundred percent sure of the actual step-by-step process."

"Atticus is going to make a supply run, but you could go with him, check out what's left in town," Heath suggested, sitting in a soccer-mom foldable chair with his feet propped on the edge of the fire pit. Lily returned, stacking the dishes near the tree house, her hair eerily white in the darkness. She dried her hands on Heath's pants until he laughed and pulled her onto his lap.

"Actually, Amelia," Lily said, "I'm hard up for radish and broccoli seeds, and I think I planted the spinach too soon. It just keeled over into a soggy mess."

Amelia's brow furrowed. "I'm sure Atticus can get whatever you need."

"Probably too much for one person to carry," Lily gently countered.

"I can go," Mabel said from where she sat on a loose stump, casually working a piece of charcoal over parchment paper, the shape of our campsite emerging from broadly sketched strokes.

"Don't you have to paint?" Amelia bristled. A flush crept into Mabel's cheeks, but she didn't respond, just turned her attention back to the charcoal drawing.

Lily interjected, sensing trouble. "What if you and Atticus left for town in the morning and Heath and I met you down at that garden center? You know the one. We could hike back together in the afternoon. That way, I can still work in the garden tomorrow morning."

"Fine," Amelia sighed. "Although I don't know what you all plan on eating for dinner tomorrow."

"Paint," Lily laughed.

The tension diffused like a popped inner tube, shoulders relaxing and grins replacing frowns. I didn't realize that I had been holding my breath.

Amelia poured her coffee alternative into enamel mugs. I took mine from her outstretched hand with trembling fingers. I sipped slowly, a smile hidden behind my cup, joy filling my chest cavity. Amelia and I together again, walking the roads just like we did when sickness and chaos first spread like a bad cough across the world. This could be what we needed to mend what was broken.

I could try to finally shake the feeling that she simply wouldn't return one day from traversing the mountain. I could stop following her, lose the fear that something so precious could vanish.

In the firelight, Lily played her violin, altering between sweet melodies and bluegrass fiddle. Amelia climbed the rope ladder to the tree house, emerging with a jeroboam of Merlot that we passed to each other with two hands, slugging it right from the bottle.

We drank, laughter growing louder, Amelia singing a sweet, campy song to Lily's bluegrass music. Mabel and Heath danced, and I sat tapping my foot contentedly.

The fire was kicked out once Heath had fallen asleep, and Amelia had broken the wine bottle, slipping from her hands as she sang animatedly.

I felt light, all infractions were forgotten for a moment. These times of merriment were new to us, the warming nights encouraging lightness. Amelia would forget sometimes all that I had done, that we had done. Times like these were simple, her lips wide with laughter, the catalog of my transgressions closed in her mind, let go like a rock from the hand.

Amelia insisted we all go up the ladder before her, afraid she'd tumble to her death. I waited with her as everyone climbed, her breath smelling of wine and her hand brushing mine in the moonlight. She met my gaze, eyelashes sweeping wide. Sorry was in my mouth, tumbling like marbles, feeling like battery acid, but she turned away, waving me up impatiently.

It was dark inside, smelling like new construction and wood smoke, the tarp above rustling in the wind. I settled into my hammock, shedding my sweat-stained clothes for the day. Amelia appeared, as if she was a nightcrawler, emerging from a hole that went down, down to the center of the earth. She staggered into the hammock next to mine.

"Leave at dawn?" she asked.

"Yes," I said, my tongue loose from alcohol. She drifted off after much rustling around to get comfortable. I wanted to reach out to her in the dark, trail my fingers down her neck, and feel the softness of her skin. But I was likely to get my hand snapped off by crocodile jaws should I stray near.

Heath and Lily whispered together, their voices dripping saccharine love. He rocked her to sleep every night, his foot pushing her hammock rhythmically.

Heath had divulged, as we hauled wooden planks through mud and raging snowmelt, how he'd met Lily. Not long after New York City had stumbled to her knees with fever, hundreds of thousands of refugees had streamed into Baltimore.

Predictably, the rumor of fever grew until it could no longer be hidden. Black vomit first filled the hospitals and then the streets. Those still healthy looked down the barrel of hunger with no stores open, and no supply lines to feed the roiling, panicked masses. Seeing the end of times, Heath rolled his dirt bike out of the shed behind his apartment complex, somehow making it through the provisional quarantine gates and out into the wild. He said he stayed those first few nights in empty warehouses along the way, following the highway northward deep into Pennsylvania. They were haunting structures, ghosts of a time when America thought of itself proudly as a titan of industry.

It was by chance that Heath stopped to siphon gas at a convenience store. Using a section of hose, he sucked gas from an abandoned Bronco. As gas poured into his tank, he heard a curious tap, tapping sound coming from a building across the street. Dead neon lights promised Naked Girls, Nude, Nude, Nude!

Heath capped his gas tank, the soft tapping making him wince as if it was a gong being struck next to his ear after the silence of days. Setting the kickstand, he walked cautiously across the road. The door had been wedged shut from the outside with a rusted crowbar. Beads of water on the doorknob from the light mist falling vibrated with every tap.

Heath rapped his knuckles on the door, and the sound stopped, a soft cry of agony taking its place. He pulled at the crowbar, cracking the front half of the wooden door into splinters.

Twisting the knob, he flung it wide open, and a slip of a woman fell out onto the pavement. A nauseating stench wafted from the dark room beyond, obscure masses rotting in chairs and on the floor.

She got to her feet slowly, knees knocking. Her hair had turned a snowy white, from shock, Heath guessed. Her eyes were like inkblots, so dark you couldn't tell the iris from the pupil. He shrugged out of his jacket and draped it over her, giving her sips of water from his pack.

She clambered onto the back of his bike, and they rode off together. "Lily," she told him when he asked her name, wind whistling in their ears.

When he finished telling me his story, I had grown quiet, humbled by a love that fell together so simply. I thought of it often.

NOW

I woke the following morning, overjoyed with anticipation of the hike into town with Amelia. It would be just us, without distractions or chores to divert attention or sow animosity.

I looked for her, peering above my blankets in the daybreak cold, but her hammock was empty. I frowned, worrying she forgot or left on an errand that would send me looking for supplies alone. Rolling to the floor, careful to be quiet, I pulled on pants, boots, and a sweater and crept through the door, climbing down to the forest floor.

Lily stood over a small cooking fire. Amelia crouched beside her, feeding the flames with bracken. They both looked up at the sound of leaves crunching beneath my boots, Lily giving a small smile, Amelia pursing her lips, and returning to her task. I sighed with relief.

We left soon after, Lily waving us on with steaming mugs of tea clasped in stiff fingers. The packs we wore were light, empty except for provisions that included smoked fish wrapped in spring greens and cold pheasant from last night's dinner. I carried my bow, Amelia her air rifle.

She wore durable hiking boots and a windbreaker that made a swish, swish sound when she walked. I followed close behind her as we scaled the rocky trail that led down the mountain. Everything was quiet and serene as the morning mist evaporated under the rising sun.

A light veil of green clung to the trees, leaves unfurling after the long winter. The forest was transforming, sprouting carpets of fiddleheads and spring ephemerals. Small flowers were emerging on the mountain laurel, bursting into all shades of pink.

Occasionally, Amelia would stop, crouching to sketch the location of blueberry bushes or apple trees in her small notebook, double-checking edibility with the field guide. Gossamer cobweb strands were caught in her hair, like a silver thread in a sea of strawberries.

Bird song filled the silence as we walked; last year's leaves crunching beneath our shoes. We soon took our jackets off, sweating from the hike. We walked on, splashing through a brook and back up its steep bank to fall again amongst the winding trail.

Amelia grew noticeably agitated the farther we walked, insisting on long pauses in which we listened for enemies, beasts in the woods. By mid-morning, we came to the derelict guard station at the entrance to the park, its roof slowly collapsing in on itself. A metal sign proclaiming, *"Welcome to Minnewaska State Park!"* swung noisily on its hinges.

The empty parking lot seemed far too exposed after the closeness of the forest, a feeling of unease settling over me. Untended new shoots of grass peppered the gravel drive. Amelia stooped low, crisscrossing the space, searching for unfamiliar footprints.

I pushed open the door to the guard's station. The air smelled stale, like dust and mouse droppings. Riffling through the neatly organized maps, I selected a topographic beauty, sealed in a protective plastic cover. Although leaving the maps for anyone to find seemed foolish, we understood that the park did not belong to us, though we had made it our home. And anyway, we knew nothing of cartography. In this world, things could be easily destroyed but never remade.

"Should we take the road?" Amelia asked, toes touching the edge of the blacktop.

"Not yet, there's a hidden trail alongside we can take first."

She nodded and followed me into the brush. The winding path was carpeted in quiet pine needles. Thick branches above blocked the sun. I felt a chill creep up my neck.

We made the final descent into the valley slowly, listening intently for any sound foreign to the chirping of birds or the wind rustling softly through the trees. We reached a wide expanse of overgrown farmland and stopped at its edge. Butterflies flitted happily amidst the flowers and grasses.

"Where do we go from here?" Amelia asked, pushing hair out of her face that had loosened from its tie.

"The trail ends here," I explained. "We'll have to take the road now."

She craned her neck, wanting to get a better view of the distance, doubting me. "The road is a complete mess, Att."

She was right, of course. Without the highway department to clean things up, storms had blown trees across the road, and flooding had caused some sections to buckle and erode. Cars and trucks were parked haphazardly on the shoulders or locked together in old accidents.

"But," she conceded, "I haven't been down here since we first went up last fall. What do I know?"

"There's nothing to worry about," I said, leaving the protection of the trees and moving onto the road. I didn't mention that every time I ventured here alone, I thought I'd snap my neck from looking around at every sound, real or imagined.

She stepped out cautiously, like a fawn taking its first look at the world.

"It'll be alright," I said, offering my hand. Amelia took it, folding hers into mine, her bones delicate beneath calloused skin.

We walked down the middle of the road, hand in hand like lovers on our way to brunch one spring morning. I closed my eyes and pictured myself in loafers and slacks, Amelia in a white summer dress.

We soon noticed buzzards circling in the distance. Amelia pointed to the sky where they swooped, as harpies would.

Rounding a bend, we saw something dead lying in the road, still far ahead. A putrid stench filled the air, like what you'd smell briefly through your car vents as you sped by roadkill. Amelia stopped, dropping my hand.

"Let's go back," she whispered.

"It's probably nothing but an animal. Let's just stay out of sight and see what it is first." Like creatures, we dropped into the road's deep ditch, making our way through brambles and muck, hidden from those higher on the food chain.

"It almost looks like a car wreck," Amelia said as we got closer. "But with no car."

A suitcase was sprung open. Its contents strewn about in the ragweed that pushed through the pavement. Amelia climbed onto the road, picking up a sneaker, its laces caked in dirt and blood. Her mouth turned down in a grimace.

A body lay crumpled a little farther away, face down, his head resting upon his arm. Blood had leaked from a belly wound, dry and flaking on the pavement. Amelia shooed the buzzards. They squawked angrily, hopping away. Their yellow eyes followed us, thinking we were here to steal their meal.

The man's right leg had been stripped to the bone; his cargo shorts soiled. Black flies crawled over everything imaginable like a moving, frantic blanket. I hooked my fingers through his belt loops, tugging. My shoulders ached, bodies being so terribly heavy.

"Oh, let him be," Amelia said. "Unless we want to dig a hole, the buzzards will just pull him back out."

I sighed but let go, the pneumatic body settling like gelatin.

"This is totally fucked. It's murder. He couldn't have been here for more than a few days. Why was he so close to the tree house?"

"I don't know, Amelia," I said. "Whoever did it is probably long gone by now."

Her face darkened. "This trip we're on for seeds and supplies is not worth our lives."

"It'll be fine. I promise," I said, exasperated, not wanting our trip to end so abruptly.

I bent over the suitcase, rummaging through things this person had thought important enough to pack. Picking a blue shirt, I held it up to examine it. The creatures from *Where the Wild Things Are* were splashed across the front, with the lettering, *"I'll eat you up, I love you so."*

Amelia looked down the road uneasily. "Att, let's move," she said, "forwards or backward, I don't care. Take what you want, and let's just go."

"That's not right," I said.

"What?" she asked, distracted.

"To steal from the dead."

She narrowed her eyes. "Everyone is dead, Atticus. I don't see factories chugging along anymore. Money is useless." She grabbed the shirt, looking at it before balling it up and throwing it back at me. "Here, it's perfect for you."

It fell near the body, sending a cloud of flies into the air. Amelia whirled off, pack bouncing as she marched down the road. I picked it up, the cotton soft to the touch, and laid it over the man's head, affording him some semblance of decency. Looking sadly at him, I wondered where his murderer now lurked and what hole they had folded their lethal limbs into. I took off after Amelia, her head held high like a righteous queen.

"Where's the nursery?" she asked when I caught up. "Can we just go there and wait for Lily and Heath?"

"I've got to get stuff for the tree house, so that means going to the hardware store in town. If you want to wait for me at the nursery, you can." I knew she wouldn't.

"Split up? This isn't an episode of *Scooby-Doo*."

"We can stop at the library and pick up new stuff to read."

She chewed the inside of her lip, but I knew that I had won. Nights spent without the dulling of a television screen were long, and our tree house library was limited to what we had carried up the mountain, straining our backs for invaluable information or just for the sake of entertainment.

"The nursery is that way." I pointed when we reached a crossroad. "We'll head there after town."

We walked until we came to New Paltz's town limits, the Wallkill River separating the land. A bridge spanned the distance. There were scour holes on the far side caused by floodwaters. It was like looking at its bones, crumbling concrete abutments exposed to the open air.

Amelia sighed, "I feel like I'm a pioneer sometimes." She looked at the bridge as if it insulted her. "Throw the rope yonder, Samuel. We'll ford this river with the cattle herd."

The water churned brown below, fed from snow melt and storm run-off. I stepped onto the bridge, listening for any cracking. I waved Amelia on when I reached the center, confident that this bridge neither knew nor cared about the extra weight.

"Is it safe?" she asked.

"I think so. Just move slowly."

She edged onto the structure, gripping the metal beams. Rust flaked onto her palms while she took calculated steps, never once looking down. She hesitated at a large car bumper, unwilling to lift her foot high enough to step over it.

"Amelia, stay there, and I'll move it," I called. I should've known she'd stop, as terrified of heights as she was. She crouched down when I drew close, her knees quaking with fear.

Stagnant water pooled in the bumper, moldy and green with squiggly mosquito larvae. I heaved it over the side. It took a second to hit the water below, floating briefly before sinking out of view.

Amelia squeezed her eyes shut. "You're making me dizzy," she said.

"What should I do?" I asked.

"Get off the fucking bridge." I retreated quickly, turning around when I reached solid ground.

She opened her eyes to confirm I was gone and began crawling on her hands and knees. A water canteen fell from her pack and clattered on the pavement as she inched forward. She ignored it entirely, shuffling slowly by it. I heaved her up by her armpits when she finally made it across.

She let out a shaky breath and wiped sweaty, dirty hands onto her pants. "Heights, man."

New Paltz looked forlorn and empty. The street curved up and away past a Japanese sushi place, a loose weathervane knocking against a wall. It had been one of those peace and love kind of towns, with a progressive college at its borders and washed-up hippies selling molded wizard candles.

We passed by Victorian homes, empty windows frowning down at us. The Savings Bank looked like it had been fortified early in the Panic but was now desolate. A tattered pride flag waved from a store-front with faded tie-dye shirts showcased in the window.

Yet for every building that still stood, many were burned to their foundations, unchecked by scream-ing fire trucks. In apocalypse movies, characters found solace in lonely homes, ate from dusty cans, and contemplated the death of materialism. This narrative was unrealistic because everyone forgot about the utility lines. Miles and miles of piping and infrastructure left to rot and rust. As the world died, no one turned the gas off, shut the water mains, or the nuclear reactors. Soon, there will be nothing but scorched concrete pads, shells of looping suburbs, and great cities reduced to ash. The particulate mat-ter made for great sunsets, though. And cancer.

Towns and cities, prone to erratic fires and spon-taneous flooding, were the catalyst that drove us into the mountains. While there was always a danger of forest fires and the like, we would at least see it com-ing and smell it in the air. We lived with no com-bustibles, however pleasant the thought of having propane heat might be. Lily had been the hardest to convince, having lived her childhood with sporadic outages in the trailer she shared with her mother in rural Pennsylvania.

The bridge experience had rattled Amelia. Quiet now, her notebook didn't reappear as we marched by overgrown gardens and yards. I pointed out a cluster of skunk cabbages, but she ignored me, soldiering on.

We passed brick storefronts painted in bright colors. The heady scent of yeast still drifted faintly from an Irish pub once frequented by girls wearing crew sweaters and guys with alt-right-inspired haircuts, waiting to try their luck with fake IDs and STDs.

Amelia began lagging, running her hands over windows, making trails in the dust. She came to a complete stop outside a hostel, cupping her hands to peer inside the front window. The structure it was lodged in appeared to have been falling apart long before the Panic, its fuchsia painting flaking, a gray watermark creeping down from the AC unit. The plants inside were dead, shriveled aloe and mother-in-law's tongue.

Bending down, Amelia picked up a heavy piece of loose asphalt, tossing it to get a feel for the weight. She marched backward before throwing it with all her might, missing the window and bouncing harmlessly to the ground.

She regarded her failed handiwork with red cheeks and a flaring nose. Fear had sloughed off her coldness, if only for a moment, and left her alive.

It was her first time seeing town since last year, over six months prior. She'd taken to the forest like a persistent mold, hard to root out. I thought she wouldn't be permeable to a ghost town atmosphere, hadn't considered her feelings and potential shock at the general barrenness of it all.

I had been conditioned for such a scenario growing up in the Catskills. That whole place was a goddamn ghost town with rundown bungalows to abandoned hotels. The winters were the harshest with hardly a soul to admire the blanket snow, the way the trees rattled after an ice storm. There was always a promise of the casinos returning, the region's knight in shining armor. People didn't think past the initial promise, the crime it would bring, the shit jobs, or even what another failure would mean.

"Where is the library?" Amelia asked. "I don't want to wander aimlessly for the day."

"Right up ahead," I said, wary of her temper.

"We'll have to carry heavy books on our backs the whole time we're here?" she asked, impatience nettling her voice. "Should we leave it till last?"

"It's a nice place to take a break. We can stash the books in a mailbox or something if you don't want to carry them."

She blew out her cheeks, conceding. "Fine," she said, "Let's go."

"Follow me."

THEN

We walked the Metro-North train tracks for nearly a week after our escape from the city, finally reaching the Poughkeepsie station, ragged and weary. Holes had appeared in the toes and heels of my socks, worn thin from miles of travel.

Amelia limped beside me. Her dress hung loosely from her frame, now torn and filthy. The only food we had eaten was what we could scavenge from train station vending machines. Our teeth ached from all the candy and soda, a gritty film of processed sugar coating our enamel.

It was like nothing I had ever experienced before, starving, and desperate, not having access to any information or communication systems. We threw our phones away on the fourth day, heavy, useless things they were. Actually, Amelia smashed hers repeatedly on a rock, only satisfied when the parts resembled nothing more than a mangled mess.

We held a fantasy that her parents were okay, that they were holed up in their home awaiting the return of their only offspring. We dreamed of salvation and safety. I had a vague plan of continuing on to my own childhood home. I hoped that seclusion had saved my parents.

Amelia had thought to follow the train tracks instead of the highways, which had quickly turned into lawless territory. Gunshots and screams could be heard when the tracks ran parallel to the grid-locked interstate. It shook me to my core until my teeth chattered, and Amelia shushed me.

Thankfully, the tracks mostly cut through forests, a gash of metal amid a dense riot of lush summer green. We'd slap at mosquitoes and listen to birdsong, our rhythmic footfalls lulling us, so we'd sometimes forget our predicament, focusing only on moving forever forward.

We saw only a handful of people on the tracks, always walking south. We'd call out to each other for news, staying cautiously apart for fear of contagion. The information was always confusing or conflicting, full of raw hysteria.

One man had melted into the tree cover after passing us, his eyes sliding over Amelia. We hid in the tree canopy that night, uncomfortable and cold. We saw him in the moonlight later, having doubled-back to waylay us in the dark. He walked with steady purpose, sporadically peering into bushes and thickets, hoping to find us. Having no luck, he continued onward. We came across his body the next afternoon, struck down by a blow to the head. He likely found something he was no match for, a leviathan to his shark.

Sometimes I thought it wasn't all that bad, following that mane of strawberry hair, a sweet song on her tongue when she wasn't black with despair. I picked bouquets of flowers that she'd twine behind her ear. It was as if I tumbled down into madness, a waking dream where my heart was soggy with love and my mind was stuttering with fear.

When we finally scrambled onto the platform in Poughkeepsie, Amelia promised that her parents' house lay just a few more miles north of town. I felt trepidation leaving the tracks and venturing into the unknown.

The train station was built with brown bricks and had large arching windows. We didn't dare to go inside because it looked like it had been a temporary Red Cross shelter. Now things were hushed, with blankets and belongings strewn across the marble floor. Bodies were left where they had fallen.

We skirted the parking lot, leery of the cars and what might be lying in wait like camel spiders in the desert sand. Great leafy oak and maple trees shaded the town below, fluorescent stripes sprayed onto front doors indicating sickness within. Gates were pulled down over storefronts, and front lawns were absent of children.

We came across a roadblock, orange sawhorses placed nose to nose. Behind them, a large military truck idled. Amelia blew out her cheeks in relief and picked up the pace. We had not seen anyone of authority since leaving the city.

Two people sat in the truck's cab in full HAZMAT suits. I feared they were dead from the way they were slumped in their seats. Amelia climbed over the roadblock and rapped her knuckles on the window.

When they didn't stir, she pulled the handle and opened the door. An awful smell wafted out, and we instinctively took a few steps back, covering our noses. The man in the driver's seat woke, eyes fluttering.

"Help us," Amelia pleaded, cheeks flushed from dehydration and sunburn.

The man was having trouble focusing. "We're supposed to tell people to turn back," he muttered, "S'not safe." His gums were bleeding, teeth tinted red as if he'd misapplied lipstick.

I peered around him to see if his passenger was also sick. Behind his mask, rivulets of blood ran down his face from where his eyes bled. He'd been dead for some time.

Instead of feeling disgusted or terrified, I felt bone-crushingly tired, resigned to horror and disappointment.

Amelia must have felt the same way because she slammed the door shut as the man said something else.

I opened the door again. "I'm sorry," I apologized. "Can you tell us what happened?" But the man collapsed forward onto the steering wheel, blood pouring from his nose after the effort of those few words. His Plexiglas mask was smeared red, his chest still.

We hadn't gotten sick. I suspected our immunity was some kind of genetic mutation, much like what saved a handful of saps during the Black Plague of the 14th century. Amelia insisted on divinity, hers specifically.

"Come on," Amelia said, pulling my arm. "Don't worry about them. What could they say that we don't already know?"

Leaving the truck behind, we walked through town, passing diners, colleges, and box stores. The sun was warm, the air humid. Cicadas rattled, and birds chirped intermittently.

By the afternoon, Amelia stopped at a snaking private driveway, complete with an empty guard house and a wrought iron gate.

It was twisted and broken, the bottom damaged where someone had driven their car against it. Hickory Hollow was written on a plaque in a calligraphic script, nailed to one of the brick pillars that stood on either side of the gate.

A stone fountain gurgled pleasantly just inside the gate. Amelia trailed her freckled fingers through the lily pad-covered surface as we passed by.

"There must still be electricity," I noted, looking at the running water.

"It's solar-powered," she said, pointing to a discreet solar panel jutting from the surrounding foliage.

Manufactured mansions stood at the end of winding driveways, screaming of new money. Each home was surrounded by a manicured acre of grass, now ankle high. Opportunistic dandelions sprouted in patches.

My skin prickled. There were no fluorescent marks on these doors like in town, yet certain smells wafted from homes, distinct the way rotting flesh can only be.

Amelia plowed on, a blister on the back of her heel looking painfully raw.

The door was locked when we arrived at her house, hungrier and dirtier than ever. Amelia pounded on the door, yelling for her mother. When no one answered, she rummaged around in a tall planter, extracting a key. With a soft snick, the door swung open, revealing a large foyer. A curved staircase climbed to the second story and a crystal chandelier dangled from above. I got the overwhelming sense of having been here before, until realizing I was thinking of the house from Jumanji.

She tore inside, racing down a dark corridor. I locked the door behind us and collapsed onto a bench, the rich leather squeaking in protest. I realized then how horrible I smelled.

The air was stale, the same type of staleness that greeted you when you returned from a long trip. It told me that Amelia's parents had not been here for a while and were unlikely to return.

"Fuck!" Amelia screamed. "They're gone."

I got back on my feet slowly, my muscles just about disintegrated. I followed her voice, finding a spacious kitchen. She stood over the table, hands splayed and head down. A crumpled note lay before her.

"They're not here," she said, lifting her head. A look not of sadness was upon her face, but of inconvenience and abandonment.

I picked up the note.

In neat handwriting, it said:

Amelia,
I'm taking your mom to the hospital. We will call you once the phones are back up. Hopefully, you're reading this and not stuck in the city. Talk to you soon.
Dad

The message was dry, with no sense of urgency or anxiety over the mother's health or the fact that they couldn't get in touch with Amelia. By my estimation, the date written in the far corner was roughly a day or so after the first night we spent in the bakery. I wondered if her father had written it before the scope of the virus was truly known, or perhaps it explained Amelia quite well.

"I'm sure they're okay and getting the help they need," I said gently.

She shrugged, as if casting off the yoke of her parents' fate didn't destroy her. Instead, she said, "There's a generator in the garage. Should we try to get it running?"

"I'd love a hot shower," I said.

The generator was a rusting behemoth that had probably seen as many winters as I had. It was quite at odds with the rest of the shining tools and gadgets that packed the neatly organized space.

"My mother insisted we take it when my grand-father passed away," Amelia explained. "I don't think they ever lost power long enough to use it."

Its gas tank was half full, and twenty minutes of picking through shelves yielded two empty gas cans and bad tempers. We moved the generator around to the side of the house and hooked it into the in-verter. I yanked the pull cord. Roaring to life, it vibrated the ground beneath our feet, and we looked around uneasily, worried that the noise would carry.

Inside, Amelia reset the breakers. "It's working," she called out. I pulled the garage door shut, its mechanics protesting the manual force.

"I'm taking a shower, Att. There are towels in the hall closet if you want to take one too."

Att. That's what she started calling me while we walked those train tracks, sometime between the terrible blackness of an endless tunnel and the wreckage of a freight train derailment, unnamed chemicals still glugging into the earth as we skirted by, our shoes squelching.

I retrieved a towel and chose a bathroom at random, my filthy feet leaving marks on the pristine white tile. I waited for the water to get hot and then stepped into what could probably be described as the best shower of my life.

Dirt swirled down the drain as I massaged shampoo into my scalp. Using a loofah, I scrubbed the rest of my body raw and shut the water off only after it had gone cold, my fingers and toes satisfactorily wrinkled.

The house was quiet when I emerged. Tying the towel around my waist, I padded through the house, searching for Amelia. I found her sleeping in a nondescript bedroom, wrapped in a robe, her wet hair soaking the pillow. I shut the door and went to find something to eat.

The kitchen pantry was orderly and enormous, filled with privileged organic-only foods like dried mangos and chia seeds. Pea chips. Coconut clusters. Cassava flour. Brown rice pasta. Something called Paleo Snacks that looked like packaged bowel movements. It was more food than I'd seen in one place besides a grocery store, and even those had become increasingly barren in the months leading up to the Panic.

I opened a box of jalapeño sprouted seed crackers and ate an entire sleeve, drinking boxed coconut water when my mouth became too dry to swallow. Next, I opened a can of beans and ate it cold, only bothering with a spoon when I couldn't reach the bottom half with my tongue.

With a full stomach, exhaustion made itself known. It took everything I had left in me to turn the generator off before finding a den with a comfortable-looking couch and laying down, falling asleep instantly.

I woke in stages the following morning, getting up briefly for a glass of water and listening for Amelia before ditching the towel and pulling a throw blanket over myself. When I couldn't sleep anymore, I found clothes in the dryer that fit and drifted outside. It felt like I was the first kid awake at a slumber party.

The kidney-shaped pool was dappled with morning light, the sun not yet high enough to crest the forest bordering the back lawn. A chlorine smell permeated the air, and with it, a freshness of summer, ripe berries, and growing grass.

I hooked my finger beneath the filter's lid and pulled, revealing dead frogs and leaves. Dumping the mess into the compost, I stopped at the garden on my way back, pushing aside chicken wire.

I gathered what I could, abandoning the filter for the sake of two hands. There was squash, cucumbers, tomatoes, green beans, and peppers. I plucked them all.

I dumped the cache onto the kitchen island, sorting and wiping the dirt and dust with a dish towel. I was ravenous for something alive after eating nothing but processed, packaged shit for a week.

I set the vegetables on the kitchen windowsill then slowly sank to the floor, my knees buckling, strength gone. My cheek against the tile, I made a strangled sound of sadness and disbelief.

I thought of my parents, and everyone I ever cared for, friends, acquaintances, even my despised co-worker, Thom. Did they all die this plague death? Why hadn't I died with them?

If I left to find my parents, it'd be real then. To find nothing but a note or to discover that they had puked their life away in arterial blood and coffee-ground emesis.

Amelia found me on the floor sometime later, my shoulder and neck sore and cramped. She sat next to me and lifted my head into her lap, fingers twirling through my hair, cool and comforting.

"Are you going to leave? Keep heading upstate?" Her expression was one of false calm.

"No," I whispered. "I'm afraid."

"I'll go with you, if you want, to find your family. You came with me to find mine. Your parents could still be alive." Her voice grew shaky. "I don't want us to be the last people left."

I sat upright and drew her close, her chin quivering with sorrow, warm tears soaking through my shirt.

She pulled away, wiping her eyes. "You found the garden?"

"A lot of the plants have wilted in the heat, and some things have already turned, but if we tend to it, it'll feed us," I said, helping her to her feet.

I handed her a cucumber, and she bit into it as one would a pickle. I ate a tomato, its juice running down my chin.

"Come on, let's see if we can find anything on TV that will tell us what's happened," Amelia said. "I turned the generator on again, but we'll have to ration the gas."

Migrating to the living room, a grand space with suede cream couches and a stone fireplace, we tried getting the television to work. It showed only a blue screen punctuated by colored bands. Sometimes a tinny sound would come through, almost like an emergency message.

Amelia fiddled with the settings on the remote before getting frustrated and throwing it at the screen, cracking it. The noise still broadcasted, taunting her in its imperceptible ghostly voice. I turned it off, and we sat in silence, the quiet overwhelming.

With nothing to do, Amelia poured us drinks from the liquor cabinet, warm whiskey from an impressive-looking bottle. "Let's go out back," she suggested. "It's getting stuffy in here without the air conditioning running."

We killed the generator before settling on wicker lounge chairs overlooking the pool. They were the expensive kind, with cushions that were supposed to be brought inside every night. The pool landscaping was professionally tended and featured feathery pampas grass, rose of Sharon shrubs, hostas, and creeping Jenny.

A high fence with a trellis ran the length of the yard on all sides, covered in thick tendrils of grape vines. We could have been anywhere in this oasis of quiet, shielded privacy. A handsome BBQ grill and a gas fireplace stood under a pergola on the far side of the pool.

"What do your parents do for work?" I asked.

"My mother was a Vice President for a conglomerate electric company. My father was a tenured professor at Marist College."

I nodded, sipping my drink.

"And I'm a fashion school dropout, so..." she let the thought linger. "We haven't gotten along too well the past few years. I took a loan from them to start my own clothing label, and if you know anything about the fashion industry, it's just a giant, wobbling bubble constantly on the verge of collapse. The collections are always out of season and plagued by markdowns.

"In my parents' eyes, I've failed twice. Unable to make the grades in college and unable to turn a profit on a fledgling label. I was using Instagram to sell whatever leftover stock I had to try to pay them back."

"I'm sure they'll come around."

She paused and took a sip of her drink. "After what just happened, what we just saw, I don't think I'll ever have to worry about their disappointments or approvals again. I'm worried you're not understanding the true scope of current events."

"How can we know that, though? There's been no way to find out what's going on. I'm betting this virus is regional. Sickness doesn't normally spread this rapidly. We'll be found and flown out to safety."

Amelia threw her head back and laughed, a full-throated roar of mirth. "I know you're saying these things, but you don't feel them here," she said, gently touching a finger to my chest. "If you're not honest with yourself, this will be a lot harder for you."

"I can't yet. We're still here, so others must be too."

She downed the rest of her whiskey. "Want another?" she asked.

We became steadily drunker as the day wound on, Amelia changing into a bathing suit by her third cocktail. Her fourth glass sunk to the bottom of the pool, breaking near the deep end. I found inflatable rafts in the shed, dusty from disuse.

Amelia hauled herself out of the pool, water shimmering off her lean body. Without bothering to dry herself off, she marched into the house, re-emerging with multiple bottles of alcohol balanced on a rolling bar cart. She grabbed a raft, Dewar's clutched in her hand.

I stripped to my boxers, well, they weren't mine, just ones I had discovered in the dryer, and followed her in.

Amelia nodded at me, holding up the Dewar's. I swam to her and rested my arms on the raft, rocking it slightly. A tiny reservoir of water pooled in the small hollow of her throat.

She watched me, her lashes casting dark shadows under her eyes. I unscrewed the cap and swigged, the liquid burning on its way down. I passed it back, and she took a deep drink, an amber drop sliding from the corner of her lips.

I reached out to wipe it away but stopped midway, thinking better of it. Instead, I drank her in as one would a glass of water after a salty meal.

I wanted to tell her I loved her, but I was afraid she'd drown me like a runt piglet. So, I said nothing, and we floated serenely beneath the woozy, numbing haze of hard liquor.

When the bottle was empty, she let it float away, and we watched as it slowly filled and sank to the bottom with a muted clunk. She slipped from the raft and wound her arms behind my neck, eyes unfocused and bleary. My stomach swooped as she pressed her mouth to mine, and I remembered the taste of her, remembered our tongues desperate for one another in a bathroom filled with graffiti, in a place a long way from here.

***

As the days stretched into weeks, that house became our sanctuary. We pulled the solar shades down on the windows to keep the heat out and barricaded all but the sliding back door that led out to the pool.

I combed through every room, from the basement to the attic, looking for survival supplies, piling whatever I found on the grand kitchen island to be sorted through and organized into hiking packs. From bandages and batteries, a camping stove with propane canisters, flashlights and sleeping bags, a tent that looked like it had been purchased twenty years prior, and other things I thought might come in useful.

I lost myself in the library, reading about different types of viruses or how to best apply medical aid for common mishaps and accidents. I organized and cataloged the food in the pantry and siphoned gas from neighborhood cars for our generator.

I felt an overwhelming compulsion to stay busy. I chalked it up to a lifetime of programming by school systems and jobs, of wanting to please.

Amelia was the opposite. She would rise around noon and make her first drink of the day, a whiskey neat, which was just a large, tepid glass of whiskey that she'd grimace through until it started to taste smooth and smoky. She lived in various bathing suits, whichever was cleanest.

Setting her drink on the lip of the pool, she'd frog kick from end to end with her hair piled on top of her head in a knot. I'd bring her a towel and help her out, unsticking wet ringlets from her neck so I could kiss it.

We'd fuck on a patio chaise lounge or if it was already too hot, I'd follow her inside, my fingers untying the knots of her bikini, our feet slipping and squeaking on the dark, polished wood floor until tumbling into one of the innumerable bedrooms, sheets still mussed from the last time we slept together.

Her eyes would often go glassy and distant, and I'd ask her if she wanted to stop, to which she'd decline. I wanted to consume her, to know her, but knowing someone's body is not the same as knowing their heart.

My desire for her was rapacious, and she accepted it onto but not into herself. The grief she felt for Bridget, her parents, for the world was a fatal wound she drowned in sex and liquor, those classic, dependable escapisms.

On what we estimated to be the Fourth of July, we lit sparklers in the twilight and roasted marshmallows over the grill. We thought we'd find comfort in tradition, but it only aided in making our pain more acute. It wasn't until much later, after falling asleep outside on pool floats, that we woke to the distant boom of a single firework, and we whooped with joy.

NOW

The shrubs that bordered the pathway leading to the library were overgrown and verdant. The door was chained shut, standing sentential over our knowledge, our stories. We tramped through the yard, now a fledgling meadow, around back where I knew there was a broken lock.

I pushed open the back door, squinting through the gloom. The cheap carpet was littered with dry dung from wintering mice and other small critters. I listened intently, Amelia peering around me to get a look.

"This place reminds me of the library I used to visit with my mom when I was little. She used to let me borrow whatever I wanted, no matter how old I was. They had a used bookstore where I'd spend my entire allowance."

Amelia stepped around me, picking up a book from the return cart. The spine creaked when she opened it, and she took a deep breath, smiling at some long-ago memory.

"The man who ran the bookstore," she continued, "sat behind an ancient desk and wore a conductor's cap. There were thousands of books, all around him, piled nearly to the ceiling, falling off shelves. It was chaos. You'd pick one of these wayward books and pay him a quarter, and he'd look at you so proud like you just adopted the oldest, most decrepit dog from the pound. I still think he was the most magical person I've ever met, as if he stepped out of a secret door from another world and decided to stay."

"Maybe he's still there," I said, feeling an ache someplace deep that held a love for my own missing mother.

"Maybe he escaped back into his own world."

It didn't appear as if anyone else had been here since the Panic. It always surprised me to think that no one would want to know how to live sustainably, how to feed yourself with other things besides Vienna sausages and spiced ham.

I wandered through the stacks, pulling survival guides and wildlife books. I thumbed through a book called Wild Sugar. Making maple syrup intrigued me, and I was happy to learn that we needed no commercialized ingredients. We would need to find a decent food thermometer and a few spigots before hiking back home.

"Amelia," I called.

"Yeah," she answered from somewhere deep in the library stacks.

I found her in the science fiction section, cradling numerous books under one arm as her finger traveled lightly over the spines of those on the shelves. Her hair was speckled with dust, making it appear gray, an old librarian helping schoolchildren find tomes on talking kangaroos or South America.

"Are you almost ready to go?" I asked.

A smile played around her lips, but she didn't answer me, meandering farther away, pulling books, and flipping to their inside covers. She was absorbed, in love with new stories.

I wandered too, finding a computer station, a row of Dells waiting for someone to restore the electricity. They had the look of a publicly used computer, with crayon scribbles, and dingy fingerprints smudging the keyboard. I pushed the power button and immediately felt foolish. The screen was ominously dark as if it was sucking the light from the few bright places left in the world.

I longed to hit a few keystrokes to read the news, scroll through Twitter. I could log in to LinkedIn, change my profession to Hunter and Gatherer, and congratulate people on their new promotions to Cannibal, Dead, or Hopeless.

A door with a black sign of stick figures stood slightly ajar. I pushed it open, hoping to rummage around for hand soap or a decent roll of toilet paper.

I had never ventured this far into the library, being so skittish on trips here alone.

I pulled my shirt over my nose at the smell, musty and fetid. A corpse lay rotting on the linoleum floor.

I gasped and drew back, feeling like I'd just fallen from a great height. The decomposition was severe, with lank black hair hanging from the skull. This was the second body we had come across in a single morning, a sign something foul was afoot.

I couldn't look away, noticing more sad details. Their hands were shackled around the toilet; one wrist with deep chunks missing as if they had tried to chew their way out. The floor was covered in old blood. A book bag lay close to the body, turned inside out on the hunt for supplies. I squinted at the body's jacket. "Matilda" was written above the breast in a slanting cursive. Her pants were tangled around her feet, filthy with grime.

I shut the door, shaking my head like a beast trying to rid itself of horseflies. A sensation slipped over me, like something weightless and wicked was crawling into my ear, down the canal, and plunging into the dark recesses of my brain.

Matilda.

Feeling disoriented, I lurched back through the library, searching for Amelia. I found her sitting inside the vestibule reading from a ratty novel. Her mouth was slightly parted as her eyes darted back and forth, devouring whatever the haughty teens pictured on the front cover had to say.

"You ready?" I asked.

"There's a smell in here. It's getting to me," she scrunched her nose, folding down the page.

A weight continued to press on my chest, my skin prickling with disquietude. I shivered, wanting to leave the darkness, close the door with a snap, and not return for another few months.

Matilda.

"Got everything you wanted?" I asked.

"I think so," she sighed. "I never learned the Dewey Decimal System."

"Did anyone? What about these books?" I asked, pointing to a sloppy pile near her feet.

"Those," she sniffed, "are drivel. I thought maybe it'd be kitsch to read dystopian fiction but seriously, who gives a shit about how they think the world ends?" She gave the books a savage kick.

We walked out into the sunshine, the backlot of the library looking more desolate than usual, what the field guide would call a waste ground.

I shut the door behind me, closing Matilda's tomb until the next time I'd wander back, seeking information on poultices or snakebite antidotes.

Heath would have buried her. He always buried the bodies he found. He said he felt the world needed to experience compassion again.

"Do you think the names of towns matter anymore?" Amelia asked as we walked, our feet crunching on the detritus scattered in the road. "If there is no more postal service and no one to visit?"

Amelia missed other people, her friends and family, people en masse, and the normality of society. I thought of all the dead hamlets, towns, and cities from here to the west coast and the types of people still living there, desperate people, like us.

"I suppose not," I answered sadly.

"Well, if the world ever goes back to the way it used to be, I'll petition to rename all these places. We'll forget the crimes committed there. I'll burn every record I find."

"You'll be destroying history."

"No one needs to know about this," she said, pointing at a slender bone lying in the dirt, picked clean. "I'd wipe out religion, too. Burn the bibles with the bank files."

"You'd be like Pol Pot," I said.

"That," she countered, "is not an accurate comparison. I think I'd be more like Thoreau."

"Thoreau's mother did his laundry for him while he lived at Walden Pond."

"How like a man," she said, "to benefit from the invisible labor of women and pretend their accomplishments are solely their own."

We marched along the road, our bags heavy with books. "Want to stash these somewhere?" I asked, adjusting my straps.

"I'm fine," she answered. Freckles were springing into being across her nose, the sunshine making her hair gleam with color.

The door to the hardware store hung crazily off its hinges, the glass panes shattered. I pushed it open, and we slipped inside. I shut it quickly and wedged a piece of wood in the frame.

The posters in the window detailing July 4th sales were faded and curling. Dust drifted lazily in the shafts of sunlight that cut through the front room. A strong smell of rot hung in the air, likely from a leak in the roof, creating a dark mold stain across the ceiling. It had that cluttered feel so typical of local hardware stores. Most of the obvious essentials had been looted, the knife case smashed.

We had left this particular hardware store relatively untouched, preferring to get building supplies from sheds and garages closer to the tree house. It was safer that way.

I poked around, sifting through overturned shelves for a spigot. Amelia sat behind the counter on a leather stool, its stuffing spilling out. Her legs were crossed, feet jangling to some unknown melody in her head.

"See if you can find mason jars," she said as an afterthought, a book propped open in front of her.

I collected bits of fishing line, a roll of twine, and a small chisel. I found two dusty cases of mason jars, Amelia grinning when I showed them to her.

I spied a plastic bin filled with spigots on a bottom shelf. They were tiny things, like something that should be attached to a hose, not sunk into a tree. I searched around for buckets, finding none. The book said you could use plastic milk cartons to collect the sap, of which there were plenty to scavenge. The world would never be rid of the plastic blight for a thousand years.

I stacked boxes of nails near the door, wood glue, screws, and everything we would need to finish constructing the tree house. The pile grew and grew, and I wondered how we'd carry all of it. The books were already heavy enough. There's no way a shopping cart would survive the trip home. Most could barely survive a spin around their own stores these days.

The sun began to set outside, our stomachs rumbling by the time I had finished. I packed and repacked our bags, fitting boxes in like puzzle pieces. A few items would have to be left for a second trip. I hid them in the ceiling, Amelia rolling her eyes at my cautiousness.

We shouldered our packs and left, chewing on smoked fish. The hours seemed to have gotten away from us. I didn't relish the thought of not making it to the nursery before dark. It would mean we'd have to camp there for the night to avoid turning an ankle or missing a trail and getting lost.

But maybe I didn't care. It would be a relief to spend a night away from the tree house, smelling everyone's farts and tripping over blankets, clothes, and tools.

"Think we'll make it to the nursery before sunset?" Amelia asked, picking her teeth with a fish bone. "Lily and Heath are probably worried."

"Probably not," I replied.

"Yeah?" she asked. "Where will we sleep?"

"We'll find something comfortable enough to sleep on, cushions or whatever." She was quiet for a beat, thinking.

"That's probably better anyway. My back is killing me."

We walked in silence. I kicked a loose stone like a soccer ball but soon quit, the empty windows of the buildings leering with lidless eyes. Long shadows intersected the road, the air cooling considerably.

A skittering noise followed by a sharp knock cut through the evening air. I whirled around, searching, but all was still.

"A raccoon?" Amelia wondered, clicking off the safety on her air rifle.

Our steps quickened. We kept to the center of the road, out of reach from hands and jaws that could spring from blackened doorways.

The trip back seemed to be taking no time at all, the bridge in sight as we rounded the curve by the sushi restaurant. It was all so familiar that I let out a breath of relief.

We jogged the rest of the way, packs bouncing heavily on our backs. With a determined look on her face, Amelia stepped onto the bridge, arms outstretched as if she was balancing on a tightrope. The nape of her neck was exposed, long and slender.

Clip clop, clip clop, clip clop.

Amelia whirled around at the sound. My heart froze, and I turned slowly, hoping it was just a wandering deer. A goat, patches of black and white across its flank, stopped a few feet away, considering me. Its eyes were yellow, the pupils oddly horizontal, like rectangles. But what made the fish churn nastily in my stomach was the red bandana tied prettily around its neck.

"Grab it!" Amelia screamed.

The goat shook its head, ears flapping merrily, and clip-clopped to the side of the road where it pulled up a mouthful of grass. Heavy pink udders swung with each step. I was in disbelief, thoughts of fresh milk and cheese filling my head.

Just as I reached my hand out tentatively, a shadow emerged from the tree cover on the far side of the bridge. It was a man. He carried no pack and was skeletally thin, skin pulled tight across his cheekbones.

I had been careless, I realized, as my legs went watery and weak. Amelia hadn't seen him yet, focused on the goat, a trap.

But the man was not looking at her. Instead, his eyes wandered to mine, an expression of polite disinterest on his face. He winked in a conspiratorial way as if we had just shared an inside joke. Then he edged onto the bridge.

I broke into a run, pounding onto the bridge, my legs working like pistons. Amelia whipped her head around at the sound, her mouth gaping. She dropped to her hunches and wrapped her arms around a steel post.

"Atticus!" she screamed. "I'll fall!"

I let out a strangled, incomprehensible yell, rolling my ankle on a rogue rock that sent me sprawling through the air. I hit the pavement with a huff that emptied my lungs, my overstuffed pack bursting open, sending nails and spigots and books flying every which way.

I scrambled to my feet, but the man had already reached his hand out. Amelia miraculously took it, gazing upwards with such trust that the breath was emptied from my lungs a second time. The man led her off the bridge, where she let out a shaky laugh.

My side was splitting with a cramp as I flew across the last few meters, running full force, and taking him out at the midsection. We tumbled off the road and down the steep embankment.

NOW

I thrashed towards the stranger on the reedy, swampy riverbank. The muck threatened to suck the boots right off my feet. I threw myself onto him, straddling him, pushing him into the mud. Dirty water pooled in his ears and crept up around his jaw.

"Atticus!" Amelia screamed. "Stop!"

Instead of struggling in the frightened rabbit way I expected, he guffawed with such merriment that I could feel his lungs emptying like bellows beneath me. I reached for the hilt of my knife, and his laughter died into burps of chuckles.

"Who the fuck are you?" I asked, blinking away blood that ran into my eyes. I glanced around, searching for other marauders.

"Roman." His breath had a stench like a swine slaughterhouse. I swallowed a gag, bile rising into my throat. A puckered scar trailed down his face from eye socket to jawbone, like he'd been mauled with a bear claw.

"And what do you want, Roman?" I pushed him deeper into the muck.

"Atticus, you're hurting him!"

A fleeting memory, a déjà vu, surfaced and rolled through me. I fought to keep it, to focus on it, but it was lost.

"I saw a billboard painted on the highway. It said all were welcome here, but here I've been for days, and there's been no one. I thought the worst until I came across the two of you."

"That welcome message has long since expired. Just no one around to paint over it."

"Oh," he smiled, seemingly content to have me sitting atop him. It suddenly felt like an unsettling perversion. I stood, every movement coming with a slurp as I struggled to free myself from the muck.

"We took some fall!" he laughed, rising to his feet. "It looks like you've got a gash on your head."

I touched the tender spot above my brow. My fingers came away bloody.

He was tall, towering even, and wore tight leather pants and a Patagonia shell jacket, an odd juxtaposition. He extended his hand out, a gesture of helpfulness, which I vehemently brushed aside. His smile never wavered.

He shrugged and started climbing the bank, his lanky body tilted nearly vertical on the slope. I followed behind him closely, spitting out dust and pebbles that came bouncing down from under his feet. I tried catching Amelia's eye, but she ignored me, her air rifle slung harmlessly over her shoulder.

She gave him a hand-up when he neared the top, leaving me to scrabble unassisted over the lip of the bank. I scowled, unhappy and suspicious of this rapid succession of events.

He didn't release Amelia's hand but instead shook it so enthusiastically you would have thought he had just sold her a used car. He rounded on me and gripped my hand, his eyes an indeterminate color.

"My name is Roman," he declared. "I haven't had a day as good as this for a while."

I smiled despite myself.

"Pleasure," Amelia said. "I'm Amelia, and the one that just pushed you down a hill is Atticus."

"And this is Peaches," Roman whistled for the goat.

It raised its head in response, bleating from the far side of the bridge, its piebald coat shining in the last of the evening sun. It clip-clopped across the bridge, stepping lightly in good humor.

"How did you come by this animal?" Amelia asked. "I haven't seen livestock in ages."

Saying we hadn't seen any livestock was a misnomer. She wasn't laying blame correctly. Suspected as vessels of the virus, domesticated farm animals were euthanized en masse during the initial wave of infection. What escaped euthanasia was quick-

ly eaten once the supply chains collapsed. Trac-
tor-trailers carrying potato flakes and frozen pizza
sat quietly on highways jammed with the dead. The
coyotes, emboldened from the vacancy of farmer's
rifles, took care of the rest.

Amelia held her hand out, and it snuffled its nose
searching for a treat.

"Peaches and I have been friends for a very long
time."

"Hi, Peaches," she said, scratching the goat's ears
and accepting the unusual answer. "Does it produce
milk?"

Looking at the goat reminded me of what it felt
like to look at extreme wealth before the Panic. New
York skyscraper penthouses with price tags of hundreds of millions of dollars that only Russian oli-
garchs could afford. Tabloid celebrities with cocaine
nose jobs and concave stomachs. Unicorn tech bil-
lionaires with awkward hairlines and backdoor con-
gressional deals.

"She sure does. Do you have a cup?"

Amelia unslung her pack and dug around, finding a collapsible camping cup.

"Hold it under her, here," he guided her hand.
With two quick squeezes, milk filled the bottom half
of the cup.

"Is it fine to drink it like this? Wasn't there always
some argument over pasteurization?" Amelia asked.

"Completely fine," Roman smiled.

She sipped cautiously. "Christ, that's good. Want to try, Att?" She handed me the cup.

Milk.

Milk.

Milk.

How grotesque to harvest mammals' milk for consumption. But the taste of it, sweet and grassy, was an ecstasy. It was nostalgia. It was fattening, most importantly.

"Want to come back to my place for the night?" Roman asked, brushing mud from his jacket. "I'm staying just down the road. I'd like to get to know you, see if we can't join up."

"Out of the question," I said automatically.

"We were on our way home," Amelia cut in, pinching me for my rudeness. "But we lost track of time in town, and well, it's getting dark."

Aghast, I turned to her, "Amelia, we don't know this man."

"I know, but I'm not walking to the nursery in the pitch dark. Especially after what we saw dead on the road this morning."

I ground my teeth in frustration. "Lily and Heath will be worried we didn't make it back. They're waiting for us."

"We weren't going to make it before dark anyway. You said it yourself. This is the first new person we've met in ages. They'll forgive our lateness, especially if Peaches comes along with us."

Milk.

Milk.

Milk.

A caloric lottery jackpot. A savior from winter-induced starvation.

"Come on. You can't hoof it far in wet boots anyway. We might as well stay with Roman tonight and dry out."

Before I could respond, Roman was offering to carry Amelia's pack, shouldering it like it weighed nothing. They set off together, leaving me forgotten.

I ran back to the center of the bridge, gathering up everything that had fallen from my pack. "Amelia!" I called, trotting to catch up, my arms full. She ignored me, her hand touching Roman's shoulder briefly in laughter.

Something writhed in the bubbling vat of my subconsciousness.

Peaches pranced happily alongside us as we broke off from the main street and ambled down a side road, the smell of the river growing stronger the further we walked. From its mad rush beneath the bridge, the water flattened out, growing shallow and murky.

The shadows grew long as the sun set behind the mountains, the air slowly losing its daytime warmth. My boots squelched with water, my jacket dripping wet. I shivered. A few of the houses we passed were old stone relics from a century past. Signs were stuck in the front yards detailing their year of construction and significance. Amelia raised her rifle and shot one, the pellet pinging off harmlessly.

"Do you know the date?" Roman asked. His hands moved with his words, long skeletal fingers with half-moon nails.

"No," Amelia replied, her eyebrow raised at the odd question. "How would we?"

"Do you still celebrate birthdays, then?"

"I haven't thought about it. What's there to celebrate?"

I was growing anxious, clipping, and unclipping the holster that held my knife. I imagined a house of horrors where we'd be chained to the floor for life or absorbed into a perverse traveling circus where we'd be forced to perform as greasepaint clowns.

I couldn't help but sneak glances at Roman. Knowing Heath and Lily, Amelia, and Mabel so well, it was jarring to see new gestures, new clothing, and hear a new voice. Amelia would want to bring him to the tree house, like a pound puppy, one with watery, sad eyes and a thumping tail that once adopted would piss all over your furniture and bite small children.

The home Roman led us to was constructed of solid stone with one of those southern wrap-around porches that movies always portrayed as desirable, where women swooned, and men made weighty decisions. If a generation far into the future restarted the electrical grid and popped a DVD into a dusty player, would they not think the women among them had experienced a type of mental evolution? They would say, goddamn, women were nothing but sexual sidekicks back then!

We trudged to the front steps, the wood squeaking under the weight of our boots. Roman pushed the door open, and we followed him across the threshold.

The front hallway opened into a spacious kitchen, complete with picturesque windows overlooking the river. The house didn't seem to have known violence. Nothing was broken, and there were no bodies decaying anywhere. It's strange, the places where people decided to finally die, whether by their own hand or by sickness. You would think they would like the comfort of their beds, but I've seen people curled in their cars, backyard jungle gyms, floating serenely in the community pool, and even in a chicken coop once.

That was at the beginning. Now, they are just gone. Eaten by time. You'll find scraps of clothes or wedding rings if you really looked, skulls still grinning if they died protected from the elements.

I don't like leaving the mountain. It's not safe in the valleys.

Amelia shrugged off her pack and leaned it against the counter. She massaged her rotator cuff and cracked her neck. "Have you stayed here long?" she asked.

"Few days since coming into town," Roman quipped, drawing up a chair. He stretched his long legs leisurely in front of him.

"Cool," she replied, leaving it at that. People had become strange since the Panic, and it was in Amelia's nature not to knock strange. "Where are you coming from?"

"I came down from the north, through Canada, following spring."

"Can't imagine the winter you must have had up there. It was horrible enough here. Snowed in for months."

She opened each cabinet successively, pulling out cans and checking the dates. I hovered near her like a moon devoted to its planet.

There was nothing that suggested he had been here long, just a simple travel bag lying innocently on the kitchen table. Nothing to indicate that he was lying.

"Can you move, Att?" Amelia asked, pointing to the cabinet behind where I stood. I stepped aside but not nearly far enough, Amelia catching her elbow in the back of my head as she reached. "Can you find a chair," she sighed with impatience.

Roman watched with interest, my cheeks growing hotter the longer I lingered. Setting my pack down, I wandered through the house, one of my boots making an embarrassing squeak that I only now noticed. The situation made me nervous, this man and his goat.

All the rooms were dark, untouched. My heartbeat rapidly, fearing a jump scare from cohorts. Amelia's laugh carried high and true. My fists curled in anger at this interloper; Amelia was suddenly impervious to the wariness of outsiders, her caginess and caution thrown aside.

I unlocked the back door and with some pulling was able to free it from its frame, swollen from rain and disuse. There was a huge BBQ grill on the back porch, made of shiny metallic steel with at least twenty different knobs. I checked the propane tank and lifted the lid, removed a nest from beneath the grate, bits of stuffing and straw all wound together. I should smother him with it.

The yard sloped steeply down to the river, overgrown with dandelions and clover. A towering oak had fallen, leaving deep groove marks on the ground where it had bounced once, twice, before coming to rest. A rabbit bounded across the yard, its coat a deep, sleek brown.

I retreated quickly into the house, finding Amelia and Roman talking animatedly.

"I was paying nearly a thousand dollars in student loans every month," Amelia said, sipping from a snifter, having found a bottle of brandy in one of the cabinets. "Living off of credit cards because the legalese in the promissory notes said that I couldn't put my loan in forbearance no matter my economic situation."

They were speaking like college freshman lovers, waxing poetic about the bubble that destroyed a generation.

"I was in Chile," Roman said, tipping his chair back casually, "When Francisco Tapia burned $500 million in student loan files."

"Really?" Amelia breathed, her eyes sparkling.

"Amelia," I said, my voice sounding hollow.

"Atticus," Amelia said jovially. "Have a brandy!"

"There are rabbits, well, at least one, out back. Get your gun."

THEN

In the end, our reverie at Amelia's parents' house was broken not by us but by outside forces beyond our control or even our comprehension.

It was August, or so we thought, not being very good at keeping track of the days. We were sleeping away the hottest part of the afternoon, tangled and sweaty in the sheets when Amelia shook me awake.

"Wake up. Does the sky look strange to you?"

I rubbed my eyes and looked out the window. Thunderclouds loomed in the distance, menacing and vast. There was a deep green tint to the roiling clouds, something I'd never seen before.

"Do you hear that?" Amelia asked, her hair mussed, and head cocked, listening intently. "It's like a low rumble."

"It's probably just a thunderstorm," I said.

Her arm flew up, her finger pointing to something out the window. "Oh god, that's a funnel!"

"A what?" I asked as she leapt from bed, pulling a loose dress over her head.

"A tornado, a tornado! Get up, we have to go!"

I threw the sheets off, grabbing clothes from the floor as we ran from the room. The rumble had turned into a low roar, like an oncoming train.

Beyond the back fence, down in the valley where town was, a twisting cone of wind was decimating everything in its path. It had no purpose other than random, devastating destruction.

We ran into the basement, pulling the door shut behind us. Without light, we fumbled down the stairs, terror rising in our throats.

"In here," Amelia said, pulling me into a linen closet. She swept folded blankets and dusty pillows from the shelves over the top of us, and we clung to each other, breathing hard.

The house creaked, then groaned, the strength of its mass production quality tested. Glass shattered somewhere above us. Then, as if an earthquake had hit, we were thrown around the closet like we weighed nothing at all.

A terrible cracking sounded, like a gunshot, followed by more crashing. I held onto Amelia, shielding her with my body as best I could. Then, just like that, it was over.

"Are you okay?" I asked, feeling for her face in the darkness.

"I think I am," she said. "I don't think the house is, though."

The closet door was wedged shut, and for a moment, I worried we were trapped. We kicked it in half and climbed out into a ruin. Half the roof had caved in, leaving a yawning hole from the basement to the sky.

The stairs were broken, so I hefted Amelia up to the first floor, and she pulled me up after. The house was almost unrecognizable, rain pitter-pattering down to destroy what was left exposed.

"What in the Kansas cornfield hell happened here?" Amelia exclaimed.

We both burst into laughter, guffawing at the sheer absurdity of it all. Amelia held her stomach, tears of laughter streaming down her face. When the armchair I was leaning on broke beneath me, we laughed in soundless shrieks, trying to catch our breath.

"Whoever wants to stomp us out is going to have to try harder," Amelia cried. "What a pair of fucking cockroaches we are!"

A sudden boom rattled the teeth in our heads, shattering what was left of the windows on the second story and sending glass raining down onto the back patio. Amelia screamed, looking around for the source of the explosion.

We raised our heads in unison, watching through the broken roof as black, traitorous smoke rolled into the sky.

"Where is it coming from?" Amelia yelled.

We stumbled around the side of the house to the front yard. Just down the street, a Spanish colonial-like estate complete with an elaborate peacock statue in the front yard had half its roof blown off. Fire licked at the exposed beams, charred black and splintered.

"Their propane tank blew," I said. The wind was blowing embers into the neighboring house, its siding already melting from the heat.

We surveyed the neighborhood. Not a single house had been left undamaged, most looked like a wrecking ball had been taken to them.

The house crackled ominously, and I watched the fire with morbid curiosity. It was as if the other houses watched with me, concerned and distressed, abandoned by those who loved them to a fate of flame and disaster.

A chill crept through me with the sudden realization that we had been living in a bubble of relative safety here. My eyes roved the rest of the street, quickly picking up odd things, spookiness in dark windows, and silent cars parked in driveways. How many people had fled? How many people were dead? I retreated, walking backward until I felt safe enough to turn and flee.

With sputtering candles, we pulled gear from the wreckage, searching for anything that could keep us alive. Everything I had previously collected had been flung and scattered by the tornado.

"Should we make the trip to your parents' house or regroup somewhere local?" Amelia asked. "I'm ready to find out, I think, what happened to them."

Amelia discovered an air rifle in what was probably once a closet. Loading pellets into the chamber, she pumped the onboard lever and raised it to her eye, shattering a vase in a burst of porcelain dust.

"My grandfather gave it to me when I was a kid," she said when I asked her about it. "I loved old western movies and used to pretend I was Barbara Stanwyck from The Furies. My mother was horrified, of course. She wanted me to play tennis, not set up a shooting range in the backyard."

"It'll come in useful," I said.

"For what?" she asked.

"For protection."

She gave me a curious look. "You're talking about murder. This is only an air rifle. Unless the bullet is well placed, like in an eye, it's not doing much besides giving them a nasty wound."

"Maybe that's all we need, though."

She leaned the gun against the wall and drifted off, finding an unbroken vodka bottle in the den. She became steadily drunker until finally passing out onto a dusty, stiff-looking chair in a sitting room where we piled the gear.

Throughout the night, ash rained upon our heads, the house, and the pool. It seemed that the town was on fire, the suburbs, even a distant black smoke plume that hinted New York City might be aflame.

In the garage, I found two bicycles and bungee corded to them an ancient tent that smelled of mildew, a battery-powered lantern, sleeping bags, a first aid kit, the air rifle, a tarp, a collapsible pot, a lighter, and two hiking packs filled with vegetables from the garden and packaged food from the pantry.

We left the following morning. Amelia sat in the long grass of the front yard, drinking vodka from the bottle, studying the wreckage of her childhood home.

I rolled a bike out for her, patting the seat hopefully. "Ready?" I asked.

"Can't we drive?"

"I don't think we'd get very far. There were a lot of stalled vehicles when we came through town, remember?"

"Hardly," she said.

We left with as little fanfare as we arrived, deserting one haven for the promise of another, but only after sucking up every available resource, like locusts.

I didn't have a map, so I tried to make sense of Amelia's slurred directions. We didn't make it far that day, maybe eight miles, before she tumbled down an embankment, scraping the skin off her arm. I washed the wound out in a rushing stream and dressed it, Amelia clutching me drunkenly.

I set the tent up right there, exhausted. Rain came, pounding on the thin fabric, one corner filling with water. Amelia didn't care, falling asleep right on the nylon floor. I sat awake, terrified that we were too close to the road. But I drifted, as one often does in times of extreme danger.

I dreamt that we followed the curving road into Wurtsboro, my hometown, bike tires bumping along on stray branches and rocks. A wooden cross hung on a telephone pole going around a hairpin turn, RIP Peter, it said, a pixelated picture in a plastic sleeve tacked beneath it.

Reaching the long straightaway of Main Street, we slowed, taking in the empty horse farm, flooded as always but without any horses whickering from a dry spot. The Harley Davidson shop had been looted, its large front window smashed. A lone hog lay on its side in the showroom, chrome glittering.

The post office sat back from the road, a squat structure with Roman columns. The swamp surrounding the parking lot was slowly retaking the property, complete with standing, stagnant water and scrub grass poking up from the crumbling blacktop. It looked as if the town had been abandoned for years, not just a couple of months.

We dismounted, leaning our bikes against the building. Near the front door, a large cork board was suspended under the eaves, hundreds of papers rustling in the breeze.

Heartbreaking messages were scrawled across them all. I searched for my mother's handwriting, large loopy letters, or my father's neat, blockish text.

"There are layers of these," Amelia said, pulling bits of paper from the board. She was even more beautiful in my dream, her eyes clear and sober, her hair washed.

"Don't lose those," I told her.

"Why?" she asked.

"There's nobody left to read them."

"But if others survived, like us, and they come here and don't see their message because you let it blow away, how will they find anyone?"

Her jaw jutted, but she secured them.

I read until my eyes watered, and my head was filled with screams. There was no note from my parents. I sat down, resting my pounding head against a column.

"No luck?" Amelia asked.

I slumped further. Dear Mr. and Mrs. Pestilence, this is your son, Atticus, and I would like to die.

She took a lighter from her pocket, flicked it, and ran the flame along the bottom of the board. The weathered papers caught fire immediately.

"You're burning somebody's last hope, Amelia."

"I don't care," she said. "If there's nothing for you, there should be nothing for anyone."

Tears leaked from my eyes as she took my hand and helped me up. "Let's check your home. They may be there."

"They're not," I said, thinking of what we would see if we were to go, cycling down the dirt road only to find an empty house at the end.

I woke up crying, tears slipping down the sides of my face. Amelia rustled beside me. "Don't worry," she whispered, draping an arm across my chest. "We don't have to go."

"Are we dreaming the same dream, Amelia?" I asked her.

"I can't tell the difference."

Thunder boomed, rolling through the valley with such violence I cowered. Afraid the pegged tent couldn't withstand the gales that sucked at the fabric like a man asphyxiating in a plastic bag, I couldn't sleep, fearing that the stream would run over its banks and drown us as we somersaulted through its churning chaos.

The foot of the sleeping bag was heavy with rainwater, my toes catching a chill that would not abate. I was worried for Amelia, that her veins were too dilated from alcohol to retain substantial body heat. I pulled a sweater from my pack, careful to keep quiet as I draped it across her shoulders. She shifted at my touch, her breath smelling of liquor.

The dream of Wurtsboro still haunted me, lingering on the periphery of memory; the desperate

notes at the post office, Amelia burning them, so
they curled and floated away as ash. It would not let
me close my eyes, the vividness returning each time
I tried, like a projector running against the insides
of my eyelids.

The night was like none I had experienced before, time stretching like taffy. I counted heartbeats,
watching as the blackness outside gave way to gray,
the sun hidden behind the last vestiges of storm
clouds. A twig snapped outside the tent that sent me
reeling into a panic. Kicking the sopping sleeping
bag off, I scrambled into a crouch, gripping the air
rifle without the faintest clue how to use it.

I reached out to wake Amelia but thought better
of it. She slept with her knees drawn up and hands
curled under her chin like an overcooked fetus.
Her skin was sallow, lips parted and cracked from
dehydration.

Gently shifting her feet from a shallow puddle, I
pulled the sleeping bag over her, thinking that even
though it was wet, it was still better than nothing.
Pausing at the tent's entrance, my fingers grasping
the zipper, I listened, but there was only bird song
and Amelia's deep breathing.

I opened the flap, half expecting to be greeted
by either the muzzle of a coyote or the muzzle of a
gun. But the clearing was empty of intruders, bees
buzzing happily around honeysuckle and Monarda
that were still dripping from the rain. Beyond a line

of trees that grew from the muddy stream bank, the water rushed by in a churning fury.

In the chaos of our arrival here, I had thrown the tarp over our bikes, thinking them safe from rain and out of sight from other possible travelers or malicious survivors. In the morning light, I realized how stupid I had been. The tarp was bright blue, a *"Hello, we're fucking here!"* sign against the green of the forest. Also, not thinking to tie it down, it had blown off into the stream, getting snagged on a drowned pine some twenty yards away.

The bags were soggy, and one had been ripped open by a critter looking for food. Plastic wrap and packaging littered the ground, and I guessed we lost almost half of what we had for the trip ahead of us. I didn't know the state of grocery stores, having avoided them until now. I chewed my nails to the quick, picking up garbage while worrying incessantly.

I noted how close we were to the road, easily making out the shiny chrome of stalled and abandoned cars. After that, paranoia eclipsed everything, and I couldn't turn my back on them, believing to catch movement from within.

I laid our belongings across various flat rocks, hoping the sun would eventually dry them out. Dreading having to wade into the stream, I procrastinated instead, watching the tent flap, waiting for Amelia to emerge.

I was cold, my back aching from sleeping all night on the ground. I'd hated camping growing up. Of course, the night before was always fun, roasting treats over an open fire, beer for days, and good laughs. You'd stumble into your cozy sleeping bag, confident the night would continue on its arc of awesomeness. But you'd awake either to the whine of mosquitoes in your ear or the yipping of coyotes. There'd be a rock in your spine and dew seeping through the sides of the tent, rendering your cozy bed a clammy nightmare.

Despite those things, I couldn't be sure I'd ever see those friends or family again. Not my roommate, who I'd known since college, who died in a utility sink, hemorrhaging blood and delirious with fever. Maybe not my parents, whom I didn't think I had the courage to find.

With my thoughts racing, I stripped my clothes, wading into the stream to get the tarp. The water was icy, the hidden rocks slippery and jagged. My lower half was numb with cold, thighs besieged in the strong current, before I was able to untangle the tarp from the tree and drag it back to the bank.

Amelia stood waiting for me, her arms crossed over a dirty t-shirt. "How does it feel?" she gestured to the stream.

"Too cold for swimming. It must be running from the mountains."

Her eyes flicked briefly to our surroundings as if trying to verify my geological claims. "Well, I stink, and my arm is all scraped up from falling off that damn bike yesterday."

I was surprised she remembered what happened as drunk as she was. She used my shoulder for balance on her way down to the water, wincing on bare feet. Wading in, she gasped at the frigid temperature. First kneeling, then rolling onto her back, the water rushed around her neck, hand holding onto an exposed root to keep from drifting downstream. I smiled at her delight.

"Is there any soap?"

I searched through the packs, finding a travel-sized shampoo. I splashed out into the water to hand it to her before retreating to the shore so I could finish repacking. After storing the tent and slipping those obnoxious poles into their bag, I gathered the clothes I had laid out, repacking the bikes as best I could. The sleeping bags were hopelessly wet, so I squeezed as much excess water out as possible and rolled them tightly, figuring we could deal with it later tonight.

Amelia floated with her eyes closed, taking deep breaths that expanded her chest above the rushing water. She was a river nymph, emerging from the depths of crystalline water to dance out of reach of her lovers, drowning them in the pebbly bottom of her world. My adoration was unintentional but ferocious, unending in its appetite. We could never be apart.

I handed Amelia a towel when she emerged shivering, lips blue and knees knocking.

"What if we headed south instead?" I asked aloud, giving the thought life. "Seems like that's where everyone was going, highways jammed with cars all going in one direction."

We sat in silence, reflecting on the trip here and what it had taken.

"No," she argued. "This emptiness here, it won't be like that down there. I bet the fever is still plowing through the population. I'd feel safer going north to your parents' house."

"It'll be fall soon."

"It won't take us but a few days of riding to get there. Come on, we can take I-84. It can't be more than fifty miles away."

I sighed in resignation and nodded my head. "How're you feeling? Want to camp out here another night?"

"I'm fine," she said, but the wound on her arm had opened again, blood mixing with water that trickled pink. She let me bandage the scrape, and I squirted extra antiseptic cream onto it, fearing blood poisoning if it were to get infected. The one hospital we had passed on our flight from the city had notified us of its location from a half-mile off, the stench of thousands of bodies unmistakable. There'd be no more doctor's visits, perhaps in a lifetime.

Amelia asked to see the map, and she traced her finger over our route. It would take us over the Mid-Hudson Bridge, a bridge more than likely packed with idle cars abandoned to rust beneath the clouds.

"Is there another way?" I asked.

"There's a walkway that runs parallel to the bridge for pedestrians. My mother took me once when I was a kid, and it was insufferable. She kept giving me roundabout advice on boys and periods, warning me about holding Bridget's hand in school. I was eleven, and already I couldn't stand the sight of her, wearing a suit with kitten heels that clicked on the pavement the entire time we walked. All the other mothers wore running sneakers and spandex. She became incensed when I asked if her mother had ever encouraged her to be a human and not a robot, oblivious to the obvious workings of the world."

I listened with genuine interest, eager to hear more about her life pre-Panic. "You two never got along then?"

"Never." She opened her mouth to say more but caught my eye and decided it wasn't such a good idea because she snapped it back closed again, frowning at me. "We should go," she finally said.

The sun arched warm over our backs as we rode in search of the bridge crossing, the miles running beneath our wheels. From ghost town suburbs, we traveled towards the heart of Poughkeepsie, the level of devastation increasing steadily. It was like in an old western film, except there was no sheriff, no vigilantes, and no villains either. The quiet of it all pressed into our eardrums, just the trill of birdsong and rustle of leaves in the brisk late summer breeze.

It made sense to stick to the highways from a logistical standpoint, but the bodies—bodies stinking, rotted, bloated in traffic jams that went on for miles. When the back roads and disused routes carried us too far from our destination, we were forced to take the Dutchess Turnpike, a cesspool of horror and catastrophe.

"Those apocalypse movies where everyone dies?" Amelia asked as we bumped along the grassy median, "They got me ready for the real thing. From a general standpoint, I mean. I'm almost disappointed it's not something beyond our imaginations, just the same shit they've been feeding us for decades." She clicked her bike into a lower gear, packs bouncing from where they were held onto the back rack with bungee cords.

"It's a tragedy on an incredible scale," I said, glancing into a car where a toddler was still strapped into a car seat, dead from internal bleeding, eyes eaten by carrion with necks long enough to reach through the window. I didn't know how to put my feelings into words, so I opted for the concerned newscaster's broadcasting opinion, something sweeping and distant. I could scream instead, but I was afraid it would continue on and on unabated.

"Of course. That's not my point. I'm saying, in the general sense, that it looks a lot like what I expected, what I've seen and read countless times. Like now, riding down a gridlocked highway, it's so cliché."

"It won't stay like this," I reassured her.

"Who's going to fix it?" her voice trembled, and she noticeably slowed, falling behind slightly, so we were no longer riding together side by side. "There's a grocery store up here. We should stop."

The sliding glass doors to the store were locked, but their glass had been shattered. A large potted plant lay on its side nearby, guilty of its crime.

I wanted nothing more than to be back at Amelia's house, dozing in the living room, a cool breeze lightly blowing the curtain. But I was here, patiently waiting for my eyes to adjust to the darkness of the store.

It struck me as an X-Files episode, one where the detectives investigate the disappearance of an entire population. They'd solve it by discovering a portal within a child's bedroom, flip a switch, and out everyone would walk. They'd be healthy and alive, complaining about missed credit card payments and vacation time squandered.

"Are you going inside or not?" Amelia called from the parking lot, feet on the ground with the bike balanced between her legs.

I held up the grocery list she had scribbled, trying to decipher what she wanted. Wine was the very first item on the list followed by peanut butter, trail mix, powdered milk, water, and granola. Chex Mix had been added as an afterthought.

I stepped through the doors, listening intently for danger before it could materialize in lethal form before me. The place appeared ransacked, but nothing worse than grocery stores usually look before snowstorms or hurricanes, except for the older man curled on the bench under a front window.

His hair was cropped close to his scalp, which was a horrid pale color shot through with disease and rot. A puddle had formed beneath him, one that had dried to a semi-sticky flake. He didn't stir. I was glad he had died facing away, not wanting to see the expression that had perished upon his face.

I shuffled further inside, noting when my feet left the last bit of sunshine splashed onto the floor. Directly before me was the produce section. Tomatoes and squash were deflated and moldy, potatoes sprouting buds that curled out of their bin. Thousands upon thousands of fruit flies scrambled over everything, delighting in the feast. I swallowed, try-ing not to gag.

I grabbed a few plastic bags and turned down the closest aisle, finding near-empty shelves of what had been over-the-counter medicine. What was left was nearly pointless, boxes of Claritin and tiger balm, which I took anyway. No aspirin or antiseptic, noth-ing for nausea or fever.

Down the next aisle, I gathered matzo meal and sardines. A stench that soon became overpowering drove me back from the end of the aisle, guessing the meat or deli section to be the culprit. Beyond that, it became too dark to see, and I started imagin-ing things moving, shadows that crept on silent feet.

I retreated, raiding the checkout treats on the way out. Peanut butter had been the only thing I found that was scribbled on the list.

"What the fuck is all this?" Amelia asked, digging through the groceries.

"That's all that was left," I said defensively.

Her lips were thin lines of disappointment as I spread the food between both bikes, balancing the weight as best I could. She kept glancing at the store as if wanting to go in herself and verify my findings. I was being second-guessed, as always.

"I'll wait if you want to check it out," I suggest-ed. Sweat trickled down my neck, the blacktop of the parking lot shimmering in the heat of the after-noon. She shook her head.

As we rode on, Amelia hummed, sometimes singing quietly under her breath, sometimes singing aloud with such heart I forgot for long moments about our predicament.

Always the same song, it came from deep within her chest, and it was powerful, and it was sorrowful, and it moved us past what was here, what was now. I asked,

"Who sings that?"

And she hummed and hummed and finally said, "Well, it's Lou Reed."

"Lou Reed died."

"Yes, he did, and so did the whole lot of them."

And I loved her truly.

NOW

W e ate on the back porch, night settling in. Mosquitoes whined in our ears, the swampy edges of the river a breeding ground for bugs. The rabbit meat was greasy and gamey. The spices Amelia had added from the pantry made me think of fine restaurants or home-cooked meals.

As we ate, I watched Roman intently, undecided in my opinion of him. He was courteous, but his insouciance about the Panic, about his history, was disquieting.

After multiple bug bites, we settled in the living room, the screen door shut against pests. Roman excused himself to hunt for candles. Peaches mounted the back steps, pawing to come inside.

"Look, she's like a dog!" Amelia slid open the back door for her. Peaches hopped onto a leather couch and settled comfortably. Roman hadn't offered us any more milk, which was notable.

I forced a grin.

Roman returned, propane lantern hissing in his grip. He set it on the coffee table and held his hand out to Amelia, holding a secret.

"What is it?" she asked, cheekbones curving into a smile.

With a flourish, he uncurled his fingers. A dozen tiny blue pills sat in his palm, the delicate cerulean of robin's eggs.

My stomach dropped, overcome by a feeling similar to when you realize your child has been far too quiet and the gate to the pool is open, when you have let danger slip by unaware.

A fleeting vision came to me of Roman holed up in various pharmacies, only moving once the pill supply had been depleted. Was that how he got his scar? A territorial knife fight squabble over an ever-dwindling supply?

Amelia reached out her freckled fingers and took a pill from Roman, smiling mischievously.

"I don't think you should take that," I said, but she ignored me, throwing it back without water. Roman held his hand out to me, but I shook my head, holding up my glass of half-finished brandy.

"So," Roman began after swallowing his pill, "you've survived this nightmare. How? What's your story?" He sat with Peaches, stroking her coarse fur.

What happened, Amelia? What did we do? The memories have evaporated to sludge, leaving nothing more than a dark spot on the basement carpet.

Roman looked at each of us expectantly, waiting.

"I remember every moment and have lived it a thousand times," Amelia finally answered, holding her hand out for another pill, which Roman quickly obliged. She crushed it with the flat edge of her knife. She bent down, hair fanning out across the coffee table, and snorted, rubbing her nose on the way up.

"Memory is a wound worth lancing," he said.

"Bridget," she began, eyes watering from buried grief. "I'd known her since elementary school. We were inseparable from the start. After high school, we moved to the city together, went to school together, and lived together. Our friendship had held up through failure, shit-head boyfriends, through rages and low times.

"It was by chance that we ended up that last night in the same bar as Atticus. I caught him stealing beer from behind the bar. I thought he'd be a fun fuck."

She glanced at me as if I would corroborate her story. I sat in stony silence, uneasy about where this was headed.

"The city ordered a sudden stay-in-place order, and it set off a chain of events that even now, I really don't understand. It was as if the virus had stealthily bubbled up beneath our feet like magma, and one wrong step had sent us straight through the earth's crust into a fucking hellscape below.

"We hid in a nearby bakery and spent the days eating sweet cakes and stale doughnuts. Atticus's roommate was the first to get sick."

She perched on the lip of the fireplace, ashing a cigarette into the cold grate. Smoke curled around her nose. We had never spoken of what happened, not even to each other. She was telling this stranger about the most personal, pivotal moments of our lives.

"We tried quarantining him, stowing him in the bathroom, but it was too late. Bridget was sick by then. I'll never forget how hot she burned with a fever. Touching her was like touching an open flame."

Roman listened with gleaming eyes, running his tongue over his teeth, hungry for more.

"Atticus's roommate, I can't even remember his name anymore, his gums started to bleed, and then his eyes. He died in gushes of blood through every orifice."

"Amelia, stop," I warned.

She glared at me and continued, snuffing at the post drip. "When the sun went down on the third or fourth day, a riot moved through the city. We could hear them coming, the wailing of people and car alarms, and gunfire getting closer until it was on top of the bakery. We were hiding in the kitchen when they came through the glass windows, I guess looking for food or just looking to destroy."

"We escaped through the back door into a side alley and out onto Seventh Avenue. It was like a half-war zone. Cops in riot gear were trying to combat the crowd, but the fucking bodega on the corner was open! I saw someone buying an e-cartridge, and another had armfuls of gallon milk jugs. The owners must have had a generator and were trying to make quick cash.

"We ran, supporting Bridget between us. She already had blood pooling in her ears and was delirious. I felt delirious. We saw people dead and dying everywhere, and the stench was unbelievable. And I thought, how could this be true? How can so many people die so fast? But so it was."

White froth was gathering at the corners of her lips. "I had this idea, fucking brilliant idea to walk the train tracks of the Metro-North out of the city. We didn't dare try the bridges. Who knew what fiefdom lord had claimed them by this point? I had my money on Chris Christie, though. Looked like a land barren, didn't he?

"You could catch the tracks in two places, either Grand Central or Harlem. Under Grand Central, there's a labyrinth of tunnels, and we couldn't hope to figure out the right way to go. Anyway, who'd want to be down in that darkness? I think I'd go insane. The Harlem station is above ground, but..." she trailed off, rubbing her nose spastically.

"It's high," I finished.

"Yes, high...Bridget fell." She stubbed out the cigarette angrily, immediately lighting a new one. "But she was so sick by then, throwing up blood everywhere. The train track had a broken sleeper, and I stumbled. I let go of Bridget as I fell to save myself, and the momentum sent her over the side. She landed on a parked car fifty feet below."

"Enough," I whispered, voice catching, "fucking enough already."

"Why can't I talk about it? Because you didn't catch her either? Imagine how I feel."

"Because it hurts."

She waved me off, sharing a conspicuous glance with Roman. "It's good to talk about these things. That tree house up there is like a strait-laced catholic church, all repentant and guilt-ridden."

She seemed to come back to herself, perhaps realizing that she had mentioned our tree house, our place of secret safety, to a stranger. We'd have to bring him now just to stop him from following at a distance, knowing what to look for.

Roman leaned back, sensing the end to her story, propping his feet on the coffee table. He drank straight from the near-empty brandy bottle, swirling the dregs at the bottom before finishing what was left. "My sincere condolences on your loss. It's a heavy burden to carry the death of a loved one."

Amelia nodded.

"But imagine the chances," Roman continued, "of you and Atticus finding each other that night, both immune to the virus."

"I think immunity was probably more widespread than it seemed," Amelia said. "After that first Panic and this last winter, I can't imagine how many have died, and not even from the virus. No medicinal supplies for diabetes and heart disease. No NICUs."

"There's not much left out there. Peaches and I have been traveling for a long time now," Roman said. "We've come across small enclaves of people, but most are sickly from famine and disease."

Amelia drew on her cigarette, but was quiet, turning over this news of the outside world. Any hope that had lingered evaporated. I could feel it sizzling off my body, sloughing a new skin of loss.

I picked at the couch's stitching, thread unraveling under my fingernail. My chest was heavy from resignation. How we ended up here, with this stranger was beyond my understanding. It had unfolded guilefully, a goat and a cheerful man with a medicine cabinet up his sleeve.

It was a party, one with no music, no friends, and nowhere to go. The night was getting tired, a time when the most fucked up stories surfaced, tears cried, and heart-to-hearts ran rampant. My head began to ache.

Amelia blew out her cheeks, purple circles sunk deep under her eyes. "I'm beat." Pinching the cherry of her cigarette between two fingers, she flicked the butt into the gaping blackness of the fireplace.

"There are bedrooms upstairs," Roman said, standing. "Or, if you want to take off, I can look for flashlights."

"I can't imagine walking that road in the dark. We came across a body on our way in, and it looked awful."

"Was it a violent death? You better stay the night, then." His expression showed neither surprise nor guilt.

Unfolding herself from the fireplace ledge, Amelia stretched, yawning widely. "Thanks. See you tomorrow." Her smile appeared, radiant as the sun.

Roman returned her smile and then nodded at me. He laid down near Peaches and dragged a blanket over himself.

I left with Amelia, knocking shins on unfamiliar furniture as we fumbled our way blindly through the house with just the propane lantern to light the way. Her boots clunked up the mahogany stairs, hips swaying as she climbed. The family portraits that hung on the wall watched her closely, their eyes following the lovely creature that dared step past their threshold.

She pushed open the door at the top of the stairs, disappearing into the master bedroom. I followed behind her, letting my eyes adjust to the dimness before securing the lock behind me.

There was a gaping hole in the ceiling, branches and bracken littering the floor where a tree must have come crashing through the roof. The beams were the only thing left, the sky visible. I tested the floor, finding the wood spongy.

Amelia walked to the window and with a great rip, pulled the curtains down, rod and all falling to the floor. It was pitch black outside except for the viscous river, ghostly in the crescent moonlight.

She crawled onto the great bed and collapsed face down in the feather blanket. Even living in the wild for nearly a year, her lustrous beauty had not dulled.

"I feel fucked up," she said, rolling over. Her pupils were hugely dilated, like a solar eclipse had moved in over her eyes, just a slight ring of color to show that she was no monster.

I sat beside her, the bed emitting a puff of mildewed air. She stood, unsteady on her feet, and walked to the closet. It was filled with shoes of all kinds, clothes waiting patiently on hangers, and silk pajamas folded delicately on shelves.

Sitting down so quickly I thought she might have fallen, she pulled off her hiking boots, sending them banging across the floor. Dragging herself up by the door frame, she wiggled out of her clothes, letting them fall in a heap as she stepped over them and into the closet, her spine like the rippled back of a sea monster.

She chose a lace nightgown, pulling it over her head. Faint shadows of her nipples could be seen through the fabric.

"Sometimes I forget that light switches don't work," she mumbled, trying on a fur coat. She dipped her hands into the pockets, pulling out crumpled tissues. Drawing the coat around her shoulders, she wobbled across the room, cursing when she stubbed her toe, and climbed in next to me.

I lifted her hair from her neck, breathing in and pulling her close. She shivered, staring silently at the night sky through the hole in the roof.

"The stars seem so much brighter than they used to be," she said quietly.

"There's no light pollution anymore. All those big cities are dark now."

She turned towards me, her nose brushing mine. Her long lashes swept almost to her eyebrows, and her eyes reflected the universe.

"I love you. Did you know?" I asked.

She was quiet for so long that I thought she didn't hear. "Is it love when there is no one else to love? The last of a mighty race of consumers left to fuck in the dirt and have your offspring die from sickness or wickedness?"

I felt myself wanting to promise her things, wanting instinctually to spread her legs and be consumed by a love I knew would never materialize. There had been hope, I remembered, fleeting instances, but perhaps I had always imagined and magnified them.

"I don't want this. Every day I'm ashamed," she said, apathetic and conditioned to hurt.

I rolled onto my back and let the little pieces of my shattered heart float up and out of the roof.

"You haunt me, Atticus."

NOW

The following morning, I woke in an empty bed with a hangover that was both searing and immediate. A lidless sun beat down upon my face from the gaping hole in the roof above, shedding light on the decaying room with its moldering silk wallpaper and wood floor disfigured by dampness.

Flashbulb memories of last night exploded behind my eyes, and with those, the titanic dredging of what Amelia's story had brought to the surface. Yanking back the bandage, she had found a festering wound flourishing in the delicate, complex folds of gray matter, ready to be called upon at our lowest. In an act of extreme urgency, I rolled to the side of the bed and puked.

There's something about certain sounds that can stay with you, burrow deep into your eardrum like an echoing phantom. For me, that sound is the grotesque whoomph of Bridget's body hitting an immovable object from a great height. The fatalistic noises of punctured organs, breaking bones, and the last utterances of her vocal folds.

There are moments that define us, at least that's what has always been said. I think that was my moment to be stronger, quicker, and braver. We had been running for our lives on the elevated train track, supporting Bridget between us, coughing through drifts of smoke and fearing the strike of stray bullets from police-issued carbines.

Bridget had been dying before she died. Her skin was slack from the hemorrhagic virus, bleeding from every orifice. She'd become a melting sack of slick tissue, a yolk held together by a fragile, degrading membrane.

I can still recall the muscle memory of her skin sliding from my hands as she fell, and if I'm being honest with myself, the feeling of letting her go and releasing her to her death.

I think Amelia knows, and that's why our love was birthed blue and still. Such potential and promise strangled by the umbilical cord of circumstance. I was the mother still clutching the dead infant, Amelia the cold doctor, exasperated with the show of illogical emotion.

With the clinical clarity of shame, I also remembered professing my love last night and being met with a resounding rebuttal that effectively fired a silver bullet into whatever delusional fantasy had been rampaging in my head about us as a couple.

Did this truth come from bubbling recollections told to a junkie stranger? Reliving those first chaotic moments must have been the push Amelia finally needed to tell me and my desperate, humiliating love to fuck off for good. The lucidity of those last cowardly, brutal moments with Bridget needed to become sharp again so she could remember who I truly was in my basest of forms.

Heaving until there was nothing left, I wiped my mouth and sat up. There was another explanation, one I could feel myself wanting to cling to because it fed on anger instead of shame. And it was: there was someone new, someone with whom she could be anyone, and cast off our shared history together with one final kick of the life raft. Goodbye, death and bleak survival. Hello, cozy tree house living with a shiny new man and a prized goat. Roman was the viable option, and it was without question he who had set this chain of events into motion.

Unrequited love notwithstanding, swiftly making its way up the list of urgent action items was getting the hell over to the nursery before Heath and Lily formed an ad hoc search party and got themselves killed by whoever had left that body in the road.

I walked downstairs, surveying the mess left over from the party. The door to the liquor cabinet was open, bottles uncorked and haphazardly replaced. Powder from crushed pills was spread over the coffee table amongst half-empty booze glasses and cigarette ashes, more than I remembered from last night.

Roman and Amelia sat outside on the back porch, smoke curling around their fingers from rolled cigarettes. I slid the back door open and joined them, choosing a stiff wooden chair.

Amelia's legs were tucked beneath her on a lounge chair, hair wrapped into a bun, and sweat beading on her upper lip. Her gaze was inculpable, a blameless babe on the tit.

"Am I joining at the end of an old party or the start of a new one?" I asked.

"What's the difference?" Amelia asked. She pulled on her cigarette, letting the smoke blow out of her nose like an industrial chimney.

"The difference is hiking out of here now to meet Heath and Lily. They're probably frantic because we didn't show up at our meeting place last night."

"I haven't been the one sleeping all day." Amelia snapped. Almost as an afterthought, she added, "Roman is coming with us."

What would she do if I said no?

"He says there are no more people left out there. We're the first he has seen in ages."

"The fact that he's here proves there are other people. He's a person," I said.

Amelia slid the ashtray along the arm of the lounge chair until it fell to the deck, cracking down the middle. She leaned forward to pick up the pieces, unfolding her legs. She still wore the diaphanous nightgown, now splotched with liquor stains. Either they had fucked, or she was high enough not to care that her breasts were visible through the fabric.

Roman sat quietly through this exchange, overly alert like a jealous boyfriend. My skin prickled.

"Can I talk to you in private?" I asked Amelia.

"No."

"Fine. I'll be waiting out front for you. You'll be quick if you want to make it to the nursery before dark."

I left, finding my pack and slamming the front door behind me. I sat on the front porch, my hands shaking from dehydration and confrontation.

They emerged a short while later, Roman carrying Amelia's pack as well as his own. She had put on a pair of leggings under the gown and wore a sweatshirt over it. The lace hem trailed in the dirt, the goat trailing behind us.

We walked for nearly an hour, leaving the town's outer limits. Sweat trickled down my back, my face sunburnt. Amelia became steadily grumpier, the journey of days finally crashing down upon her willpower. Her freckles multiplied in the sun, making her face a lovely celestial sky of tawny pinpricks.

Had we been home, we would have enjoyed these first days of warmth by gathering mushrooms and new shoots, the humidity less of a drag under the cool mountain shade.

Roman had long ago picked up the goat, slinging Peaches over his shoulders and grasping her front and back legs in his hands. She seemed content, her head bobbing with every step. She'd nibble occasionally on his shirt, tearing a hole on the neckline.

We reached the last crossroads as the sun was setting, kicking up a chill breeze that set us shivering. I rummaged through my pack, finding a small whistle. It used to hang from a keychain, along with keys to an apartment, keys to a life wholly different from this one. I blew into it, playing four shrill notes. Heath, hear me.

Roman was solemn, his moment of judgment coming close. He had lost the jubilation he'd initially had when we first met him on the bridge. It seemed as if his laughter was harder to extract the next time around, finite, like a tube of toothpaste.

Turning from the road that would take us home, we veered left, walking for maybe another quarter mile before finding the nursery. The low building was set back from the road, abandoned and forlorn. The owners seemed to have made a hasty retreat, messily stacking plant pots behind a metal grate pulled over the front entrance. A gnome figurine leaned drunkenly to the side, doffing his hat to no one in particular.

Sitting out front were Heath and Lily, shielding their eyes from the setting sun. "Amelia!" Lily called. The relief in her voice was apparent even from a distance. She rose and ran down the driveway, strides stuttering slightly as her eyes lighted upon Roman.

She collided with Amelia in a hug, grasping her tightly. "Hurry! Let's get inside. There are coyotes nearby."

Roman started down the drive without hesitation, kicking up a small plume of dust that blew sideways with the wind. He cut a terribly romantic figure in the twilight with his tall frame and goat shawl. I glanced at Amelia before following him.

"Over here," Heath said, indicating a door around the side of the building. "I'm not sure the goat will make it through. There's broken concrete that won't allow it to open all the way."

A haunting howl rose, high and wavering. Lily screamed and ran for the door.

Roman set Peaches down and grabbed a rock that was painted with a faded cartoon frog. He brought it down hard, again and again, on the padlock holding the front gate shut. A loud ping, ping, ping cut through the air, and I looked around anxiously, knowing the sound would draw the coyotes straight to us.

The lock finally gave way. We linked our fingers through the gate and pulled, it's paint flaking off on to my skin, my shoes. It relented with a screech and jammed just as quickly.

Roman wiggled under the gate. I threw my pack in after him and crawled inside on my belly. Amelia and Heath followed. Peaches bleated nervously before bending her delicate knees and squirming in after us. We pulled the gate closed, and Heath wedged the side door with a wooden shim.

We looked at each other and collectively laughed. Heath clapped me on the back and pulled me in for a hug. "God fucking damn it, you're late!"

"But who's this?" Lily asked, her ink-black eyes taking in the lanky stranger.

"Lily," Amelia said, "This is Roman. He'll be around for a bit, I think?"

Roman nodded, extending his hand for Lily to shake.

"Hello," she said shyly. "Is that a goat?"

"Sure is," he said good-naturedly. "Her name is Peaches."

On cue, Peaches bowed, her curly beard sweeping the ground.

Lily smiled and held out her hand tentatively. "Wish I had sugar for her."

"Nice to meet you, Roman. My name is Heath," he said, extending his hand for Roman to shake. "We haven't had a new person around for some time. Nice to see a new face."

"You can't imagine my elation yesterday after coming across these two in town," Roman said, gesturing towards Amelia and me. "I was hoping to spend some time with your group and help out where I can."

"I don't know how much Amelia and Atticus told you, but we sure can use a hand. I'm dog-tired every day," said Lily. "We have a house to build, a garden to work, and food to get on the table."

"I can lend a hand with all that and sweeten the pot too," he said, taking a cup from his bag and squirting warm milk from Peaches' udders in it, handing it to Lily to drink.

"I've never had goat's milk before!" she exclaimed, taking a small sip. "It's delicious."

"We're set up in the courtyard this way," Heath said. "Follow me."

The rambling store was filled with trowels, birdseed, and fertilizer. Wind chimes tinkled softly as we brushed past. The back of the building was constructed of large windows and a sliding glass door. I clicked the lock and slid it open, looking out onto an inner courtyard. A moldy angel stood stoically from the center of a small man-made pond, choked with water lilies and slime.

The courtyard was overrun with twisting vines, bursting with bright reds and yellows of tulips and daffodils. The evening sky yawned above, pale wisps of clouds gliding over the moon.

"It's lovely," Amelia said while twirling, her arms outstretched in delight.

Peaches bleated as if agreeing, bouncing happily to tear up the succulent grasses that grew between cobblestones.

"It's a shame no one found this place to hunker down. It's a haven," said Lily, picking a flower from a blossoming dogwood tree, its roots having broken the large ceramic pot that held it.

I thought of poor Matilda, murdered in a bathroom not far from here. Setting my pack down, I started piling bracken in the far corner of the courtyard to make a fire.

Heath helped, bending low and close to murmur, "Who's the tramp?"

"He came out of nowhere, literally," I whispered. "We were crossing the bridge in town, and he just appeared as if lying in wait for us. Amelia thinks he's some harmless wanderer roaming the wilderness."

"This was yesterday? How come you didn't make it here until today?"

"He suggested we stay the night at his camp, and Amelia didn't even think twice about it. She followed him as if she knew him all her life."

Heath scratched at his beard, a thick carpet that extended ear to ear. "He's here to stay?"

"Put him to work. See how long he sticks around."

Roman appeared a few minutes later, hauling a plastic jug filled with water. "Found a stream along the side of the building," he said. "There's fish, too. Little ones, but they'll do if you have fishing poles in those packs of yours."

"We don't," I said dryly.

"Roman," Amelia smiled, "if you're up for soup, we don't have to worry about fishing."

Once a fire was going, Amelia filled the travel kettle with water and started gathering things to make dinner. In went dandelion roots, milkweed shoots, and chicken of the woods mushrooms she found clinging to a spongy stump.

She pulled water lilies from the scummy pond, plucking off their unrolled leaves and flower buds and adding them to the boiling water. Rinsing the silt from the tubers that grew among their roots, she diced them into potato-sized wedges, dropping them in the kettle with a little splash.

To answer Roman's polite questions regarding each plant, Amelia retrieved the field guide and explained their edible intricacies. I added a pinch of salt that I kept in a small container in my pack and stirred the soup before removing it to cool.

Heath pulled out folding chairs and sat them around the fire. Lily disappeared into the store, emerging after a few minutes with star-spangled banner-themed plastic bowls. Relics left over from the holiday that would never be celebrated again.

"No spoons to be found, fellas," Lily said, divvying up the soup. I slurped mine immediately, scorching my tongue. The water lilies carried a fishy tang.

Roman sipped his soup slowly, closing his eyes in enjoyment. "Before last night, I'll tell you the last hot meal I had," he said, smacking his lips. "But I'd rather not, seeing how depressing it is."

"What have you been eating then?" Amelia asked.

"Mostly stuff from cans."

"Why not cook a meal?" Lily asked curiously.

"Fire draws the eye," Roman answered. "And I didn't know I could eat all these plants. I thought they were just weeds."

His boisterousness had receded somewhat since yesterday, but with an opioid hangover, it wasn't that surprising.

Roxys had hit the market when I was in elementary school. The doctors, no better than common drug dealers, peddled them out to high-risk and low-risk individuals alike, regardless of what was detailed in their medical history questionnaire. The doctors didn't care, the pharmaceutical companies were making money by the billions and in turn, padding the doctor's pockets as much as they were loath to admit.

We drank the rest of our soup in silence with the occasional hoot of an owl or the yips and yowls of the coyote pack. I drew my coat around my shoulders, sunburn sending chills down into my bones. Firelight danced over Amelia's face, exhausted and careworn.

"Roman," Heath asked, setting his empty bowl aside, "what's your story?"

Roman's eyes gleamed from across the fire, something canine in his face. "I guess I should start from the beginning," he said, clearing his throat after a moment. "My family moved to Quebec when I was small," he said. "When I quit high school, my parents kicked me out, and I lived on the streets most of the time. I saw people getting sick and thought it was only a matter of time before I caught it, except I never did. I can't quite say much more about any of it."

"Where were you when the Panic happened?" Heath asked.

Roman smiled, "I was in a court-ordered detox facility when everything burned out like a fucking firework."

"For what?" Amelia asked, stirring the coals. "Heroin," he smiled sheepishly.

"Vices, am I right?" Amelia said, pushing her chair back. "What did you sleep on last night?" she asked Lily. "Patio cushions. There's more over there."

Amelia left to examine a jumbled stack of lawn furniture under the eaves of the building. She pulled a few long cushions from the pile and scrutinized them closely. Stuffing puffed out through holes where mice had eaten through the material, but they looked relatively clean and dry. I helped her drag them over to the fire.

I put the kettle into the coals, boiling the rest of the water Roman had collected. Amelia added a few sprigs of dried herbs to make tea. We watched the fire die down, yawns cracking our jaws. We brushed skeletal spiders and mealy worms off the cushions before lying down for the night. The hot coals warmed our faces pleasantly, the sound of crickets lulling us to sleep.

I woke later that night unbelievably cold, the fire nothing but embers. Heath and Lily huddled together sleeping, his arm draped around her for warmth. Roman was snoring loudly, arms outstretched like he'd been espaliered. My fingers itched to turn out his pockets and uncover his secrets.

Amelia was gone.

I rose hurriedly, stalking silently through the courtyard and into the store, listening intently for anything unusual. Amelia stood near the front gate, staring silently out into the dark. The moon drenched the fields surrounding the nursery in silver light as if nature suddenly lost its CMYK and switched to grayscale.

I stood beside her, and she gave a little nod, holding her finger to her lips. I followed her gaze. Sleek shapes darted through the long grass that bordered the driveway, bushy tails tucked low, muzzles to the ground.

"Why are they after us?" Amelia whispered.

Coyotes were pack hunters, generally taking down lame deer or small mammals.

"I'm not sure. With all the other wildlife out there, it's unusual for them to keep circling back here."

"They've got us trapped," she said, rattling the gate. They scattered but circled to get a better handle on what they'd caught. More of the pack slipped from the undergrowth and advanced. They moved like a band of outlaw murderers, communicating seamlessly and succinctly.

"They've completely lost their fear of humans," Amelia sighed.

"Without cars and trappers to keep their numbers in check, we'll have a problem. The wolves and big cats will start moving back down from the north, picking off every slow-moving human for thousands of miles."

"And I'm glad. It's the way things were always supposed to be."

The coyotes circled, paws treading lightly over the stone driveway. Their legs were as thin and delicate as deer legs. They got ever closer, snarling, until one lunged at the gate, snapping its jaws.

Amelia bared her teeth and spread her arms wide like a grizzly bear.

"Come on," I said, pulling lightly on her shirt. "Let's find useful things for the tree house."

I picked up a grocery basket and hung it from my arm, just a suburban dad getting ready to plant his raised bed garden that would most likely shrivel

and die before producing so much as a single tomato. We strolled past dry fish tanks, their dead inhabitants stuck to the gravelly bottom like paper-mâché.
I plucked packages of vegetable seeds from a dusty
display case and put them in the basket.

"I always wanted one of these," Amelia said, holding up a glass orb. She peered inside it, fine wrinkles
creasing around her eyes.

"What is it?"

"A lawn decoration," she said. "You've never seen
one of these before?"

"It looks like a crystal ball."

"People used to stick them in their yards. I always
thought if I ever left the city and bought a house,
I'd have an absolutely insane front lawn filled with
tchotchkes."

"If I lived on the same street as you, I'd complain
to the HOA about what an eyesore it all was."

"You fucking would," she laughed, putting the
orb back on the shelf. "It's too heavy to carry back
to the tree house."

"I'm sorry."

She waved her hand. "Don't be."

We ambled through the store, stopping only
when Amelia placed something else in the basket.
Lily needed seeds, starter pots, and fertilizer. The
way she had asked over dinner the other night had
introduced a flicker of worry in me. She'd been
growing seedlings since the tail end of winter, ar-

ranging them on shelves around the fireplace in the tree house to keep them from freezing.

When the frosts subsided, there'd been a few days when we helped her hand plow a field roughly half a mile from the tree house. It was sunny, the soil showing good possibility with the berry bushes that flourished there. We helped plant most of the seedlings, leaving a few of the newer ones to continue growing inside. Lily spent her days caring for the new crops, asking for little assistance. It hadn't occurred to me that things could be going wrong.

"Let's find Lily something special," Amelia said, eyes roving the space. "I missed her last night. I can't remember spending this much time apart since we first met them. Can you?"

"In the winter."

She grew serious. "But they were always there."

"How about a wind chime? There are a few by the front door." I led her to the stand that held them, their metal flutes silent in this windless place.

"This one is nice," she said, pointing to a pleasant one with a smiling sun and animated spring tulips and crocuses. She touched it, and it tinkled softly.

"That's the best one," I agreed.

"Let's leave a list at the register of what we took," Amelia said.

I set the basket on the counter, and Amelia scooted behind the register, pulling the cash drawer open. "I wish we could leave the owners something," she said, counting the bills.

"They're not coming back, so what does it matter?" They were probably rotting silently in their beds if the fever took them or dead out on the highways if it didn't.

Finding a scrap piece of paper and a pencil nub, she proceeded to list every item in the basket, even though there was never any way we could bring it all home. I watched her with amusement.

Feeling my eyes on her, she looked up, setting the pencil down. "Oh, Atticus...," she said, reaching for my hand, her skin callused, and not at all the way it used to be, softer than velveteen.

"Roman will be a big help to us. You'll see. I don't want us to be at odds anymore over this."

But I didn't like the way she held my hand like I was a patient at a sick ward and she, a celebrity, on a publicity tour.

"I don't think he should come back with us. Something about him sets my nerves," I said, bracing for an argument.

"Don't be a callous dick, Att. You can't throw aside a human life just because you don't like him. Roman has been nothing but nice since we met him."

"He's a drug addict."

She waved her hand as if physically brushing aside my words. "It's not your problem to worry about."

"I'm worried about you."

She released my hand. "I know it hurts, but I stand by what I said last night. There's nothing left between us," she said, suppressing a small smile that played around her lips, attempting to conceal the revelry she was feeling. My devotion gave her power in a world where everything was bent on crushing her.

"If you're saying whatever we've had is over, then I respect your decision to end it."

"I thought you'd put up more of a fight."

I shrugged, "What do you want me to say? If it's done, it's done. But that means you need to be done too."

"What's that supposed to mean?"

"I think you know what it means," I said, gathering up the stuff we were going to bring home.

"Have it your way," she said, walking back towards the courtyard.

We slipped into our beds, the cushions now slick with dew. Dawn was reassuringly near. I scooted my cushion closer to the fire, closing my eyes and willing her to crawl over, fit herself into me like she used to. The sun rose as I waited while Amelia breathed lightly just across the fire.

When I finally slept, I dreamt of the dead woman from the library. She floated on display in the liquid amphitheater of my brain. Her black hair hung limp, and her eye sockets glittered from within like shiny coins at the bottom of a well. She was naked from the waist down, wearing just the Dickies jacket I had found her in.

Hello, Atticus, she murmured without moving a single muscle in her ruined face.

Matilda?

That's as good a name as any, she said.

Who murdered you?

A man. Men. A long time ago.

Did those same men kill the person we found on the road? Are they coming for us too?

They're always coming.

How did you die?

Gruesomely. If only there hadn't been water in the toilet I was handcuffed to, I would have died in a matter of days. I couldn't help myself. So I starved instead. I tried eating my way out towards the end. She held her wrists up so I could see the mangled tendons where she'd chewed them.

I wish I knew you were there. I could have freed you.

But you did free me, and now we can be the best of friends. It seems like you need one of those right now.

I choked down a sob.

Later that morning, after a breakfast of protein bars courtesy of Lily, I walked through the store and pulled the front gate up as much as I could by myself. I wiggled under and began searching for coyote tracks.

It seemed they had paced long after we retreated, relentlessly searching for a way inside. My skin prickled, and I knew they couldn't be far. I eyed the overgrown grasses and wildflowers that had taken up residency around the nursery. They seemed to beckon, waving gently in the wind. Certain death waited in there.

Great thunderclouds were building in the distance, getting ready for war with the mountains. The long stretch of road was empty, nothing but great buckles of blacktop and detritus.

Back inside, Amelia and Lily were stuffing as many things as possible into their packs. Roman sat in a folding chair milking Peaches.

I kicked out what was left of the fire and stacked the cushions. We left not long after to bring a stranger home.

THEN

The nearer we got to the bridge, the more chaotic the abandoned traffic became. There were deep tire marks alongside the road, some of the smaller cars getting stuck in the mud on their desperate flight. Others had tried driving on the wrong side of the road, an accident involving multiple vehicles and a tractor-trailer was evidence of their idiocy. The fire from the wreckage had husked everything to a shell, gobbling flesh, belongings, and seat cushioning until there was nothing left but metal, charred black. There had been no fire trucks and no rescue operation.

The bridge came into view towards the evening hours, the setting sun glittering on the Hudson River below. Wide enough for six cruise ships to easily sail through together; the water was a deep blue, nearly purple with a murky brown that ran along its edges. Various boats floated unmoored, a few were dashed upon rocks and jutting docks.

"It always surprises me how big the river is after not seeing it for some time," Amelia said, worry etched in her face.

We stopped beneath an overpass to rest, faint from overexertion and hunger. Swallows dove from muddy nests at the sound of our approach, fluffy heads of chicks peeking out at us curiously.

The steep concrete sides of the overpass sported colorful graffiti. The artwork depicted the president giving that last televised speech from his bunker, the one where he had urged forceful calmness in the face of calamity. Instead of a podium, he stood upon a pile of bodies. Sprayed flowers erupted from their mouths, so life-like that I touched one—but only the rough feel of the concrete met my fingers.

I ate a packet of peanuts from the grocery story haul, savoring their salty goodness. I studied the bridge from afar, majestic and serene in the way only mammoth structures can be. The pedestrian walkway was farther north still, but not by much. It was much smaller than the Mid-Hudson Bridge, mimicking the look of a train trestle.

"How do you get onto the walkway?" I asked, shading my eyes against the setting sun.

"I have a vague recollection. I figured once we got close, it'd be obvious."

"Look how it comes in off the shore," I said, making a line with my hand. "It doesn't look like we can get on from the highway. Its elevated way into the city."

"Should we cross it in the dark? We're better off camping here for the night," Amelia said.

I studied the opposite shoreline. "It's wooded on the other side. I'd feel better sleeping there than on concrete."

"We don't need to sleep outside. There are plenty of storefronts, apartments, or whatever we can find that would keep us just as safe, if not safer, than sleeping in a tent."

"If you're tired, we don't have to cross tonight. Whatever you want to do," I acquiesced.

She paused for a long time, looking out over the river. "No, let's go before it gets too dark."

In the fading light, we mounted our bikes once more, the seat of my ass sore from riding. Amelia no longer sang, instead, she hummed a scale of four notes that grew maddening in its repetition.

She led us through a maze of streets that featured multi-family houses with cheap siding and sagging porches. Smoke rose in the distance, but we saw no fire. On one lonesome street, a car was crumpled against a hydrant. Water glugged out in waves, creating an artificial stream that disappeared down a storm drain.

The walkway touched down behind a nondescript intersection, shielded by trees and businesses that had been abandoned long before the Panic.

Giant box stores and behemoth online shopping sites had destroyed downtown America.

Slowing to a stop at the walkway's entrance, I dismounted my bike, rubbing my calf muscles to ease cramping. An outdoor shelter made of steel and glass stood nearby, offering pamphlets, paper maps, and general safety tips for enjoying the walkway.

We sipped from our water canteens and began walking our bikes—the tires tick, ticking.

"I had friends here once," sighed Amelia. "We'd go apple picking and drink shitty wine, complain about the bloat in our stomachs."

She began humming again, those four notes in a row. Her eyes were glassy, like a weasel in headlights. We soon left the buildings behind, the walkway climbing higher over the city below, the banks of the great river fast approaching.

I paused, gauging the distance. An American flag whipped near the bridge's center, standing tall and true over the river. The railings were waist high with interspaced banners that said, *"Walkway over the Hudson."*

I started across, eager to reach the other side to set up the tent and collapse with exhaustion. I soon slowed, stopping altogether when I realized Amelia wasn't following.

She crouched by her bike, one hand trying to balance the weight while the other was wrapped tightly around her knees. Amelia's hair blew into her eyes, into her mouth, sticking on Chapstick lips.

"What's wrong?" I called.

"I'll fall." She said it halfheartedly like she wasn't sure if it was imminent or just a possibility.

I put the kickstand out and went back to her, gently taking her bike and leaning it against the railing. "You came once with your mom. Remember? The story you told me?"

"That was different."

"Why?"

"Because there wasn't a man living under the bridge then."

"What man?"

"There's a nest, like an eagle's nest, with bones from voles and rabbits strewn about in it. He built it under the bridge. It's where he lives."

Her words had a dizzying effect, spooky and untrue. The walkway was empty, save for an overturned garbage can that rolled in the stronger gusts of wind, a hollow, tinny sound reaching our ears. My skin crawled, and I suddenly felt less sure that everything was indeed okay.

"Amelia, why would someone do that? Live in a bird's nest beneath a well-traveled pedestrian walkway?"

"I don't know, but he's here now."

"So, you aren't scared of falling?" I asked.

"I'm scared of that, too. Bridget fell. I didn't catch her. I could have, but I didn't."

"She was sick, and it was dark, and we were fleeing on elevated train tracks. It was an accident."

Tears clumped her eyelashes together. "You didn't catch her either," she accused.

"I'll always regret it." I took her hand, clammy and trembling.

"Fuck you."

"Is there another way to cross?"

"There's something under the bridge," she said, her teeth chattering.

I was afraid she was having a panic attack, a misfiring in her skull. "If it's too much pressure, we can turn back, try again..."

She leaned in to whisper in my ear, "He lives under the bridge."

"Who does?"

"He eats animals. The farmers try to kill him, but he always gets away."

I studied her, dread enveloping me like a mildewed towel. There was no alcohol on her breath, and I couldn't imagine where she'd find drugs.

"Did you take something today? Medicine of any kind?"

She ignored me, choosing instead to stare blankly ahead, tears falling from her eyes and landing on her lap so that the green khakis she wore darkened with tiny splashes.

"You have to decide, Amelia. We can't stay here much longer." I had forgotten how quickly summer nights began to end, disbelief that anything so sweet could give way to snowdrifts and frigid temperatures. I'd even seen trees turning, fire orange and communist red. They were traitors, and I wished I could fell each of them, striking fear into the forest to remain summer green forever.

"How about you shut the fuck up?" Her face twisted with rage, transformed into that of a gargoyle.

I jerked back as if she'd slapped me, completely taken aback by her sudden, inexplicable anger.

Rising shakily to her feet, Amelia stepped slowly to the railing, leaning over to glance beneath the bridge. I stood, unsure what she'd do, ready to close the distance should she decide to leap over the side.

I opened my mouth, maybe to try calming her, but she spun around, finger pressed to her lips. "Be quiet, Atticus. He doesn't know we're here." She slid slowly to the ground, the heels of her boots scraping along the concrete.

"You look like a marionette doll sitting like that."

"Didn't I say we had to be quiet?"

"Yes."

"Then why are you speaking?"

"Why are you speaking?" I retorted, not bothering to keep my voice down. I crouched next to her once more, seeing that her hair had blown into her eyes, and she hadn't bothered to pull the strands free. She blinked normally, but both eyes appeared goopy, like a dog just rising in the morning, boogers trailing down the insides of their eyes.

I'd always have to find a paper towel to wipe them from my childhood dog before she could put her head in my lap, begging for breakfast crumbs. Her name was Biscuit, and she died when I was still in high school. There was a wooden cross in the backyard. No, there'd been three wooden crosses. We put stones on top so the coyotes couldn't dig up our deceased pets. Reburying the dead was a smelly, heart-hurting business.

I plucked the hair slowly from her eyes, strands sliding grossly across her pupils. I tucked the flyaway pieces into her shirt collar, unsure how to secure them properly.

She cupped her hands to her ears. "You've woken him."

"Stop it."

"He's crawling from his nest. He'll eat us. He'll eat us!" Her last sentence rose in volume to an unimaginable pitch, an opera singer breaking wine glasses, enough to drive a person mad.

I clamped my hand over her mouth, fright sidling up the back of my neck like a cold draft. "What's wrong? Why are you acting like this?"

Her tongue wiggled out between my fingers like a fat maggot, and I drew it away in disgust, wiping it dry on my pants.

"He'll scuttle like a lizard," she giggled. "With a chameleon's tongue, he'll stick you good, then chomp your bones. Your bones!" she emphasized, laughing hysterically.

The bridge, I realized. She's scared of the height of it, post-traumatic stress from when Bridget fell. I pulled her upright, but she was like a child being removed from their favorite toy store, refusing to stand on her own.

And then there was a noise, a rustle, like a bird fanning its wings, and a splash. Amelia fainted at the sound, her eyes rolling into whites. Her weight pulled us both to the ground, and in the twilight came the sound of treading water below and the soft rustle of leaves as whatever it was left the river and started climbing the bank.

A small part of me knew it was probably a duck or some other creature and not a man leaving a nest of bones to devour us, but I was blinded with fright. I shook Amelia's shoulders until she mumbled, and her pupils reappeared.

"Amelia," I grunted as she slumped back into my arms again. "We've got to get out of here." Her legs kept buckling, her head lolling.

Over the wind, a curious sound came from the bridge's entrance; a tip-tap, like a boogeyman, stealing across the basement floor with exaggerated steps. The moon above was obscured by clouds, hiding whatever it was that hunted us.

I grabbed the gun from Amelia's pack and slung it over my shoulder. I balanced her on my bike seat, then stood on the pedals and pumped furiously. We wobbled, and I shouted for Amelia to hold onto me. Her arms snaked across my stomach and locked together.

"It's coming," Amelia screamed, and I could hear footfalls fast approaching from behind. Or maybe I imagined them, I don't know. With my chest heaving, we raced across the walkway, and I envisioned us as a zipping dragonfly attempting escape from sharp talons that beat on merciless wings.

Ahead, the concrete bridge gave way to a paved path that twisted away into the darkness of a dense forest. Trees towered overhead, impenetrable and mighty. It was wild, this place, far different than the ordered chaos of the city we just left behind.

The tires left the bridge with a whir, hitting the blacktop so hard that I struggled to keep us upright. Without warning, Amelia set her feet down, boots skidding along the pavement. I lost my balance, and we went careening into the bordering trees. She fell with a scream, tumbling away into a ditch filled with brambles that reached for her with thorny fingers.

With a death squeal of broken spokes, the front tire of the bike smashed into a rock, catapulting me down a steep ravine. My head slammed into the ground, and light exploded behind my eyes, my body going limp from the pain.

I came to rest in a small brook, cold water trickling around me and filling my shoes. The mangled bike lay a few feet away, its front tire destroyed. Our belongings were scattered everywhere.

The crickets were deafening, a cacophony of synchronized sound. It cradled me, this noise. It was a comfort from summers when I was small, the window thrown open against the heat, the sound of crickets keeping me company as I made shadow puppets with the flashlight I kept tucked between my mattress and the wall.

"Atticus?" Amelia called out.

I closed my mouth from the warm, penny-tasting blood that flowed from my nose.

"Where are you?" Her voice still had an odd lilt, like she was trying to keep from laughing. "You've got the gun?"

She slipped down the ravine towards me, giggling to herself quietly, hysterically.

The gun was flat black, its metal consuming what little moonlight there was. Amelia's groping fingers found it, bone white and starvation thin. She pulled it to her shoulder, climbing back to where we had crashed.

"You come for me, I come for you!" she yelled.

"Hide, Amelia," I croaked, spitting blood.

A whirring noise cut through the crickets. It was the wheels of the bike we had left behind, spinning at a higher speed than ever I would dare to go in this darkness. Amelia laughed out loud as she pumped the rifle.

I tried moving my pinky fingers first, then my toes and hands. When I sat upright, it felt like a breeze was blowing into the cavities of my skull. Blood soaked the back of my shirt and mixed with the mud that covered me entirely.

Clawing up the ravine over nettles that stung and false footholds that sent me sliding backward, I found Amelia kneeling behind a tree whose roots grew octopus-like around a jutting boulder.

If our purgatory was an island instead of drab suburbs, I would spend my days netting those deep-sea beasts to drape their tentacles around Amelia's shoulders like a fox stole. I'd use its ink to draw curlicue henna on the backs of her hands. Its beak would get lodged in my intestines, and I would die of diverticulosis.

I threw up my dinner of chewed peanuts and beef jerky. It came gurgling with swallowed blood and bile. "Is there anyone?" I asked, looking out onto the empty bike path. It twisted off into the distance like a snake. The bridge arched up and away, suspiciously benign.

"I missed."

The blood pouring from my nose was beginning to slow, hardening on my upper lip. I wiped it with my shirt sleeve and winced at the ache. Deciding against examining the back of my head, I feared I'd find a horribleness that would be impossible to fix. I slumped to the ground, and Amelia plucked dead leaves from my clothes, her fingers nervous and restless.

"Did you get hurt?" I asked.

"I don't think so."

I soon fell into the forbidden sleep of concussions where I dreamt of the scream of a cornered beast, of a rabbit that's been caught around the neck by a dog. I knew it was Amelia, and I swear I didn't care, laying there in my own blood and vomit.

My breath was visible in the early morning cold, the day just light enough to assure you that the sun was once again rising. She stood on the bike path, facing toward the pedestrian bridge with her hands bunched into fists at her sides and jaw hanging loose. With cheeks red from cold, a latticework of scratches varying in severity covered her face and neck.

We watched her, us creatures of the woods, the birds silent, the squirrels with ears flat to their backs, the deer quaking with fear at her animosity and terror.

Then she ran.

NOW

"Not much farther," Amelia said, wiping the sweat from her brow. "Stay on the trail. It's easy to get turned around."

Roman fell in line. Peaches stepped tiredly behind him with her head hung low. Whenever she lagged, he'd make a sharp tisk noise, and she would be right back at his heels.

"Where are we?" Roman asked, looking around.

"It's a state park. Well, I guess it used to be a state park," Amelia said. "It'll probably take you time to figure out all the trails. There are over 50 miles of them. The ranger's station has maps, but they won't be much help because we pried off most of the trail markers near the tree house to make it harder for strangers to find us."

"This trail is called Blueberry Run," Lily said. Her fingers grabbed at the short blueberry bushes as evidence. "It's the main trail we use to go up and down the mountain."

We had hiked through the morning after leaving the nursery, Amelia leading us back home. The forest listened, suspicious of another human spoiling its virginal flower. Birds settled on low branches to gawk at the procession. Squirrels sat on their hind legs, nuts forgotten. A fawn, hidden in green brambles by its mother, turned its long face to the side, watching us through an innocent eye. No, the forest did not approve.

I could feel it, too, as if Roman was a shrimping boat trawling a fishing net behind him, collecting all the malicious things left to cause harm and chaos.

Without television or the Internet, the world expanded exponentially again. Mysticism had crept back to its throne, laughing at us for having the audacity to think we could escape. I imagined it as a thing of slime with an infinite number of tentacles, pulling on strings of madness. Jesus Christ was its greatest creation, subjecting humanity to thousands of years of old men raping children and women laid low as second-class citizens.

"Can we take a quick break? I'm not used to all this walking," Lily said.

We rested on a jutting rock that overlooked a grove of oak trees and drank from our canteens. Amelia doled out the last of the smoked fish she'd brought though it tasted like cinder.

"I felt a raindrop," Heath said. "Let's get going before we get soaked."

We gathered our packs and set off. From Blueberry Run, Amelia led us off a side path that plunged us deeper into the forest. The final miles were hiked in near silence except for the fruitless swatting at a stinging horsefly that delighted in our sweat.

Nothing good will come of this, Matilda whispered.

I know, I said, *but I don't have a choice.*

He'll hurt you.

I'm afraid Amelia would leave with him. That would be catastrophic. I'll never be able to find her again.

The wind picked up, swaying the trees and exposing their leaves' underbellies. Thunder rumbled from massive cumulonimbus clouds that flattened themselves against the stratosphere. We made a last, courageous dash to the tree house as the sky opened and hail thundered down, bouncing and breaking through the forest canopy.

"I thought you were all dead!" Mabel exclaimed while she helped us up through the door. "Never again am I staying here by myself. I've been a wreck thinking about all the ways you could've been killed out there. And what's this? A goat?"

Roman pushed Peaches through the door and followed in after her. She shook the rain from her fur and found a warm spot in front of the fireplace to lay down.

"Hi, I'm Roman," he said, extending his hand.

"Another person? I don't believe this. We usually try to hide from people as a general rule."

"Mabel, maybe stop for a breath?" Amelia said.

"It's nice to meet you," Roman said. "I didn't know there was someone else living here too."

"No one told him about me? Did anyone miss me? I was worrying myself sick, and no one even tells the new guy I exist?"

"We missed you so much," Lily said, wrapping her arms around Mabel. "Don't fret. We're all home safe now."

Backpacks were unloaded, boxes and books stacked near the stone fireplace to be pawed through and coveted, and like the stolen possessions of magpies, squirreled away into respective nests.

Lily's cheeks flushed when Amelia presented her with the wind chime from the nursery. Her eyes glistened over at the small act of kindness.

"It reminds me of my ma," she said, holding it to her chest. "There were half a dozen hanging from our front porch. I'd go to sleep in the summer listening to them."

"I'm glad you like it," Amelia said, embracing her.

"I made dinner for everyone," Mabel said. "I don't know how good it'll taste, but it's something."

"You did?" Amelia asked, lifting the lid on the cast iron pot. "What is it?"

"Fiddlehead ferns and a can of roast beef hash."

"I thought fiddleheads were poisonous?" Heath asked, squinting suspiciously at a furled frond that sat haplessly in the weak broth.

"They are, but if you swap out the water a few times while boiling, they're fine to eat. They also contain fatty acids and antioxidants and are high in potassium." Amelia said, quoting from the field guide.

"Did you swap out the water?" Heath asked, staring intently at Mabel.

Mabel laughed, "Of course, I read about it in one of the books. I thought everyone would appreciate a warm meal. I tried my best, though it doesn't look appetizing, does it?"

"It's fine, Mabel, thank you," Amelia said, smiling.

After dinner, a bottle of bourbon was introduced, and shots were poured in a bored celebratory kind of way, having gone through these same motions many times over.

Roman draped his arm lazily over Amelia's shoulder, a casual sign of possession. She leaned into him nonchalantly, folding him into her life in the tenderest of ways.

From the moment Roman had stepped out onto the bridge, my relationship with Amelia had gone from a complicated coupledom to third-wheel abandonment. Whatever had been holding us together was finally broken, and I was helpless to salvage it.

What could be said about this crushing sadness? I had known it was coming, must be coming. She hated me for a long time now. Death had followed on our heels since that very first night we met, from Bridget falling to Pepper dying in the snow outside our door. And Piper was dead when we found her, but I have let the guilt of her death settle upon me like fine silt.

Beneath the table, I grasped Mabel's hand during a moment's lull in the conversation. I traced the pale Vitiligo pattern on her palm with my fingers. At first startled, she smiled timidly, eyes flicking briefly in Amelia's direction.

I whispered to her about a robin's nest I had found in the forest. The newly hatched chicks were nothing but urgent, moving throats. She tittered and Amelia stared at us in stony silence, Roman's arm now forgotten.

"The rain stopped. How'd you like a tour, Roman?" Amelia asked.

Agreeing, they disappeared outside with the practiced stealth of drug addicts. The rest of us retired upstairs without comment.

Matilda, it hurts.

***

Shedding his ridiculous leather pants for work trousers, Roman took to the tree house like a carpenter ant. Heath showed him the construction plans and how things should be built.

With the last of the lumber used to make Peaches a pen in the Great Meadow, the three of us hiked to an extensive grove of evergreens. It was a place of heebie-jeebies. They are dark, these pine forests, unnaturally so. And quiet, the needles muffling the footsteps of predators.

With gas being so challenging to come by, we used crosscut saws, big, rusted things with rough wooden handles. We rolled what we cut into the stream, where it was carried by the water until snagging on a convenient bend near the tree house. From there, we lugged the pieces onto the muddy bank and sawed them further into planks. The wood was roughly hewn but strong. It was hard, satisfying work.

In less than a fortnight, the second floor was completed. The girls took to meandering in and out of the rooms, swirling wine in their glasses. For Mabel, hers was a room on top of a short set of stairs that folded open for canned food storage. Her arched windows faced west, overlooking the mountain range.

Amelia's room was more compact with a round porthole-like window. She said she preferred to think she was underwater, not suspended in the air. The room faced south, the waterfall visible below, mist rising through the tree canopy.

Heath's and Lily's room was slightly larger than all the rest. Their windows faced east, the sunrise visible when not obstructed by the dissipating fog over the mountains. It all looked so wild, the expanse of it all unimaginable, like trying to speculate on the enormity of space.

My room, right off the staircase, was perhaps seven feet long and five feet wide. It was just large enough for a twin bed and a built-in closet. My window, pried from a house in the valley, had multiple panes and opened on a hinge. It looked out to the north, to the ridge far above.

Roman politely refused to sleep inside, preferring a foldable cot pulled near the fire. The tree house made him claustrophobic, he said. The closeness of the walls pressed upon his breast in a suffocating way.

And through these weeks, I grew increasingly paranoid. A rattle began in my chest that would not abate, a cough that went on and on until I was hoarse. I noticed little looks that they gave each other, Roman and Amelia, seeing them touch lightly throughout the day, a brush of fingers, a hand held momentarily at the small of her back.

Most nights, I stayed awake until the early hours, listening intently for the sound of Roman slipping into Amelia's bedroom.

Matilda, always my friend, agreed that this was a thing of great concern.

Amelia denied it whenever asked, and even Lily was kept in the dark. I told everyone but Amelia that it didn't bother me, that she had made her feelings clear towards me and she could do as she pleased.

This statement elicited pitiful nods and reassurances that made my stomach churn.

We finished the roof in time for the spring rain, torrents of water that plinked against the corrugated metal and melted the last vestiges of snow hidden in high hollows. The stream became impetuous, churning brown water running over its banks. The waterfall was so thunderous that it shook our windows, a sound of tinkling glass forever in our eardrums like two wine glasses set too close together.

This rain drove us inside, including Roman, who fidgeted incessantly, peering from the window in Peaches' direction. She didn't mind the water, happy to eat grass whether rain or shine.

Lily tended to her seedlings, bean sprouts, creeping strawberries, and squash. She mixed fertilizer and consulted with gardening books while Mabel argued passively with her on the harmful effects of chemical fertilizer.

Health tinkered with a large solar panel he pulled from a house the mountain over. Working to mend the stripped wires, he spliced and repaired, eliciting a cheer from the group when, on the third day, lights sprung to life inside, albeit dimly with a side-eye perceivable waver.

Amelia placed a lamp on the push pedal sewing machine that took up an entire hexagonal wall. It had resided in one of the abandoned shacks, someone's prized family heirloom that they had lugged from who knew where.

Amelia had been irate with Heath after he refused to retrieve it. But like tissue in gale force winds, he could not have withstood her determination, finally hiking down to the parking lot and jump-starting a jeep that had sat there since the early days of the Panic. Valiantly, he made it as far as the mouth of Blueberry Run before getting it fatally stuck in the mud. From there, we hauled it, Amelia helping us, faces slicked with dirt and sweat.

It was a Singer, made from iron and hundred-year-old wood. One of the table's feet had been knocked off, Amelia cramming books beneath it to help with the wobble. She sat, head down, foot pumping rhythmically. From rabbit skins to socks, Amelia mended and sewed, occasionally presenting creations for Lily's opinion.

At night, we drank and attempted dinner, abandoning the fire pit for the cast iron stove that sat in the kitchen, experimenting with pheasant pie or thin fish soup. The stove had a nasty scrape down the side from where it had toppled into a shallow ravine as we hauled it from the ranger's cabin, but other than that, it functioned handsomely.

It was a relief to be able to eat inside again. I didn't have to constantly look over my shoulder for stealth attacks. Gnats didn't gather around my face, no danger from ticks crawling under my pant legs.

***

In the quiet that proceeds at dawn, I woke to an unexpected sound of crinkling paper. I started from the bed, my chest still warm where her hand had lingered. A slip of paper had been forced under the door. I bent to grab it, unfolding the message.

Come out, was written in a tidy script.

"What does it say?" Mabel asked, gathering the blankets over her heavy breasts.

I put my finger to my lips, reaching to hand her the note, which she read quickly and crumpled in a burst of tense nervousness. We had perfected silent love, Mabel and I, our breath never more than soundless gasps, our hands moving to cover mouths when it became too much.

"You don't have to go," she whispered, a subtle tremble to her chin. For a moment, I considered it. Then a soft melody began being hummed, a lilting song like the sad warble of a caged songbird.

I got dressed and left, closing the door behind me with finality. Amelia was a dark silhouette lingering on the landing, faint light from the stained-glass window illuminating the crown of her head.

"Liar," she dragged the word until she lost her breath on it.

I burned inside, fire licking my face, my eyes, so that I thought I'd melt from shame.

Amelia was the one who ended things, not you, Matilda whispered, urging obstinance in my time of judgment.

Amelia shook as if she had a fever, teeth chattering, and kneecaps jumping. Advancing, she pointed a finger at me, "You said you loved me."

"You said it was over between us."

Her hand snatched at my shirt, gripping tightly. I grabbed her wrist, afraid of a hidden blade.

"Stop it," I whispered through gritted teeth.

Dragging me forward into my room, she let go of my shirt and pushed me so hard that I stumbled. With a force that rattled the windows, she slammed the door shut and spun to face me, dim moonlight showing tracts of tears down her cheeks. She slid down the wall and wiped her nose on the collar of her shirt.

"If you love me, then why are you in Mabel's room in the middle of the night?"

"You slept with Roman the first night we met him, didn't you?"

"I did, and it felt primal and urgent. It promised to satisfy these empty places here," Amelia said, pointing to her heart.

"Fuck, Am," I said, sliding down the wall, joining her. "I have always loved you, but I think you metastasize it for a sense of power."

"It's not that. You are wrapped in the death throes of the world with me, reliving them as nightmares.

To think of you is to think of the clop of hooves on a highway."

I went rigid, fear uncurling from my center like a spinning conch shell. "That wasn't real."

She smiled sadly, "But wasn't it?" Her fingertips touched mine, and I had an overwhelming urge to pull my fingers to safety.

"If you think you can eat pills to escape from it, you're wrong, and like every addict who needs a reason to self-destruct. Do you think Roman is any different from me? Have you asked him how he managed to scrape by? You don't think he's done awful things to survive too?"

"You kept your relationship with Mabel hidden from me because you knew it was wrong."

"If she's wrong, then so is Roman."

She stood but lingered by the door. "My great grandfather," she said, "lived through the Second World War, but just barely. He was mangled with shrapnel from a bomb that killed half his platoon. When he came home, my grandmother told me she could feel those pieces under his skin that the doctors couldn't remove. He died three years later."

"From what?" I asked.

"Lead poisoning from the shrapnel. Left nine children behind. I think about this all the time, how I can almost feel the lumps beneath his skin with my own fingers, like a phantom feeling.

Because he won the war but still paid with his life. Like us, Att. We made it all this way to go no further."

NOW

Shelves lined the walls of Mabel's room, each crammed with fabric, glass bottles, and art supplies. Dried flowers and herbs hung from the low ceiling. A braided rug lay on the floor, turquoise, lilac, and indigo all wound together.

Mabel sat on a stool near the window, dipping a paintbrush into one of the mason jars Amelia and I had salvaged from town. I wanted to remind her to rinse it and put it back in the cabinet, knowing Amelia would miss it when we started canning berries and tomatoes in the summer, but I didn't.

Mabel had asked me here. I hadn't been able to look her in the eyes in the days since Amelia had discovered my duplicity, feeling sorry for myself, and feeling even worse for Mabel.

"You've never been in here during the day," she stated matter-of-factly, not looking up from her work.

It felt like a judgment against me, and it was. That deep furnace of shame I kept within my belly burned anew at how inconsequential I must have made Mabel feel for my own benefit. I could fuck her in the dark but couldn't be bothered to kiss her in the light. And now, Amelia had laid it all bare with seething rage.

I shook my head, "No, it's beautiful, though. My room seems pale by comparison."

I picked up a pheasant feather and twirled it between my fingers. "Sometimes, I wonder how we managed to build this hulking tree house."

"To be fair, there's a draftiness about it, and some of the windows rattle where they don't fit their frame. The floor beams give you splinters, and carpenter ants have already invaded the kitchen," Mabel said.

"We aren't professionals, but it's working, isn't it?" I asked.

"It is, for now."

I spun the feather, not meeting her eyes. "I shouldn't have kept us a secret these last few weeks or maybe...not done it to begin with. I'm so sorry."

She smiled sadly. "Amelia has been downright vicious since she found out. This morning when I was eating breakfast, I dropped my glass of goat's milk all over the floor, and instead of helping me clean up, she told me to stop being such a clumsy bitch. Her exact words."

"None of this is your fault," I said. "Amelia thinks I belong in her gravitational orbit regardless of our relationship status. She's possessive and jealous."

"I guess I understand." She swirled her paintbrush in the murky brown water, letting it come up for air so she could dip it again in her pallet. "I'd probably act the same way if Charlie were still here."

"How so?"

"Charlie," she sighed reverently. "I met them at the ice cream shop in town after I had gone out in search of a distraction from finals week. I'd like to go back there someday soon so I can relive that most beautiful moment again. Pretend like the Panic never happened.

"I was sleeping when they wandered out into the cold last winter. I don't think they wanted me to catch whatever sickness they had. Charlie wasn't long for this world anyway. Nothing that creates such happiness ever is. It's been difficult to move on with my heart still set on an ice cream stand and a person lost in the snow. It seems like I never did make it out of those shacks."

"I know what you mean." A memory surfaced of placing Piper on the pyre, still frozen to her crib mattress, and how I had wanted to climb onto those burning logs with her so she wouldn't be alone in death.

Mabel stood and faced me, pulling her tattered shirt over her head. Vitiligo patches extended down from her face, hooking under her left breast. She had the look of someone who was once ample but had been starved.

She stepped between my outstretched legs, and I placed my hands softly on her hips. I liked the weight, the warmth of her body. I slid my hands upwards, following the tracks of unpigmented skin. My breath caught when I thought of all the times I did not get to see such beauty as we hid together in the dark.

Wrapping her arms around my neck, she drew me close and kissed me lightly. Her soft lips tasted like mint. I felt a swooping sensation in my stomach, and for a moment, I forgot.

"Can you ever move on?" she asked, pulling away. "Can you let Amelia go?"

"No," I answered bitterly, "she eclipses an entire life lived."

"I guess it's over, then," Mabel said sadly.

***

I apologized to Amelia, but of course, she didn't care. She had left my bedroom the night she found out about Mabel in a resigned fury. What sway she thought she had over me had not been true. At least, that seemed to be her thinking now.

The balance of power had shifted ever so slightly between us. Instead of attempting to keep what was between her and Roman a secret, she didn't even feign it now.

In the face of this burgeoning love, I found within myself a new, deeper well of self-loathing, and I sank below its surface with glee.

I started stealing CDs on forays from the tree house, rationalizing these trips by bringing back small furniture, cookery, door hinges, and anything we could use. From dusty home offices to teenager's bedrooms painted black, I crept like a Grinch in beggar's clothes.

There would only always be four or five CDs together at once, archaic compared to the digital download. Sometimes I'd rummage around finding a portable radio, jamming batteries in their undersides until music filled the room.

I often wondered why it didn't feel like stealing when I took things like screwdrivers or those push-button stick-on lights. I felt like a thief taking things that weren't necessarily necessary, that did not have that survivor label. I wondered about the people who had bought these things, loved these things. Sometimes I'd ask them as they moldered on the bed, on their floor, wherever they had died.

Matilda would whisper words to me, filling my head with agonizing murmurings of doom.

At home, I squirreled away the disks under my bed, removing their booklets and underlining lyrics. The cases piled up so that I had to start burning them, the plastic smell curling up my nose, spreading through my bloodstream in the form of cancerous free radicals.

I developed a nervous habit of running my tongue over my top lip, chapping both the lip and the delicate area between the nose and mouth. I thought of stealing Chapstick from the houses I raided, but instead, I stole them from Amelia.

But I'd only steal from her when I had a booklet completed, leaving them beneath her pillow, a transaction, if you will. I constructed beautiful poems for her from dead musicians, using their words to wind together a timeless love story, one of bitter rejection and creeping madness. If she read them, I never knew. Perhaps she had bonfires of her own where she fed the fire with dozens of these scribbled-on scribes.

I realized once that I had never thought to give Mabel one, but then I never thought of it again. She would eventually get sucked into the furnace that burned and burned for Amelia, just like everything else.

While I wandered, conversations with Matilda filling my time, Roman wandered too. Within a few weeks of the tree house being completed, Roman disappeared for nearly two days. Heath and Amelia had gone out searching for him that first night, to no avail. I hoped his foot was caught in an old bear trap, far away from here.

He finally came tramping back through our small clearing as the sun was setting on the second day. He looked like a gloating crocodile stuffed full of squirming fish.

"Where have you been?" Amelia demanded, throwing down a rabbit skin she'd been stitching into soft moccasins.

Roman caught her and gave her a twirl. "Everywhere!" he sang in a light-hearted twang.

"No, really," Amelia said, mouth set tight.

"I've discovered a paradise, a mansion set upon a mountain ridge."

"The Wadchu Hotel?" I asked dryly, discreetly slicing my palm open with the knife I was using to strip arrows from sticks. The blood welled and then dripped onto the ground.

"This place has pools and fountains and insulation," Roman continued, ignoring me.

"We could have picked any dozen places to live, luxurious places, but we choose to live here, where it's hidden and protected," Amelia said, dropping his hand. "Anyway, who knows how many corpses are stinking up that place."

Matilda suspected Roman knew the exact count as he plundered room after room for pills, booze, and D-R-U-G-S. I eyed his pockets, seeing no suspicious bulges.

They soon disappeared into the twilight together, walking giddily through the Great Meadow,

Amelia quickly forgiving his wrongs. Her long hair swept down her back, a mess of tangles and waves. I watched them melt away beneath the eaves of the forest, her linen shorts the last thing I saw before they faded into the gloom altogether.

They had not asked me to join, leaving me alone to contemplate my bleeding hand and pathetic heart. Matilda wept and squeezed furiously at the squishy parts of my brain.

Lily tramped home shortly after, covered in dirt from the garden. Tucked into the crook of her arm was a crisp head of lettuce. She eyed my hand wordlessly, pushing me off the stump, up the rope ladder, and into the kitchen.

"Roman is back," I muttered.

She nodded, understanding. "I hoped he had left for good," Lily said, pouring peroxide over the cut. "I can't get used to him, always seems to be underfoot or missing since we finished the house. That's how some people are, restless and into trouble if there are no tasks at hand."

I was quiet as she peeled a bandage over my palm.

"Where's Heath?" she asked. "And Mabel?"

I shrugged.

She sighed. "Girl is like the grasshopper in that children's story. The one where it sings all summer? And the ant prepares for the winter? She's in the clouds. But my ma said those creative types are like that, living only in the present."

She leaned back against the counter, crossing her arms over her chest. "She said my daddy was like that. He was a drummer in a local band that played at weddings and bars. Never knew how to keep money, pissing it away on trivialities."

"Did you know him?" I asked, cradling my injured hand.

"For a little while. I remember he smelled like old cigarettes, a cancerous smell. He left when I was still young, moving on to more failure in a different town. I probably had brothers and sisters all over Pennsylvania. Some might have been pretty, some dumb, but all disappointed in that idiot."

"I'm disappointed too."

Lily looked at me the way people look when they don't want to break bad news. "You and Amelia can have your love quarrels, but I can't have it infecting the rest of us, especially Mabel. We're held together so delicately as it is. This is all we have."

"Whatever Mabel and I had is over now."

She nodded and cleaved the lettuce into pieces. "Keep that hand clean."

I climbed the spiral stairs into my room, watching night fall from the window. I heard Lily making dinner and the low murmurings of conversation with the others. The shadows grew long, the night cold.

Roman and Amelia returned later that night, banging the front door open and tripping over things downstairs before closing her bedroom door tight. The snick of the lock crushed the breath from my lungs. And from there, sounds of them fucking, Amelia moaning, and Roman grunting.

Can I die in that bathroom instead of you, Matilda? We can switch places. You'll live here, in this tree house, and I'll be set free.

Such a kindness, she croaked.

I woke the following morning to Heath's knuckles rapping loudly on my bedroom door.

"You up?" he asked. "I need your help."

"Yes," I wheezed, bad breath enveloping my head like a poisonous gas. "Give me a few minutes."

"We got digging to do!"

"What are you talking about?" I yawned, rolling from the bed, and opening the door.

Pulling a creased piece of paper from his pocket, Heath unfolded it and waved it around. It was plans of some sort, drawn and erased and drawn again. "A root cellar," he said.

He held it from my reaching hand and pocketed it. "I'll show it to you outside. Get ready," he turned away impatiently, clomping down the stairs. The front door slammed shut, leaving behind a vacuum of silence.

Sighing, I rummaged through my wardrobe, pulling on a pair of thick jeans and wool socks, first brushing stray particles of sawdust from my feet.

Across the landing, Amelia's closed door pulled my eyes like a magnet. Was she in there with him? I slipped on boots and walked softly to her door, holding my breath to see if I could hear hers. My hand smarted as I flipped open my knife, the cut beginning to bleed fresh through the bandage. Amelia, I carved into the door frame, the wood yielding easily to the blade.

How much better would it have looked on Roman's forehead instead? Pain is a multiplier, I would tell him as he howled, holding his head steady between my knees.

I brushed curled wood shavings from the carving, admiring my work. Amelia would only notice if she stopped to inspect the door. I hoped she'd see. We could have a pleasant conversation about my desire to flay Roman's face.

I found Heath hunched over the fire pit, coaxing a flame to life beneath the coffee percolator.

"You haven't got a shirt on," he said.

"I've got shoes on," I said.

His eyebrows knitted in confusion when I didn't offer anything more. "You've got to let it be," he said, "You can't be crying over a girl who doesn't want you. Don't get weird now, not after everything we've gone through already."

I set my jaw and nodded, thinking he was right but that I was a long way from being all right.

"Okay, well, the root cellar is going to be over by the falls. The humidity level has to be high, so the vegetables don't wither over time. Usually, you'd dig the cellar directly into the ground, but I found a nice hillock that'll do just fine. Roman is over there now putting together shelves."

I started at Roman's name, a little jolt of electricity through my heart. "I thought he was still upstairs," I mumbled.

"No, only you." Heath poured out two mugs of coffee, bitter and acidic. "Now get it together." He held out a steaming enamel mug. I took it, careful not to slosh it down the front of me.

The coffee was disgusting, strong, and made from dandelion roots. Heath kicked out the flames, and we took the rocky trail down to the waterfall.

Heath cleared his throat, "I can't do this without you. I know how selfish that sounds but it's true."

"Do what?" I asked, distracted by my own thoughts.

"This," he gestured around him. "Whatever you're feeling right now is temporary. It'll pass. I know you love Amelia, but the rest of us love you too."

"No, you're right. I'll pull my head out of my ass," I said, grateful for Heath's compassion.

Moss thrived in the mist from the waterfall, the trail becoming slick with slime the farther we walked.

"Over there," Heath pointed. "Good spot for a fridge, right?"

Roman appeared before us, off to the side of Heath's hillock, bringing the hammer down on new pine shelves. He wore a headband, long hair pushed back off his brow and twisted into a bun. With better meals, he seemed to have filled out some, no more the walking famine that had accosted us on the bridge. I wondered how Heath would feel if I bricked Roman inside the root cellar alive.

"I marked out the area," Heath said as we approached, pointing to a homemade surveyor flag stuck haphazardly into the hill. Roman looked up at the sound of Heath's voice, giving a curt nod before turning back to the shelves. The roar of the waterfall behind us made it hard to hear.

Two shovels were leaning against a tree, the pointed metal kind that could crush skulls. I picked the heavier one, the wooden handle worrying the cut on my palm.

I could knock him to the ground and dig out his heart, my foot pushing down on the shovel as it sliced through his breastbone. Heath would be disappointed with my behavior.

We dug through the morning and into the early afternoon, the root cellar taking on a rectangular shape. With the extra boards, Roman worked behind us to create a support structure, like the inside of a ribcage.

When we could not pry a massive rock from its grave, we rested within our hole.

"We should make a round door, like in The Hobbit," I said, rubbing dirt between my fingers and letting it fall back to the earth.

"Hobbit?" Heath asked, drinking long from a canteen.

But I could not remember either.

We left soon after, leaving the finishing touches for another day. Roman and Heath walked together back towards the tree house, but being petty, I decided to take another route, my feet following the trail on their own accord, weaving between wild mountain laurel and tree trunks.

I hiked until I reached a small wooden bridge we had repaired over the stream. I sat, letting my feet dangle over the side. Tiny trout darted in and out of the shadows, gobbling larvae and gnats.

My reflection stared back at me from the water, distorting my image. I flicked a spider that had been creeping towards me into the stream where it swirled, swirled, until a fish sped upwards, swallowing it whole.

I imagined a monster peering up at me through the wood slats of the bridge, the same monster that had desired the Three Billy Goats, and from somewhere deep in my mind, a memory of a creature that pursued us all that time ago, that nested under bridges.

The hairs on the back of my neck rose. I heaved myself to my feet and started up the mountain, not daring to look back. I walked until I came across a wild glen, snowdrops in full bloom, with the buzz of bees in the wind. I waded through the long grass and threw myself down once I had reached the middle of the clearing.

I stared upwards, wondering what it would be like if the earth suddenly lost its center of gravity and how I would fall forever into that azure place until my head expanded and finally exploded.

"Atticus!"

I jumped to my feet, spinning around.

"Amelia," I said, spotting her sitting beyond the trail in a shady grove.

"Come here. I want to talk to you," Amelia said.

"Is everything alright?" I asked, walking towards her. Perhaps she would eat me alive, my legs still kicking as I was swallowed down her gullet, feeding her interminable appetite for misery.

I held my hand out to help her stand, but she waved it away weakly. Instead, she plucked at my pant leg with fingernails that had half-moons of dirt beneath them.

"Sit with me?"

"What are you doing out here?" I asked, looking around for her foraging basket. I sat next to her, my bones cracking in protest after a day spent digging.

"What happened to your hand?" she asked, eyeing the loose, filthy bandage Lily had tied yesterday.

"I cut myself."

"On purpose?"

"No."

Her eyelids fluttered heavily, and she fell backward amongst the undergrowth. She wore the same linen shorts as yesterday, and her feet were bare.

"Are you high?" I asked with mounting dread.

"I can't hear her when I'm high."

"What can't you hear?"

"It began as a soft babble of intermittent white noise, so slight at first that I thought I had a form of tinnitus. I even asked Lily to look in my ears, afraid I blew an eardrum or had some sort of infection. Then I realized, when everything was quiet, that I could pick out certain words or find understanding on the current of its strengthening crescendo."

"You need to stop taking painkillers. What you're saying doesn't make any sense."

"And like an epiphany, I finally grasped what was happening. I feel her flutter sometimes here," she said, cupping her stomach.

The day slowed to a crawl, time becoming taffy-like stretchable. Seething, churning hate blurred the edges of my vision. Relief would come only from pulping Roman's brains.

"What are you saying? That you're pregnant? We don't have a clue how to deliver a baby, Amelia. It'll be a miracle if you make it through labor alive."

"But Piper will," she said. "She'll be born anew, like some Christian fable knockoff."

"Piper died," I said, my voice thick. "To think she'll return as your child is a ludicrous idea. She's gone."

"Because of Mabel," Amelia cried, winnowing her acrimonious grief. "Had Mabel not been so fucking distracted by Charlie's disappearance, she would have noticed Pepper leaving the goddamn shack. How long did Piper cry? Hours? While Mabel was out wandering around in the snow looking for someone who didn't want to be found. Piper died alone and distraught because of Mabel."

"You are not pregnant with Piper, Amelia, even if you are pregnant."

"But I see her," she placed a finger on her temple. "In my mind. Her lips are blue from the cold."

I got to my feet, a wave of recognition washing over me. I had a resident, too, didn't I? A murdered gas station corpse that waded through my cerebrum.

"Don't you get it? We've been miraculously given another chance to be better people and do the right thing. I'll be a sow and raise a litter right here in the forest, a rutting primordial beast of licentiousness.

I was wrong before when I said children shouldn't be born into this world. There are so many souls clamoring to return, and they all need vessels, don't they?"

I fled into the forest, not wanting to take part anymore in her opioid-induced ranting. I could not bear witness to whatever was driving this madness.

THEN

"Amelia!" I screamed. The force of my terror took me to my knees at times. I'd hold my breath and listen intently for any sign of her. The surrounding forest was impossibly dark, with the faint light of the moon rarely making it beyond the tree canopy. I fell time and again, tripping on roots or stumbling into unseen holes. "Amelia!" My ears rang with her name, my voice ragged and hysterical.

I feared no one and nothing, not caring who heard me as long as I found her. If I came across this monster that haunted the bridge, I'd bulldoze through the motherfucker, my fury making me into a giant, able to obliterate anything that separated me from her.

Earlier that night, after waking from a concussed sleep, I'd seen her standing on the bike path, watching the pedestrian bridge, convinced of the man living beneath. Still thinking that the gaping gash on the back of my skull was the worst of our worries, I had gotten up to go to her and pull her out of sight.

And like a pistol fired, she fled, boots pounding the pavement before making a sudden turn into the woods.

Instead of following her at that crucial moment, I grabbed the gun, checking to see if there were any bullets left before running after her. By then, she was only a distant crash far ahead, and I, a moron, attempted to follow her in unfamiliar woods.

I was lost and bleeding profusely from more cuts and scratches than I could count. My grip was slick on the gun, and I imagined jamming the metal down my throat and pulling the trigger. I'd think of Amelia in a sparkly dress on that first night we met against a graffiti-covered wall. I'd think of my tenth birthday, with my parents standing proud and my friends crowding a flaming cake. I'd think of my roommate on the day we moved into our apartment, eating take-out, and laughing amongst boxes and disassembled furniture. And things wouldn't hurt anymore.

It had been fucked from the start. We hadn't been prepared, didn't anticipate the long dick of unpredictability and insanity outside the bubble of her parents' house. PPP, my father would have said, piss poor planning leads to piss poor results. Where he originally heard this, I knew not, but it had been a constant mantra growing up.

I tried to calm down and think clearly, but I was hyperventilating, gasping, and wheezing. It's always advised to stay in one place if ever lost in the woods. It was easier to be found if you stayed put, which gave you better odds of surviving. Instead of breaking your neck in an unseen gorge, you were supposed to build a shelter and start a fire. Bear Grylls was a master at this, using creative ways to snare some poor creature for dinner. Of course, I'd done none of this.

It was lighter up ahead, and I could see an opening through the trees. There was a meadow; its long grass starting to turn the color of fall's spun gold. Wading through this gently waving sea, I tramped to an apple tree that grew in the middle, spindly branches reaching upwards like a witch's fingers. I sat with my back to it, wiping sweat and blood from my cheeks. Apples dotted the ground, filling the air with a stench of sweet rot. There were still ripe ones hanging. I'd have breakfast, at least.

I toyed with the gun's safety, thinking of what to do. All the supplies were scattered, left on the bridge or in the woods, and I couldn't hope to find my way back. Thirst was a real issue in addition to being completely, devastatingly alone.

The last person we saw alive had been that government employee, sitting in an idling truck while his co-worker bled out beside him. How is it possible that there was nobody else? Poughkeepsie was a city, not a major one, but the population was large enough that you would expect to see survivors. I worried over these details, the terror of losing Amelia becoming more manageable.

Tentatively, I reached behind my head, touching the wound. It wasn't as bad as I expected, a flap of loose flesh with crusts of blood matted into my hair. If I could find a roll of gauze and anti-bacterial ointment, it could be fixable. Infection was a major concern, especially considering I hadn't properly bathed in at least a week.

I took my t-shirt off, then my undershirt to wrap around my head. Would flies lay eggs in open cuts? Putting my t-shirt back on, I pulled up dry grass and piled it on my body to make an itchy blanket. It was cold, my breath puffing out into the crisp air. With my back still to the tree, I slept, dreaming of all the places Amelia could be.

With a sharp tug, the shirt that was wrapped around my head was pulled off. The bright sunshine was blinding as I sat up dazedly, fumbling for the gun.

"It's only me," Amelia said, crouching low to the ground. Her khakis were covered in mud, hair hanging in knots with bits of sticks and leaves stuck here and there.

I pulled her into a tight hug, sobbing and laughing all at once. It felt so good to hold her. Her arms snaked around my neck, smiling so that our eyes crinkled, and our cheeks ached, like when posing for a picture too long. "How did you find me?" I cried.

Untangling herself from me, she sat cross-legged. There were deep bruise-like circles beneath her eyes, and her clothes hung from her frame with dampness and filth. "You snore like a freight train. It echoed through the trees like a beacon." She smiled playfully, but it wasn't the truth, and I didn't join in her mirth. Her grin died. "You feel clammy."

I nodded, lying back down. "I don't feel well," I said. Coldness had crept into my bones during the night, fanning an ember of fever that grew and grew, burning with false hotness.

She flipped her hair and settled next to me, our heads in the grass, nose to nose. I trailed my thumb lightly over her face, her freckles. She was streaked with dirt, clean only where her tears had rolled down, and there was a deep cut on her temple that looked raw and irritated. But her eyes were clear and focused, her mind sound once more. Her fingers moved in semi-circles on my chest, a feeling both relaxing and soft.

"You're burning up, I think. I can never tell whether or not someone has a fever. But you're shivering." She turned over, curling my arm around her.

"I wish for floss so I could tie one end to your belt loop. I'd never lose you," I whispered into the back of her head, shaking and shaking until finally falling into a fitful sleep.

I dreamt of thirst, a terrible thirst that strangled my throat with sand and turned my tongue into a shriveled corpse. In my dream, I walked an empty road, and when I thought thirst would crush me, I tried for a respite in the shade of an oak, but thirst was all-encompassing and would not let me rest.

And when I woke, thirst was sitting upon my chest, and I could not think of anything else. "Amelia," I said, shaking her awake. "We've got to find water."

It took her a minute to wake, her eyes fluttering first, licking chapped lips before sitting up. "Where?"

"I'm not sure. Even if we come across a stream, we can't drink from it without boiling it first and that means finding a kettle or a pot." My head pounded with pain, and coldness moved over my body in waves.

"If the water isn't stagnant, why would we still have to boil it? Where's the danger?"

"With all these bodies, someone could have died upstream, or waste plants could be offline, pumping sewage freely into the water. The contamination will probably be extensive over the next few months."

"Didn't we have water? Where are our packs?"

"Back by the bike. Where the bike is, I don't know."

She sighed and ran her fingers through the tangles in her hair. "Alright, well, this is a park of some sort. There's a grassy path about three hundred yards that way," she said, pointing to an indiscriminate section of the forest.

"How do you know?"

"I found it when I was looking for you last night. I'm hoping if we follow it, it'll lead us back to the highway."

"Let's go while we still can. It'll be dark again soon." The sky above was changing to a deep indigo, tapering with perfection to sunset orange on the horizon. I helped her to her feet and brushed off the back of her clothes, bits of leaves and grass falling to the ground.

"Check me for ticks?" she asked, lifting the back of her shirt. I scrutinized her from head to toe, picking off a spider that had been scurrying down the seam of her pants.

"Before we go, give me a lift into the tree." She stepped lightly into my cupped hands, shaking a branch so that apples rained to the ground. They were tart, more like crab apples than the ones you'd find for sale in grocery stores. But they were still juicy and piquant, my stomach cramping from not having eaten anything in a long while. Amelia squealed after finding a worm in hers, throwing it away and refusing to eat anymore. I filled my pockets, knowing we'd soon be hungry again.

Finding a winding deer trail, we walked in the general direction Amelia had advised. Freshly fallen leaves littered the ground, the distinctive smell of fall in the air. For the trees that had turned, I could not remember witnessing more vibrant colors. From deep reds to bright yellows, they stood out like tropical fish amongst the lingering green of summer. It reminded me of returning to school, of Halloween parties where girls in polyester costumes shivered like Chihuahuas, and the frothy creaminess of seasonal drinks.

Within a few minutes, we came to the path Amelia had promised was there. It was more like a service road for the park, a way for caretakers to get from one place to another quickly. It was rutted with dried puddles, a straightaway in both directions that faded into the trees before twisting gently around a distant bend.

"Which way?" I asked.

"Hush, let me think." She sat on a decaying log and put her head in her hands. I didn't understand and was getting steadily more impatient and thirstier as I stood there, shivering with fever and fatigue.

"Okay, left." She didn't wait for a response, and I was too tired anyway to discuss the trivialities of her choice. It was a relief when the forest finally thinned, and the shine of cars could be seen on the road beyond.

Amelia didn't bother to survey the situation, just stepped out onto the highway without a nervous glance. She feared no one because there was no one left to fear. I supposed what took hold of her last night on the pedestrian bridge had been temporarily forgotten. But it would come back. Insanity like that was never far away.

It wasn't long before the ground became unsteady beneath my weary feet, rocking like a narrow dock. The trees and surrounding cars soon followed, confusing up with down. Amelia walked before me, sure-footed and confident in this spinning world.

Black spots spread across my vision, like amoebas, unstoppable and illusive. My arms hung like trunks, my tongue sandpaper in my dehydrated mouth.

The day was cold, with a layer of cirrostratus clouds obscuring the sun. The wind rippled our light summer clothing, and Amelia hugged her arms to her chest, goosebumps standing at attention.

There was a gas station that we raided, stepping over bodies that slumped between aisles. The attendant had been shot in the face, and he lay like I remembered that murdered kid from Kent State lying in that iconic picture, board straight. It was a fever dream, so I imagined that they spoke, and told me the mistakes of their lives, their sins. I placed my hands on their heads, feeling stringy hair and loose flesh. "You are forgiven," I said.

"You're not the goddamn pope," Amelia snapped. "Let's go, this place is cleaned out."

"Your face is melting, Amelia. Dali said he fucked you on a clock while a starved horse watched."

"What is wrong with you?" Her words expanded into bubbles that wrapped around her head and suffocated her. "Don't fucking do this!"

She was screaming, screaming, screaming so that I held my hands to my ears which felt hot enough to melt clocks. I tried to tell her this, but it came out garbled and backward.

She was behind the counter, rifling through one-dose pill packets. "What are you sick with? Is it an infection? You were just fine yesterday!"

My teeth chattered uncontrollably. "You left me behind. In the woods. Last night. You left me."

"I'm sorry, Att. I really am. I lost my head, is all. Have you got a fever? You're shaking and sweating." Her voice was pinched and hysterical.

"Here." She dropped two pills into my hand. "Take them with this. It was an opened Gatorade that smelled too sweet, sickly sweet. I took the pills and swallowed down the drink, which I then promptly puked up again, splashing my shoes with half-digested apples and bile.

"Jesus, you've got to keep the medicine down." Amelia picked the pills from the mess and made me take them again.

"We'll have to find water elsewhere. There's none left here."

"I need to rest, just for a minute."

"No, Att," she said, grabbing my hand. "I'm thirsty, and you're feverish. There's no reason to rest here.

We've got to find another store, or maybe a house would be better?" She dragged me along like a child, scolding and supposing.

Back on the highway, light rain started to fall. Dark spots marked where raindrops fell on our shirts, quickly becoming wet in a full-force downpour. A blister burst on the back of my heel, and my boot felt oddly warm and slimy.

"Start opening cars," Amelia ordered, dropping my hand. "There's got to be water in one of these vehicles."

We pulled handles, looking for cars that were empty, but sometimes you misjudged, and the corpse of someone left dead in the back seat would surprise you with a stench, like opening a long-forgotten Tupperware of spoiled food. If they died sitting upright, their jaws were open, revealing a dark cavity that would suck you down if you weren't careful.

"Here! I found some!" Amelia called, running with a gallon jug of water. "It's unopened."

She unscrewed the cap and drank in deep gulps, water running down the sides of her mouth. She handed me the jug, gasping. I drank and drank and drank, my stomach cramping. My head felt clearer, but my fever felt worse.

"What are your symptoms?" She peeled my eyelids up, peering at them like they'd tell her everything. "The cut on your head must be infected."

"We're going to die," I said. "We're ten generations removed from being able to survive on our
own."

"That's because we're going about this backward.
We need to find new camping gear. A pot to boil
water, fishing poles, and a shelter."

"I've tried."

"I know you have, and I know I fucked it all up.
It's my fault and I'm sorry." Her face was long with
worry. "Here," she said, pulling open the door to an
SUV, "Get in. We shouldn't get caught in the rain
like this."

We crawled into the backseat together, Amelia
pushing me from behind. The seat was made of soft
brown leather, the smell of a new car about us. A
man's glasses rested on the front dash; a purse was
left abandoned in the center console. Amelia rifled
through its contents, finding a bottle of Tylenol that
shook with fullness.

"Open up," she ordered, popping four pills into
my mouth.

"It's too much, Amelia. I just took some."

"We don't have doctors. It isn't too much. Now
relax."

I laid on my back, wet clothes sticking to my
skin, and drifted, being too wary to fully sleep. She
moved to the driver's seat, chin resting on the wheel,
contemplating. I thought I heard the door open at

one point, but when I opened my eyes, she hadn't moved.

The rain came forever, pitter-pattering on the roof in a soothing rhythm. The windows fogged with our breath as the night became cooler, and the crickets could be heard faintly through the closed doors.

But the calm gave me chills, and I kept thinking that we weren't far from the pedestrian walkway at all, a few miles at most after being delayed in the woods last night and with the onset of sickness today.

In a voice that sounded altogether paranoid, I asked Amelia to lock the doors. She raised her head to glance at me, probably making sure it wasn't a fever dream request before hitting the button and settling back down, adjusting the seat and curling into a comfortable position, breathing slower and steadier as she fell asleep. Being completely enervated, I struggled to stay awake, but the dread that cloaked me was no match for the pharmacy Amelia had made me ingest.

And then it was here. Standing at the back of the SUV as a silhouette beyond the foggy windows. A thing of malice. It was equine in a way I couldn't explain, perhaps the way it bobbed its head like a horse tired of its reins. And it spoke of pestilence and apocalypse, and my blood moved in rhythm with its words. It wanted to frighten, to seize power.

But for all its wickedness, I felt nothing but disgust, and the harder I focused, the less sway its murmurings had over me until I opened my eyes. Not in the normal way you'd open them, but like I was a dog, only opening the inner lid with the outer still shut.

In this world, Amelia no longer slept soundly in the front seat. The door was ajar, and the overhead light was on, casting a halo over what I had lost. I pushed forward, knowing perhaps that this wasn't real either.

I woke with a gasp, like a man half-drowned. Amelia still slept, grinding her teeth at whatever haunted her dreams.

A deep feeling of guilt settled over me. The kind of guilt you feel as the sun is cresting the horizon, but the party has died down, and you're all alone, sucking back the last vestiges of cocaine from your nasal cavity. And all you can think about is what a fucking piece of shit you've been your whole life.

"Maybe we should turn back, Amelia," I told her as we sat in the car later that morning. She had woken a few minutes before, eyes unfocused and sleepy. Her hands were between her thighs to keep them warm.

"I can't face the walkway again," she said, yawning.

"We can find a different way."

She sighed, tired of this argument. "I left myself on the other side. I don't want to go back for it. Don't want to see what's become of it."

I thought of the equine monster, feasting with block teeth on Amelia's spirit as it screamed and struggled. But in the end, devoured, always devoured.

"Let's get to New Paltz. Regroup. It's a hippy-happy place. There'll be camping gear we can scavenge. We can find a decent place to lay low for a few days until you feel better."

"Okay," I agreed, though I didn't want to. I didn't want to leave this backseat. I wanted to rewind time, watch it as you would a videotape of us walking backward, mouths yammering silently as we spoke, of us running wildly through the woods, of us fleeing madly over the walkway. There, I'd stop the tape and point to a shadow on the screen, proof of the monster on the walkway with us. Now that it's been confirmed, I can rewind all the way to back to before the quarantine announcement stating we were forever fucked.

"Come on," Amelia said, opening the door and stretching. "Sun's out!"

As we walked, Amelia sang. It was prophetic and filled up an empty place. Her voice was rounded and beautiful, ending sometimes in a falsetto. And the birds listened, and the crickets listened, and everything that believed in song listened to her as we traveled. The music carried us as we moved forever forward, my fever forgotten momentarily, shivering only sometimes when the wind cut through the sun's warmth upon our faces.

"Look," Amelia squealed, pointing ahead.

I squinted into the sunlight, shading my eyes. A billboard loomed large down the highway, a behemoth with its post the size of a large tree trunk. *"Welcome!"* was written in swirling paint, each letter at least six feet in height. Upon hearing Amelia's shout, two people, wearing smocks and holding paint brushes, turned around on the narrow platform and hailed us.

Amelia collapsed, and I was too slow to grab her. With fists clenched, she screamed, "thankyouthankyouthankyouthankyouthankyouthankyouthankyouthankyou," over and over until the words ran together.

Unfurling a rope ladder, the two painters descended and approached us, slightly wary.

"Hi," Amelia called to them, getting to her feet.

"Hi," one of them said, their hair cut short and dyed electric red. Their eyes were ringed by shimmering eyeshadow, their lips stained crimson.

"Ziggy Stardust, then?" Amelia asked, smiling.

"Charlie, actually," they said, introducing themself. "My pronouns are they/them."

"And I'm Mabel," the other person said, somewhat dreamily. "Mine are she/her."

They were both covered in paint splatter but looking a hell of a lot better than we were.

"My name is Amelia, and this is Atticus. She/her and he/him. It's great to meet you. You're the first people we've talked to since the Panic."

"Panic?" Charlie echoed.

"Oh, I guess that's just what we call it. Do you have a name for it? Does it have an official name?"

They both shrugged. "Everyone has a different name for it."

Amelia's brow furrowed ever so slightly. "Do you have any food or medicine?"

"We don't," Mabel said, "but if you continue on about another mile, you'll run into Lou. He runs the welcome stand. He'll get you settled."

"Thanks," Amelia said. "Is it like a survivor's enclave or something?"

Charlie nodded. "Yeah, and it's a good one too. Glad you found us."

We thanked them and started walking. Soon enough, a lemonade-like stand came into view. Painted on the front was a big welcome sign. A man with his feet propped up, dozing in the sunshine, sat behind it. He wore a cowboy hat over sleek black hair, pulled back into a ponytail.

Amelia rapped her knuckles on the wood, waking him, which he did with a start.

"Oh, hello! Sorry, I must have dozed off. Not too much action these days," he said, standing. "I'm Llewellyn, but you can call me Lou."

Amelia introduced us. "Have you got any food or medicine?"

"Are you sick?"

"Atticus has a bad cut on the back of his head that's become infected. He's feverish."

"Can I ask you both a few questions first?" Lou asked, picking up a clipboard.

Amelia shrugged. "Sure, I guess."

"Have you been exposed to the viral hemorrhagic fever?"

"Yes, we were," Amelia said.

"Did you experience symptoms and recover, or are you immune?"

"No symptoms, probably immune. Have you met anyone that's recovered?"

"No, but I still like to ask. You never know."

"Our friends died."

"I'm sorry to hear that. Before everything went dark, the news reported that the virus had an incubation period of only twelve hours and a mortality rate of 97%."

"We've been cut off from any kind of news for a very long time," I said.

"That's a real shame. Always like when newcomers bring updates from the big beyond."

Amelia scoffed, "it's nothing but the big empty now."

"There's a hostel up the road there," Lou pointed. "A young lady there will get you checked in. I'll be up in an hour or two. Let's talk more then."

NOW

L eaving Amelia to her raving, I hiked down the mountain towards the abandoned shacks in a moment of urgent compulsion to confirm that the dead had stayed dead. I imagined blackened bodies clawing up through the mud, mouths gasping for air after having been incinerated. Their molecules pulled from the muck and dust to recreate what had burned on the pyre.

The shacks turned out to be much the same as we had left them. Forlorn and rotting, they were, in reality, nothing but walls of cracked plywood and corrugated metal roofs. A fungus, or maybe it was a mold, crept up the wood, giving it a sickly green tint.

We called them pods at first because pod had been a more palatable name when deciding to winter in them rather than calling them what they truly were. Of all the mistakes Amelia and I made in those first few chaotic months of the Panic, deciding to live here was the one I probably regretted the most.

Amelia wanted to burn them once we had awoken from our stupor of horror. Lily wouldn't hear of it, insisting they stand as a memorial to those that had perished.

I touched the doorframe of the nearest one and peered inside. Various bits of detritus lay on the floor, the inner sole of a sneaker, a scrap of a dirty blanket, and a tiny bone of unknown origin. A phantom feeling of coldness crept into my toes, and I curled them inwards, alarmed.

This is a bad place, Matilda whispered. *A relic of suffering will beget more suffering.*

Beyond the shacks lay an area of scorched earth. Wood anemones and bloodroot pushed through the soil in vivid brilliance, the ashes providing nutrients to aid in their delicate show of beauty.

I kneeled in the dirt and pressed my forehead into the ground. I wept silently, great shuddering breaths wracking my body. Amelia's pregnancy was a watermelon seed of despair growing in my own belly, forcing its twisting vines up through my throat, threatening to burst from my mouth. I tried to keep my teeth shut tight, my molars screaming from the pressure.

There was no one to help us. Death was predicated on happenstance and fortuity now. There were no gleaming hospital rooms with beeping machines monitoring our vitals. We lived in a forest, alone, like animals.

When I finally lifted my head to wipe the snot trickling from my nose, I realized how dark it had gotten. The sun had disappeared behind the mountains casting the world into deep, velvety twilight. I rose to my feet, cursing myself for lingering so long. To be outside at night was perilous. I thought of the coyotes that had so aggressively hunted us at the nursery.

From the corner of my eye, a shift in movement, and an impression of a colossal mass beyond a grove of birch trees. I froze, my heart thundering in my chest. The shifting shadows of the trees made it hard to discern if I had just imagined something.

I didn't even have a weapon, let alone a shirt, having left the tree house this morning with Heath to dig the cellar in what seemed like a lifetime ago.

A crisp crack of a branch cut through the quietness.

Run, Matilda urged.

I took off running, my heavy boots churning up packed dirt on the trail. A scream, like that of a bobcat, rent the air. There was fury in that sound. I didn't slow or look back, so frightened of what I'd see.

It was night by the time I reached the tree house, and I could barely see my hand in front of my face. In the time it had taken me to get home, I convinced myself that whatever I had heard was a trick of the senses, the culmination of a long day. With my legs and lungs burning, I climbed the ladder and banged open the front door, pulling myself inside.

Amelia lay on the couch, shoulders rounded against the cushions and feet propped on the opposite armrest. A steaming mug was balanced on her stomach, the tiniest hint of a rounded belly just starting to show.

I turned the wick up on the oil lamp in the kitchen, casting warm light into the room. Her eyes never wavered from the stained-glass window near the ceiling, the one that looked upwards into the mountains through a painted religious setting of Jesus putting his pious hands on so-called sinners. I thought it would be kitsch, so we stole it from a nearby church, leaving a gaping invitation for the critters to come pray.

"Where is everyone?" I asked.

Amelia giggled to herself. The high-pitched, hysterical giggle that I associated with manic moments. It sent chills up my spine. I walked around the coffee table to look her full in the face. She smiled widely and giggled again, tea slopping over the rim of the mug and dampening her shirt. It was buttoned wrong, with the very top button closed around her throat, and the rest so mismatched her undershirt was visible beneath.

That wasn't even the worst of it. Her teeth were tinted black. I thought it was a trick of the light, but I moved closer, lifting the mug from her hands to smell its contents. It was sweet but powerful, like something slightly rancid.

"What is this?" I asked warily.

"Tea," she laughed, her face arranged around a mischievous smile. She reached for it, but I held it aloof, waiting for her to answer me truthfully.

"Fairy candle. Now give it back. I'm supposed to drink this four times a day."

"Why?" She giggled again, and I didn't like how fake it sounded, like suppressed animosity.

"It's making your teeth black."

"It's doing much more than that. Give it back to me."

I handed it back, unable to ascertain what was pulling her into that scary place she sometimes went.

"Atticus?" Lily called from upstairs.

"Yeah?" I answered, taking the steps two at a time. I pushed open their bedroom door. Heath was in bed reading, and Lily was sorting through her lock-box of seed packets. A candle burned merrily on the nightstand.

"You're home late. We were starting to worry. We ate dinner already and everything."

"I know, I lost track of time. Did Amelia eat with you tonight? She seems off."

"No, she came in late after we'd come up here. Did something happen?" Lily asked.

"She's drinking some sort of tea. It's sweet-smelling but foul, and it's turned her teeth black."

Lily's lips disappeared into a grim line, heavy eyebrows knitted tightly beneath her white hair. "I saw her drinking tea yesterday before Roman came back. I asked her what it was because I'm so used to her drinking coffee that it was unusual enough to notice."

"What did she say it was?" I asked.

"She didn't, just kind of ignored me and gave it a stir with a finger."

Heath set his book down. "What's so wrong with drinking tea?"

"She has that laugh, the weird one, and her shirt is buttoned wrong," I said.

"Can you come back downstairs with me?" A knot had tightened in my chest, a toy car whose wheels had been pulled back too far. "Something's not right."

"Is she high?" Heath asked.

"Probably," I said. Do I tell them that she's pregnant? What right did I have to share someone else's monumental news? None, I decided.

"You're scaring me, Atticus," Lily said, setting down the seed packets. "Where's Mabel? Is she in her room?"

"I don't know," I said, thinking backward frantically. I remembered seeing Mabel yesterday, crushing smooth sumac in a wooden bowl, its reddish color dusting the light patches on her hands. She'd been experimenting lately with natural dyes for our clothes and her paints. "What does it matter?"

"I'm not a doctor."

"Neither is Mabel!"

"Come on, then." She pushed me by the small of my back, and we clattered down the stairs together.

Amelia took no notice of our arrival. She hadn't moved since I left, continuing to look through the stained-glass window with her feet propped up on the couch.

Lily observed Amelia like one would a prized horse after a nasty fall. You hope for the best, but in your heart, you know it'll come up lame.

"What's going on?" Lily coaxed.

Amelia giggled, bared her black teeth, and cocked her head like a puppy. "Whatever do you mean?" she asked.

Lily went to her, kneeling so that they were at eye level. She gasped and drew back, the kneecaps of her pants darkened with a dripping liquid. She slapped the mug away from Amelia, and it went tumbling across the living room, the tea leaving droplets on the walls.

"Ah fuck, Amelia, what did you do?" Lily moaned, pulling Amelia's arm until she rolled haplessly to the floor. The couch was soaked with blood, metallic-smelling blood that tickled my nostrils.

Amelia pulled herself back onto the couch, spreading her legs so that her skirt rode up past her thighs. She was hemorrhaging. Lily screamed in distress, and Amelia screamed along with her in mock seriousness.

"Heath! Get down here!" Lily yelled. "Are you having a miscarriage, Amelia?"

"Gauze! We need gauze!" I yelled, flinging open the pantry door and pulling out bags of rice, gardening tools, and sacks of potatoes that had halfway rotted with eyes the size of my forearm. "Where's the first aid kit, Lily?"

"Check the bottom shelf. By the wine!"

There it was, in all its rusted tin glory. We had a more extensive cache of medical supplies, but I couldn't remember where it was stashed. Not right now. I wrenched the lid off and grabbed rolls of gauze.

Lily took it from me, packing it between Amelia's legs. The amount of blood was unbelievable, the floor slick with it, the couch sodden.

Heath ran down the stairs, stopping in his tracks at the sight in front of him. "Is Amelia hurt?" he asked, then immediately sprinted to the sink to puke up his dinner.

"How long have you been bleeding?" Lily asked.

I held Amelia's head steady while her eyes rolled in all directions, and she laughed with those black teeth. Her hand snaked up, and I thought for a moment that she meant to caress Lily's face, but instead, she raked her nails across her cheek with such violence I blanched, while Lily howled and stumbled back.

Amelia was on Lily with cat-like reflexes, tearing, biting, and slapping. I leapt on her from behind and dragged her backward by the neck while she kicked and laughed like we were part of a comic troupe putting on a show, and this was all part of it, wink wink.

Lily rolled in pain, both hands covering her injured face, groaning.

"How bad is it, Lily?" I called over the writhing body of Amelia.

A door banged open above and Mabel came careening down the stairs, pausing at the scene before her.

"The zip ties, Mabel! In the cabinet to the right of the sink," I called.

To her credit, Mabel didn't stop to ask questions, just slipped and skidded on the blood into the kitchen, pulling the bag of zip ties down so fast that they scattered everywhere.

I wrestled with Amelia, forcing her on her stomach and her hands behind her back. Pinning her, I tied her hands together, zipping that tiny piece of plastic tight against her wrists. Amelia slammed her head on the floor over and over.

"Stop fighting, we're just trying to help you," I begged.

She struggled once more but then went limp in my hands, her fingers already turning eggplant purple.

Heath examined Lily's face, his hands shaking. "Can someone please tell me what's happening?"

"It's not really Piper, Atticus," Amelia said. "It was only pretending to be her."

"Piper?" Mabel asked. "What are you talking about?"

"Amelia must have induced an abortion," I said, picking her up in my arms. She squeezed her eyes shut and tears leaked from the corners. "We need to stop the bleeding, or she'll die."

I carried Amelia to her room and set her in bed. I cut the zip ties and messaged her hands to stimulate circulation. Lily rummaged through our first aid kit of scavenged medicine and made Amelia take whatever she thought would be helpful. The blood was seditious, seeping through towels and sheets, relentless in its want of release.

The fear of losing Amelia was sickeningly palpable. For it to end like this, after all we had suffered and survived through was incomprehensible.

You should have never left her after what she told you, Matilda hissed. *Your rejection of the pregnancy was the catalyst for this act. Your love for her isn't deep or true. It's just a fallacy of lust.*

With a bandage stuck to her cheek that oozed hydrocortisone, Lily thought to open the field guide to see if there was some sort of herb that would help, only to discover that it had been hollowed out. Amelia had carved a square so deep that it went through the entire book. Housing a multitude of pills of all shapes and colors, we looked upon her with renewed worry. To have destroyed *Henderson's*...we could not fathom what was driving her.

From there, we systematically combed through her room, finding similar caches. There was no doubt any longer the purpose of Roman's frequent disappearances. Only Heath put up a small protest against going through Amelia's things and invading her privacy. The rest of us gave it no thought, fingers roving in all directions with bright, anxious eyes, finding pills in drawers and socks and under floorboards.

The extent of it was ludicrous and we all wanted to blame the other for not understanding the scope of her addiction. Where had Roman gotten it all? Most of the hospitals ran out of medication in those first few weeks trying to battle the fever. They had all become tombs in the end. And all the pharmacies had their front windows smashed in, people desperate for a cure or at least to stop the torrent of black puke that poured from themselves or their loved ones.

Cars, maybe. Or from the pockets of the rotting dead that were lucky enough not to die out in the elements. It was alarming to think of Roman going from house to house, car to car, turning out pockets, and rifling through purses.

We put all the pills into a stockpot and stared at the multi-colored contents with trepidation. The silence of Amelia's room was deafening. Lily got her fiddle and played a low, hauntingly beautiful piece of Appalachia music to fill our minds with something other than terror.

We took Amelia's temperature when we noticed the magnitude of heat radiating from her body. The small glass thermometer read 104 degrees. Amelia, unconscious, tossed with fever dreams. I held her burning hand and wept, distraught and helpless. Heath's arm fell across my shoulders, comforting me when I deserved no such grace.

The front door opened below. Roman was home. A surge of rage filled my body like I had been struck by lightning. I stood, hands tightening into fists as he climbed the stairs.

"What happened?" Roman asked, stooping his large frame beneath Amelia's door. "There's blood all over the floor downstairs."

"Amelia had an abortion and nearly died, might still die," I said.

His lips pulled back over his teeth, and I thought he might hit me. "That was my baby. She had no right to do that. It's outlawed."

"Says who? In this community, we believe in freedom for all." Lily said bravely. "Amelia can do whatever she wants with her body."

"One murder begets another." Roman seemed to grow taller within the crowded room, an optical illusion doubling and redoubling until it seemed his head would touch the ceiling. He moved towards Amelia, but Heath blocked him.

"The fuck it does! You're no longer welcome here. Take your painkillers and go," Heath said, shoving the stockpot into Roman's hands.

A preternatural smile crept across his face. "See you around, then," he said, before turning to leave. "I didn't think you were the type to throw a man out on the street with nothing, and you know, if I go, so does Peaches and your milk supply."

"Leave with what you came with, it's only fair," Heath said.

With that, he fled, and we watched him go from the window. Unlatching Peaches' pen, he whistled, and she trotted out behind him, into the darkness.

Later that night, Heath woke me from where I slept in the high-backed chair in Amelia's room, his finger to his lips. He gestured for me to follow him downstairs and crept to the window, pointing. I followed its line of direction to the Great Meadow.

A figure stood, bathed in moonlight. It was Roman, his face an immovable stone as he watched the tree house. He wore fur draped over his head and shoulders, dangling down his back. With grim understanding, I realized it was Peaches, skinned. Bile rose into my throat, and I clamped my hand over my mouth to keep from throwing up.

Malice radiated from his stance. In his hand, he held a long knife, one stolen from the kitchen. The metal shined dully each time he shifted his weight.

Heath pumped Amelia's air rifle, but I reached out, guiding the nose of the gun to the floor. Even at close range, it would be difficult to kill someone with such a low caliber. If Heath shot and missed, Roman would know we had tried to kill him. It was a far shot, far enough where he could easily slip into the forest and disappear, us hopelessly hunting in the dark. It was too risky.

Roman stayed like this for over an hour, until the moon began to set, and the first warblers woke the world. Before turning to leave, he winked, the right side of his face crumpling to his eye in exaggeration, so that we'd be sure to see it from this distance.

***

Over the next few nights, we set up a watch. I took most shifts, having trouble sleeping knowing Roman was out there unhinged. The living room offered the best vantage point, with windows facing in nearly every direction. I kept one cracked, my ear sensitive to any rustle.

I sat before the fireplace, wrapped in a tattered blanket, absently stirring the coals. It crackled and danced, warm and welcoming compared to the cold night outside. It was a relief to escape the confines of my room. I had woken with a start by a nightmare, soaked with sweat. Coming downstairs, I tapped Lily to bed.

I had dreamt of Amelia. She was balancing on top of a rusty gate, honeysuckle and wild hedgerows tumbling around her, deep greens and bright yellows. She wore only a crop top, her belly rounded with pregnancy, a globe of freckles.

The sun was high, the air thick with humidity and alive with the sound of cicadas and the chirping of birds.

I watched her from across the span of a lush meadow. She hummed and twirled a piece of hair between two fingers, staring dreamily at nothing in particular. I lifted my foot to take a step towards her but was held in place by deep muck. Caught fast, I struggled with mounting dread. A green mist of pestilence began to rise, enveloping me in a fog.

It became hard to breathe, my lungs filling quickly with what appeared to be blood as it trickled from my mouth. I screamed horrid screams that gurgled, and wailed for Amelia to help me, to kill me.

She watched with an indifference that chilled me, swatting casually at a bug that circled her. My vision grew cloudy as blood vessels burst, but I still saw when she turned away, swinging her legs over the fence, disappearing into a sea of grass and brambles.

Matilda comforted my heart as it went into arrest, hushing me in my last death throes.

It's a monster, she whispered, *what's in her belly is a monster with goat eyes.*

We do not dream the same dream anymore.

No, she agreed.

The house settled into the night, creaking in the wind with mice skittering between the walls. In these lonesome times, it seemed like we had become Robinson Crusoe figures. I habitually thought of that term, not just because of the irony, but because Robinson Crusoe was utterly stuck, surrounded by a vast ocean.

We were similarly stuck. Not with just a forest, but also by the emptiness of it all. We were a lone satellite, fruitlessly pinging an abandoned space center. But there were surely others out there, there had to be. I imagined a peaceful society working towards the greater good in temperate climates; I imagined thousands in chains along the beaches, digging for clams; I imagined a network of huts hidden in the bayou, where children fished from rafts and died from snake bites. Yet here we stuck our flag and here we stay.

A door creaked high above, and footsteps padded softly down the stairs. I waited, watching a dark figure come spiraling down.

"Hello, Atticus," Mabel said, moving into the firelight. She walked quietly to stand next to me, hardly making a sound across the wooden floor.

"Did I wake you?" I asked.

"No, I couldn't sleep," she said, sitting next to me and warming her hands in the merry flames. "Fires like these always remind me of roasting marshmallows."

"You must always think of them then, we have a fire going nearly all the time."

The corners of her mouth drooped and I'm afraid I've hurt her in some way. We sit quietly and I sneak a sidelong look at her, the fire reflected in her eyes.

"Atticus," she started, "Do you ever feel as if the music has stopped and we're the only ones left trying to find a chair?"

"I feel—"

A blast erupted from the mountain over, a fiery demon rising into the night sky. The sound didn't hit us until a moment later, rattling the windows violently.

"Atticus!" Mabel screamed.

I grabbed her around the middle and dove into the pantry, shutting the door with a snap. We sat breathing heavily in the darkness listening to rolling booms that seemed to shake my very heart. Someone came clattering down the stairs. I pushed open the door. It was Heath, rubbing the sleep from his eyes with a knife at his side. Lily peered through the step slats, high above, an owl face of concern.

"Was that an explosion?" Heath asked, staring hard into the darkness beyond the window. "Should we worry about the forest burning around us?"

In the distance, a brightness shone, brighter than anything I had seen since the Panic. Smoke, blacker than the night, rose into the sky.

"I bet anything the Wadchu Hotel just exploded," I said with conviction.

"Gas, you think?" Heath asked.

We stood huddled together, the four of us, looking out the window. I remembered back to a time when Roman had gone missing, how he had stridden into our clearing so proud, like a peacock, to tell us about his discovery of the hotel. Had this fire been an accident? Was it a malevolent scheme to lure us away from the tree house? I hoped he had blown himself up in the process. Perhaps he had nothing to do with it at all.

"I need to check on Amelia," I said, climbing the stairs. A guttering candle cast weak light on her sleeping form. Her bleeding had finally slowed to a stop the day before, but she was left pale and shaking. The fever persisted, not as high as it had been that first night, but a fever, nonetheless. She murmured in her sleep, restless and clammy.

A plate of food sat untouched on her nightstand, uneaten from this morning. She hadn't stirred then, and she didn't stir now. I resisted the urge to check her pulse.

Back downstairs, I stirred up the coals in the fire and added an extra log, there'd be no rest tonight.

"Is anyone hungry?" Lily asked, stepping over to the stove.

"What are you making?" Heath asked, pulling on a knit hat against the cold.

"Soup," she replied, piling kindling into the bottom and striking a thing of flint. She coaxed an ember into life and soon snapped the door closed, the heat warming the room pleasantly.

"What kind of soup?" Heath asked suspiciously. "We haven't left the tree house in days. We've eaten all the fresh food."

"Cup Noodles!" she exclaimed happily, rummaging around in the cabinet. She pulled out the Styrofoam cups with a flourish.

"There's no way I'm eating those," Heath said. "They remind me too much of being on the road during the Panic."

An awkward pause. We rarely spoke of those desperate times right after the Panic, preferring to keep it light with post-shack era topics. It hurt less.

"Well, I'm starving, and I don't feel like eating tinned peaches," she said, checking the date. "Still good."

"They're freeze-dried, aren't they?" Mabel asked. "As long as no bugs have gotten inside the packaging, it should be fine."

Lily pulled a pot down from the rack and filled it from the plastic water tank above the sink. She set it on the stove to boil, soon spooning out three bowls and set them steaming on the coffee table. I threw a couch cushion on the floor and scooted over to a bowl.

Mabel came and picked hers up, sitting near the fire with the bowl balanced on her lap. Lily came to sit next to me, swirling her noodles around, letting them cool first. I blew on mine, taking a tentative sip. Flavor bloomed in my mouth.

"Sure, you don't want some, Heath?" Lily asked.

"No, it does smell wonderful though," he replied, leaning against the kitchen counter. "Assuming that the Wadchu Hotel did catch on fire, are we also assuming this was Roman's doing? I know he'd go up there from time to time, wouldn't say what for, but I knew."

"It's some treachery, whatever it is," Lily said. "It's good we've had quite a bit of rain and all the rivers and streams are still running heavy from the winter snows."

"Can't we still do something to protect the tree house in case the fire does jump?" asked Mabel.

Heath shrugged. "Like what? It's risky venturing out right now, getting caught in the fire, or worse, running into Roman."

Mabel frowned. "He's upset about Amelia, sure, but he wouldn't hurt us."

We hadn't told Lily and Mabel yet, or even Amelia, that Heath and I saw that brute wearing his pet's skin in the moonlight. Let Amelia get better first, we agreed, keeping our patriarchal secrets close.

"Did you hear what he said about it being his baby?" Mabel asked. "I refuse to let that kind of mentality get indoctrinated into this new world, whatever that means for the future. Fuck that, women have suffered enough under the thumb of men."

"Hear, hear," said Heath. "We should draw up a proclamation setting equal rights and bodily autonomy that applies to all, not just white Christian males."

"That would mean setting up a provisional government with borders, and thus owners," Lily said. "Land should have no owners, only guardians."

"Do you ever wonder if remote indigenous people know what's happened?" Mabel asked. "It must feel like such a reprieve from all our pollution and climate-changing ways."

"Speaking of climate change, it seems too cold for spring. It must be close to freezing outside right now," Heath said.

"Oh, please don't say that," Lily pleaded. "All the cool weather crops will be killed if it gets below freezing."

We watched the fire until dawn, heads eventually nodding into chests. The fire didn't seem to be spreading, but it was hard to tell from this distance. We didn't speak of what would happen if it did. We had no plan.

NOW

By morning, the tree house stunk like a campfire left burning. Even with the windows latched tight, smoke hung in the air, visible near the push-button lights. We watched the fire's progress diligently from the living room windows, much like we used to watch breaking news, with a semi-removed air. We were Americans after all.

We stoked the fireplace after clouds moved in, the temperature falling rapidly. We draped ourselves in blankets and sweatshirts. Amelia finally found the strength to get out of bed, dragging her blankets downstairs where it was warmer.

Lily tried to coax vegetable broth into her, but she refused, leaving the steaming bowl to grow cold. She shuffled back and forth from the chemical toilet to the couch, a shadow about her. Deep, black circles ringed her eyes, and her lips were chapped and peeling from dehydration.

Lily grew increasingly anxious about the cold weather affecting the garden. Her nails, normally black with dirt, were chewed to the quick, ragged, and painful looking.

To comfort her, and because she probably still felt bad for scratching her, Amelia asked Lily to sit before her so she could braid and re-braid her hair, deft fingers unsnarling and smoothing. They murmured together in quiet conversation.

Mabel sat with her back to the fire, quietly observing Lily, sketching her in charcoal. I watched her progress, becoming more alarmed as Lily was transformed into a human-like ember, her white hair represented as twisting smoke above her anguished expression, both hands held up, fingers gone.

"Everything will work out, Lily," Heath said. "The garden will make it through the cold snap."

"Not with this rain moving in. I'm afraid it'll freeze, and the weight from the ice will break the stems," said Lily. "I knew I should have kept the row covers on. I didn't expect cold weather so far into spring."

"Where are the row covers?" I asked. "I can get them set up before it starts raining."

"I used the netting as a weed control barrier in the tomato and cucumber garden. I feel so stupid," Lily cried, holding her head in her hands. "If we lose the garden, it'll be my fault."

"I hate to bring it up again, but we've run out of all the fresh food we have in the tree house. Unless we want to get into the canned goods we have saved, we need to figure something out. We can't hide inside from Roman forever," I said.

Amelia glanced at me but said nothing. Since her fever broke, she hasn't spoken about what happened. She seemed more upset about losing Peaches than Roman.

The rest of us had been having the same looping conversation for days. It was starting to drive me mad. Was Roman going to harm us? Was he gone for good? How do we go about our lives again knowing he could be out there, waiting to pick us off one by one in the forest? Would he come back for Amelia?

To prove to them, or perhaps to myself, that Roman didn't intimidate me, I shrugged on my raincoat and left with my bow, anxious faces watching from the windows. Once outside, it dawned on me how stir-crazy I'd been these last few days, tired of my own thoughts and longing for a distraction. We understood each other's absences as something needed, a coping mechanism. We all found solace in different things.

With our meat stockpiles gone, I embarked on a hunt, first checking traps (empty) before setting off to find bigger game. The day began to darken, and a light mist of rain started to fall. Chilled, I zipped my coat to my chin, my breath visible as I traversed the mountain.

I dove under a towering hemlock tree once the sky opened and rain fell in torrents, making myself comfortable in the dry needles that littered the ground. A thin sheet of ice started to form on the tree branches.

After some time, a small doe picked her way down the trail, head hung low in the rain. Letting an arrow fly, it pierced her jugular, and she careened through the underbrush in a panicked dash.

I kicked the ground in frustration and set off after her, tracking the droplets of blood on the ground. I had meant to hit her in the heart for a clean kill. It was monstrous to make her suffer like this.

I followed her into the dense pine forest, the ice on the tree branches creaking ominously. She died in a small clearing, blood coating her neck and forming a pool beneath her. I had no right to take her life.

With a piece of rope tied around her back hooves, I hauled the carcass into a pine tree to gut it. Blood dripped, dripped onto the ground making little rivulets that ran like a red spring down the mountainside.

I worked until sweat beaded on my forehead. I loosened my jacket. A growing pile of meat sat steaming on a rack I constructed from bendable saplings. The forest was quiet today, the pines enclosing me in muffled silence, smoke hanging like a haze.

A feeling of being watched stole over me, similar to what I had felt down at the shacks. I paused but could hear little over the falling rain, now sleet, bouncing off the crust of ice that blanketed everything.

Could it be a bear? But no, the wild bears of North America had finally succumbed to overhunting and vehicular collisions, their human-like bodies left to decompose on the sides of the roads.

When zoos were outlawed, animals were sold piecemeal to the highest bidder, those usually being illegal circuses or the private cages of the ultra-rich. You'd catch a shaky video sometimes on social media of bears dancing with an iron ring around their necks, the intelligence in their eyes dimmed by the trauma of forced captivity.

Many of the big mammals had said their final goodbyes over the last five years or so. The elephants and rhinos died, alongside the Ugandans and Kenyans, in a bloody war with the People's Republic of China when they tried to annex a large swath of eastern Africa for control of the uranium mines. The United Nations wrung their hands publicly at the carnage but hung the taxidermied animal heads in their baobab-paneled studies.

They would have died anyway, the world leaders reasoned, from cataclysmic drought and desertification caused by nations half a world away. As long as it wasn't happening to the wealthy, was it even a problem?

I worked quickly, hacking off the last of the meat and wiping the blood from my hands. I untied the rope, letting the carcass slump to the ground. Perhaps whatever stalked me would want to tear at the remains first. Wiping my knife, I sheathed it and grabbed hold of the rack, dragging it behind me. My pants had frozen, my feet numb and blistered in wet boots.

The way home was difficult, with rocky outcrops and ledges that I hefted and heaved the rack down, skidding and slipping on the icy ground. From time to time, I thought I heard the parallel crunching of footsteps but couldn't be sure.

Is it Roman, Matilda? I asked, but she was curiously absent.

Ahead, a dark lump blocked the trail, and I struggled to make out what it was through the sleet. I approached warily, my knife at the ready. I drew closer and closer, suddenly recognizing the curls, now matted and sodden. I dropped the rack and ran to her.

"Mabel!" I shouted, shaking her shoulder roughly. She was cold, too cold. She looked up at me slowly, her eyelashes heavy with frost.

"Atticus?" she asked, her voice thick.

"Let's get you out of here," I said, lifting her slowly. She struggled to her feet, her stare faraway and empty. "Can you walk? Are you hurt?"

"They've come back, Atticus," Mabel replied dreamily.

"Who?" I asked, rubbing my hands up and down her arms and blowing hot air into her frozen hands. "We have to move. We can't stay here." I slung her arm around my neck, and half carried her, pulling the rack behind us.

"We needed more water, so I went down to the stream to fill the portable tank. There were fresh footprints on the muddy bank, barefoot and small."

Her head lolled, and I hoisted her back up. A shadow mimicked our movement, keeping abreast, but hidden within the pine boughs. I thought I saw the gleam of a wicked smile, one that curled far too high.

Frightened, I pulled a torch from my rucksack and lit it, the flame whooshing to life in a merry crackle of warmth and light that spit and spat. It was made of animal fat and rags, the wetness no match for it. The shadow sank back into the protection of the forest.

"They were Charlie's. I feel it in my heart. After all this time, I finally found their footprints. Charlie is trying to find their way back to me."

The wind carried a new sound, that of yipping coyotes. They were tracking us, drawn to the scent of blood and weakness. Mabel stumbled beside me. Her hair was saturated corkscrews that bounced with every step.

"Not too far now," I said, seeing the slight curl of smoke from our fireplace over the trees.

They're coming, Matilda warned.

Gleaming sets of eyes reflected the firelight, flanking us. I grabbed a hunk of venison from the rack and stuffed it into my coat pocket, heaving Mabel over my shoulders. Leaving the rack, I held the torch high, a beacon of safety as I navigated the icy trail. Snarling and snapping rent the air as the coyotes descended upon the meat.

At last, we broke through the trees and came down through the Great Meadow. "Save us!" I cried over and over until I grew hoarse. Lights began to grow in the tree house, and the front door was thrown open. Heath climbed to the ground, quickly followed by Lily, each bearing flashlights and weapons. They rushed to my aid, Heath taking Mabel and Lily grabbing my arm to help me escape into the copse of trees where our home stood sentinel over the wild forest.

Heath heaved Mabel up the ladder and through the door. Lily pushed me through, and I fell onto the floor. Amelia slammed the door shut and barred it with the heavy oak slab. She held the rifle at her side, her face drawn with distress, the first lucid expression I had seen in some time. I smiled. I couldn't help it.

In the sobering safety of the tree house, Mabel explained that she'd just gotten turned around in the sleet, that maybe it had been a walking night-mare. She was no worse for the wear, shaken a bit, but had no apparent injuries.

Lily, eyes puffy from crying, checked all Mabel's appendages for frostbite and sat her close to the fire with a hot cup of tea. "Mabel, we thought you fell into the stream and went over the falls. I cannot explain to you how sick with worry I've been."

"Are you sure you saw footprints?" Amelia asked. "Heath said there was only one set of prints, yours, leading straight into the water."

"I thought Charlie had come back," Mabel said miserably.

Amelia stiffened at this. "Charlie died last winter."

"No," Mabel said, "they disappeared last winter."

They glared at one another from across the room. Lily chewed her lip at the tension.

As I cubed the hunk of venison to make a stew, I mulled over what Mabel thought she saw by the stream. There had been something within the pines watching me, I was sure of it, and not just the coyotes. A coil of anxiety kept tightening in my chest the more I thought about it.

"Either way, I think we should only leave the tree house in pairs for now," Heath said. "It feels like we're on our last goddamn legs."

"That's ridiculous," Amelia said. "How are we supposed to get anything done?"

"I'm not saying it has to be forever. We need to look out for each other."

"You're trying to keep tabs on me. That's what this is all about, isn't it?" Amelia asked, anger straining her voice.

Mabel sighed. "Why does everything have to be about you? We were attacked by coyotes, and you want to make this about your abortion? You get to decide that, yes, but you don't get to undermine Heath's practical plan to keep us safe."

Amelia shrugged, already disengaging from the conversation. "Fine, you're right. I'm too tired to argue."

Later that night, with stomachs full of venison stew (stew being relative since the only other ingredient was a single, precious can of creamed corn), we peeled ourselves from the warmth of the fireplace to retire to our respective bedrooms. Heath would be taking the first watch of the night.

"Can you help me up the stairs, Att?" Amelia asked. "I still feel weak."

"You lost a lot of blood. You're lucky to be alive," I said, taking hold of her arm.

"I'm a New York City cockroach. Of course I'm alive," she smiled.

We stopped before her door. "Want to come in for a little while? I don't want to be alone."

"Yeah, okay," I said. "Are you sure?"

She must have seen doubt cross my face. "Jesus, yes, come on." She slipped underneath her covers and held them open for me to join. "It's cold."

Kicking my shoes off, I climbed into her bed. Amelia pulled the covers to our chins and snaked an arm across my chest. The weight of her gave me pure, unalloyed happiness. The night was bright, so bright I could make out the hollows of her cheekbones. I breathed her in, grateful she was still here.

"Can you tell me a story?" she asked.

"What kind of story?"

"I don't know. Anything that comes to mind."

I thought for a moment. "There's a town in Virginia named Amelia."

"Really? You've been there? What was it like?" she asked, settling in to hear my story. Her index finger drew lazy concentric circles across my chest as she listened.

"It was desolate even before the Panic. The air was heavy with humidity, and thick vegetation grew all over everything. Many of the houses there were made of cinder block, whitewashed and shabby, with too many toys strewn about the yards. An abandoned mechanic's shop was called Amelia's Auto Body. It had big plate glass windows and sat right up against the road. It probably smelled like old grease with outdated tools still hanging from hooks."

"Do you think anyone still lives there?"

"Maybe they were spared and just kept living a humdrum life. Ate their own crops instead of selling them to big conglomerates. Used their horses for tilling, oil lamps for light."

"We should visit. Stay awhile."

"Alright," I agreed.

"We can fly. Commandeer one of those small Cessnas. Enough with this walking everywhere bullshit. I don't care if we're seen by anyone. We can write hopeless messages on little slips of paper and throw them down when people come running from hovels."

"You've got an evil heart, Amelia."

"I know," she sighed. "It's what I like best about myself."

I drew her close, her head resting upon my heart. "Would we bring everyone? On this trip to Amelia?"

"Why? Can't live without Mabel?" She pulled herself onto her elbows.

"What about Mabel?"

"I'm asking, if we left, would you insist Mabel come with us?"

"I only insist that you come with me."

This seemed to pacify her. "Would the townspeople think I'm faking my name? I lost my wallet a long time ago. I think I left it at my parents' house."

"I could vouch." I paused, my eyes unfocused as I tried to remember. "Did I know your last name?"

"I don't know yours. It's lovelier this way."

"Amelia?"

"Hmm?"

"Please don't hurt yourself anymore."

"I can try."

She fell asleep soon after and I carefully untangled myself from her arms, tucking the blankets around her, and slipping out of her bedroom and into mine.

The following morning brought a warm sun that went to work melting the ice in drips and trickles. Lily and Heath left at first light to hike up to the garden and brought back grim news—all the seedlings were damaged by the ice and would have to be regrown. That would cut our overall harvest this year by quite a bit with the bullish outlook that the next round of plantings wouldn't get taken out by deer or bugs or fungus or any number of blights.

"We'll have to smoke fish and venison, make supply runs for canned goods wherever we haven't already cleared," Amelia said. "There will be wild blueberries and blackberries we can harvest. We can even eat cattails if we get desperate. They apparently taste a lot like potatoes."

"I can go fishing today," I said. "The marsh isn't too far from here."

"No," Mabel said forcefully. "Heath we should stick together in pairs."

"Do you want to come with me, then?"

"I can't. Amelia asked me to help her sort through a garbage bag full of knotted yarn so she can start mending and sewing again."

"Heath?"

"I've got to get the rest of these seedlings to the garden for Lily. She wants to replant as soon as possible. Take the canoe. Do you remember where to find it? Coyotes can't get to you out on the water."

"You sure?" I asked.

He raised his hands defeatedly. "Bring your knife and the whistle, too. If you get into trouble, call for us and we'll come running."

***

The marsh stretched before me, a plain of bright water that reflected the afternoon sun. Mountains loomed all around, their roots drinking in the sweet muddiness of the mire. Small birds twittered and flitted through the grassland, their tiny wings beating, their songs mellifluous on the breeze as they snapped up bugs and grubs.

I uncovered the canoe that lay hidden in the scrub. An ancient heavy thing, its red paint chipped. Names were carved on the inside with a penknife. *Catherine,* it said, in square-like letters. *Mary,* said another.

I imagined them as sisters, legs hanging over the side, toes trailing in the water on lazy summer days. Days, when days were still counted, and Monday came to ruin weekends like a faceless monster of re-sponsibility. They'd brush out their tangles and slip into pencil skirts for a tedious week filled with paper pushing or test-taking, all the while daydreaming of freedom.

Sliding the canoe into the water, I pushed off the bank, steadying myself with the oars as I sat on the rotting wooden seat. Wasn't it funny how things that seemed of monumental importance could be so quickly forgotten? Weekdays. I didn't have a fucking clue what day of the week it was, it didn't touch me. I could still recall the feeling of facing a new week though, that trepidation. Monday. A new name for a legion of children so we could forget what it ever meant to us, and fold into the lexicon like Amanda or Samantha, those bland names parents selected for their precious gestating offspring.

The marsh water was so clear you could see the bottom. Rainbow trout basked in the sun's rays, their caudal fins rippling in the current. The close banks supported heavy vegetation. Sedges grew thick and wild with splashes of color from marsh marigolds and swamp roses. Tulips lifted their purple spring flowers over the tangle of greenery.

Gliding along slowly, I followed the twists and turns of a deep channel that wound its way through the marsh. The oars made hardly a sound as I rowed. I kept watch for Roman, the specter that had skinned his prized goat.

Heath and I didn't know what Peaches' death meant, whether it was a senseless act of rage or perhaps something more sinister, unimaginable until the final act.

I hadn't given poor Peaches much thought until now, possibly because she had been the catalyst in us allowing Roman into our enclave. She had minded herself in the little movable wooden enclosure, cropping grasses and wild weeds with incessantly chewing jaws, a constant sight in the Great Meadow.

I slid off the canoe seat and stretched out, content to let the current sweep me slowly further. I closed my eyes and listened to the melody of bullfrogs croaking, insects buzzing, and the soft sound of wind through the cattails.

I dreamt that I paddled the canoe with fervor, the early morning sun glinting off the water making it hard to see. I searched the banks as I paddled, peering through the thick vegetation. I spotted a flash of color as Amelia went careening through the swamp, muck up to her thighs.

"Amelia!" I called, ramming the canoe into the bank. I leaped onto the ground, sending birds skyward in fright. I lost my shoes to the mud, yet I did not stop. Her dress whipped in and out of view as I struggled to keep up. With a burst of speed that sent pain up the side of my chest, I grabbed her hand. She let out a shriek and spun around. I stumbled back in fright. Lips were bared over fangs, and her eyes glinted yellow through matted hair.

I woke suddenly, my eyes flying open. The canoe had become lodged on a fallen tree and was rocking gently. The sky was shot through with color, curtains of orange and pink. I must have slept for hours. Peepers and crickets were making a deafening racket.

That dream felt so real, I said to Matilda.

It was nothing more than that, she replied, floating serenely in the blackness of my mind. *Whatever made you fall asleep? If you don't catch anything soon, there will be nothing to eat for dinner.*

I gave the tree trunk a heave and continued further into the marsh. I took a torch from my pack and blew on it softly, coaxing the burning ember that lived at the center. It whooshed to life, and I wedged it near the stern. The fire burned merrily, happy with its watery reflection.

I untangled my fishing line and baited it, choosing a fat maggot out of many that I had found in a rotting log. I tossed the line into the water and reeled slowly, the spool making a satisfying click, click, click sound.

I drifted slowly, impatience mounting as my line got snagged over and over and not a single fish was tempted by the bait. The current pushed me into a wide pool where the water became shallower, and the underwater vegetation made it nearly impossible to catch anything but weeds. I sighed, gazing around, searching for darker, deeper water that trout and bass loved.

I gasped. Not thirty feet away, Roman stood in the muck up to his ankles in galoshes he must have swiped from town. He grinned, his hands on his hips. Peaches' coat was tied nonchalantly around his waist.

"Hello, Atticus," Roman said, waving. Dried blood ringed his nose, a leftover from a nosebleed he must not have cared to staunch. His beard was chopped in ragged tufts.

Immediately, I reached for the whistle that should have been around my neck. I'd forgotten it, leaving it hanging on its hook near the front door.

"Roman," I said, acknowledging him. As calmly as I could, I reversed course by paddling backward, sending small eddies whirling in his direction. My fishing line snagged, and I paddled harder, the pole bending under competing forces.

"Aren't you going to ask where I've been?" Roman asked.

"I've never cared where you've been. You're no longer welcome here."

His grin widened. "I can always count on you for the hard truth."

"Amelia almost died because of you."

"I can always count on you to know about Amelia, too, isn't that right? Seems to me like there might be too many roosters in the hen house."

"I never thought you cared much about the hen house, Roman. You were off scheming most of the time anyway."

"Scheming," he echoed. "Not me."

With a swift motion, I cut the fishing line with my pocketknife and the canoe was free. "It's time for you to leave."

He laughed. "There's no more hiding. The wolves have found a way in."

I paddled backward, never taking my eyes off him. Roman followed my progress, walking along the shore, crashing through the growth and mud in his rubber boots. His forehead seemed to bulge like something was straining from his skull. It gave him a warped, melted look.

Without hesitation, Roman leapt from the shore, his face a mask of animalistic rage. The impact of his weight tipped the canoe, dumping us into the water. The torch went out with a hiss. My feet found purchase on the muddy bottom, and I stood, gasping for air, losing my knife.

Roman broke the surface with a surge. Weeds hung from him, and mud was smeared across his face. He lunged. I tried to scramble out of reach, but my feet slipped on the slick rocks. His pupils were black abysses of lunacy.

I desperately felt around the bottom of the marsh, searching for my lost knife, crashing and splashing. I felt like I was a water buffalo and he, a crocodile, brutal and calculating. Images of primal beasts getting dragged to a horrifying watery death kept looping in my head. Roman seemed intent on locking onto my neck for a death roll.

My hand closed around the fishing pole, and I hurled it spear-like into his eye. Screams filled the air, the kind that draws scavengers. I dragged him towards me in his pain, the fishing pole straining under the pressure. My stomach somersaulted as I saw his eye up close, oozing a mixture of corneal jelly and blood.

He grabbed the floating oar in a last-ditch attempt, swinging it wildly. It connected with the side of my head, and my vision went black and I struggled to stay upright. He jumped onto me, sending us underwater, where we twisted and fought. The fishing line was wrapped around his neck in a floating haze of silver. I yanked on it, sending air bubbles spewing from his mouth. Grabbing a rock, he brought it down wherever he could on my hands, arms, and face.

I broke the surface, my lungs consumed by fire. The fishing line was slicing my hands as I pulled it tighter. Blood was running into my eyes. I held Roman under until his thrashing and kicking grew more laborious until it stopped altogether.

I dove under, visibility low from the silt and debris that had been kicked up. Roman floated facedown, neck bulging where the fishing line had strangled him. His body slowly turned with the current, like that of the last monstrous dinosaurs that would become buried in mud only to be uncovered and fawned over by archeologists in a millennium.

I scrambled onto a nearby bank where I lay gasping, trying to make sense of what just happened.

Murderer, Matilda hissed.

THEN

The façade of the hostel was painted a cheerful fuchsia. Flower boxes were attached to the upper-story windows and held overflowing licorice vines and pink petunias. A stone patio was off to one side, home to a dozen metal folding chairs and a young woman bouncing an infant on her leg. She was pulling hard on a cigarette, blowing the smoke forcefully through her nose before stubbing the butt in an ashtray.

"Hi!" she said, smiling in that way people have when they're embarrassed by their teeth. "Lou radioed up and told me you were on your way here." She stood, switching the baby to her hip. Her only articles of clothing were a crop top and spandex shorts, and a silver belly button ring that shimmered and shined in the sun. Goosebumps stood up along her skin, cold in the chill breeze.

She couldn't have been more seventeen years old, with that rural look that some girls have upstate. They'd have a mess of kids before age twenty-five, getting caught up in the sticky red tape of the local justice system for petty crimes or addiction.

"I'm Pepper, and this is Piper." She wiggled the baby until her mouth opened in laughter. "And you're Amelia, and you're Atticus," she said, matter-of-factly, lips trying to hide an overbite.

"Yes, it's a pleasure to meet you," Amelia said. "And this precious babe!"

Pepper looked at me expectantly, so I cleared my throat, finding my voice. "Hello, nice to meet you."

Amelia rolled her eyes. "Excuse him. He's got an infection that's cooking his brain."

After a pregnant pause, Pepper said, "Well, I'll show you to your rooms. Do you want two separate rooms or a room with two beds?"

"A queen-size bed if you have it," Amelia replied.

"I can do that! Besides you two, it's only me and Piper and Lou. All the others have gone up to the state park."

"Others?" Amelia asked. "There were about twenty, last time I knew. But people cycle in and out. They're building little cabins. Pods, they call them, for the winter. Lou and I stay here to catch anyone passing through."

"And have there been a lot of people?"

She paused, "Not so many, no."

"I'm surprised there are any at all," Amelia said.

"Well, come on inside. There are hot showers if you want them," Pepper said, opening the front door and leading us inside. "We have a bit of pro-pane heat left, and this place has a huge generator that Lou keeps running."

The front room doubled as a reception area and a lounge, decorated in the usual hostel fare of world maps pinned to the walls, overstuffed couches, and racks of travel magazines.

"The showers are down the hall, just there," she pointed. "I'll give you towels if I can find them." Rummaging behind the front desk with one hand, she pulled rough white towels from a bin and gave them a smell. "These will do."

I took them from her and gave a small nod of thanks.

"Does he talk much?" she asked Amelia pointed-ly. "We had a kid like that in my school who didn't speak, so I know a touch of sign language."

"He talks. He's just not feeling well. You wouldn't have anything for a fever on hand, would you?"

"Oh, sure, but I'd have to look. Why don't you get settled and come back down for something to eat in a bit? Should have something by then."

"Okay," Amelia agreed. "We probably look like vagrants."

And we did, clothes in tatters, boots caked with mud, and stinking like decomposing animals. It must be the norm, people coming in half-dead, the way Pepper treated us with such passivity.

"So, your room number is," she paused, selecting a room key from behind the desk, "six. Just jiggle the key. They tend to get stuck in the locks. And this room has an ensuite bathroom, I think."

Amelia took the key from her gratefully, and we turned to go.

"Oh, and also," she called out to our retreating backs, "just remember that me and Piper are here for you. Lou used to run the hostel, but there were a few incidents. Lou said babies give people hope, so now he's at the welcome stand, and I'm here."

Incidents. I mouthed the word.

Our room was up a narrow set of stairs, the wood worn from thousands of footsteps. The place had a quiet hush about it, missing its broke patrons and their noisy delight and raucousness. The key did indeed get stuck in the lock, and I had to force my weight on it before it opened with a click of protest. The room was small, with just a bed on a simple metal frame and a side table. The walls were papered in lime green with a subtle pattern of geometric shapes.

Amelia opened the door to the connected bathroom. "Not bad."

"Do you want to go first?" I asked. "I can just use the showers downstairs."

"You sure?" She held her towel to her chest, face streaked with dirt, sweat, and scabs.

"I don't mind." I pocketed the room key and left, walking back downstairs, and searching for the bathroom, hoping to avoid Pepper. I caught a glimpse of her, back outside with another lit cigarette in her hand, bouncing Piper absentmindedly.

I found the men's bathroom, flicking the light onto a white-tiled room with toilet stalls on one side and an open shower on the other side, a half dozen shower heads sticking out awkwardly from the wall.

I hung my towel and stripped, kicking off my destroyed clothes. Turning the water on, I stood beneath the hot stream. A soap-on-a-rope hung from the knob, and I lathered slowly, my body sore and aching. I cleaned the half-moons of dirt packed beneath my nails and gently scrubbed the dried blood from the back of my head. I picked a sharp splinter from the wound, releasing foul yellow pus.

How long ago had we left Amelia's parents' house? Two weeks? Two days? I shook my head like a dog looking for the answer, but it would not come.

I breathed deep, trying to relax but sounds reverberated off the tile, reminding me of a particularly nasty childhood fear of a clown that lived in the drains. And I thought of our very own monster, the one who lived under a bridge and clopped on equine hooves.

Shutting the water off and wrapping the towel around my waist, I hurried back upstairs, not bothering to turn the light off in the bathroom. Pepper had since come by the room, guessing by the random assortment of folded clothes on the bed. I selected a pair of sweatpants and a t-shirt, clothes that looked like they had seen the washing machine a touch too much. But they were comfortable and clean, smelling of detergent.

Amelia was still in the bathroom, light spilling from beneath the door. There was no sound of running water, and I wondered if she had decided on a bath instead. Was there a tub? I never looked.

"Are you alright?" I asked, my mouth pressed to the door. Pepper's comment about previous incidents resonated deeply, and I worried for Amelia. It was Schroder's Box, but instead of a dead cat, I'd open the door onto a scarlet tub, Amelia's wrists cut to ribbons with a razor blade, its cheerfully colored handle lying discarded on the floor.

Perhaps I'd ask if her last act of life would be to drown me. I wouldn't struggle but instead breathe in the red water with glee. The anxieties that plagued us would no longer have authority, and the beast that hunted us could not reach into the complete blankness of death.

"Yeah?" Amelia called.

"It's me."

"I know it's you. Come in and sit. There's a chair."

I opened the door, relieved to hear her voice. The bathroom was painted light pink and had a distinct early 90s feel. A fake fern hung from a dusty pot in one corner, and yellowed pictures showing sketches of chaste girls in towels were interspaced along the wall. Amelia floated in a claw foot tub, bubbles in peaks and plains around her. Just her head and toes peeked out, and on her face was a look of pure serenity.

"Are you feeling better?" she asked.

"Tired," I said, pushing her clothes from the chair so I could sit. It was a small wingback, the seat uncomfortable with broken springs.

"You know what I could go for right now? A butterbeer." She looked at me expectantly.

"What's that?"

"They're delightful, like warm, golden syrup. I visited Florida when I was a kid and went to the Wizarding World there. Do you think we could make it down that far? I've always had this secret wish, burning even through adulthood, that I could live at Disney World. Those little houses you were never allowed in were always so quaint and perfect. They'd be at odd angles and have the most beautiful details and colors. We could live above Weasley's Wizard Wheezes and wave wands and wear capes. Teach our children that kelpies and kappas were real."

"We'd have children?" I grinned.

She splashed water at me playfully. "No, I was just dreaming."

"I didn't peg you as the Disney adult type," I laughed.

"I am not!" she smiled. "Don't you dare call me that. Anyway, Weasley's is at Universal."

"Your hands are like prunes. How much longer are you staying in there?" I asked.

She hid them beneath the water. "As long as I want to be. This tap right here," she tapped with her foot, "spits out hot water on demand, and Pepper hasn't said anything yet, so I plan on staying in for quite a bit."

I leaned back, crossing my feet in front of me. The air was humid and heavy, the light fixture above buzzing with a steady hum of electricity. I closed my eyes lazily, listening to the occasional slosh of bathwater.

"Have you always been this quiet?" Amelia asked suddenly.

"I've never felt the need for constant chatter."

"It makes people worry. I can see it in their faces, you know."

"Why should they care?" I asked, opening my eyes again.

She held my gaze steady, a serious set to her jaw. "Because these people don't know anything about us. You've got to make an effort."

"Why? I don't care about them."

"You've got to. They're helping us, Att."

"We won't be here long, so why does it matter?"

Amelia leaned her head back, her long neck exposed. "What if we die trying to reach your parents? We couldn't even get to New Paltz without a major catastrophe."

And I wanted to point out that she had been that catastrophe. Instead, I said, "Let me think about it, okay?" I let the resentment slide down my throat and into my stomach, where it churned and churned in acid.

She sighed, unhappy with the unfinished argument. "Whenever I was told 'let me think about it,' the answer was always no."

"I won't leave you," I said. "So if you don't want to go, we won't."

"That's unfair." She fidgeted uncomfortably, the corners of her mouth pulled down with unhappiness. "But you'll make an effort to be friendly while we're here?" she asked.

"I never spoke much to begin with."

"You must feel very misunderstood." She rested her chin on the side of the tub, no longer covered in dirt and blood. The fine scratches and cuts that crisscrossed her face were nearly invisible now.

"People talk, but in trivialities. Is there a difference?" I asked.

Amelia ignored me, "Can you hand me that towel there?" She pointed to a ratty cotton towel hanging from a hook. "And don't look!"

The bedroom was dark when we emerged, Amelia leaving damp footprints across the floorboards. She chose a sarong and a fleece zip-up from the clothes Pepper had left for us.

Pulling back the covers, I climbed into bed. The sheets were cool and comforting against my skin. The sun had set, throwing the room into darkness. I flicked the bedside light on and rolled onto my side to bask in the soft glow.

Amelia toweled her hair and then left, promising to come back with dinner and medicine. Longing desperately for a book, I settled on flipping through the Yellow Pages, studying the ads for local businesses. I waited for what seemed like a long time, trying to decide if I should look for her.

I fell asleep waiting, woken with some confusion by Amelia much later with cold toast on a napkin and a gel cap, which I took dry. Amelia settled in next to me, and I drifted off to the sound of her soft snoring.

The next day after a hasty shower, I went downstairs, finding Pepper outside smoking. Piper was wearing an oversized puff jacket with pink, sparkly leggings, stuck resolutely on Pepper's bouncing leg.

"Oh, hey," Pepper grinned.

"Good morning," I said. "Have you seen Amelia?"

"She went down to the welcome stand with Lou. He came back early this morning with your backpacks. Said someone leaned them up against the stand. He and Amelia are riding around in the golf cart to see if they can find them. It happens sometimes, people come through, and we miss them. They end up wandering in the wrong direction, never knowing where we are."

"Why don't you just leave directions at the stand?"

"We'd prefer not to be snuck up on at night," she winked at me.

I nodded, attempting to look agreeable. "I'm just going to look for Amelia."

"Of course," she said, lighting another cigarette with a Bic lighter, a Playboy bunny stamped across the side.

I took off down the sidewalk, my hands buried deep in the pockets of my sweatpants against the cold. It was a short walk to the welcome stand, much shorter than I remembered just the day before. Had it only been a day? I felt completely new, refreshed even.

"Atticus," Lou called, seeing me.

Amelia looked up, pausing the rifling she was doing through the contents of one of our packs. Her hair was twisted into an elegant knot on the top of her head, and she wore a new windbreaker, lips shiny with Chapstick. Seeing her like this, healthy-looking, made me want to kindly ask Lou if I could borrow the golf cart and leave with her, confident that we could reach the Catskills unscathed. This whole thing seemed like an inconvenient pit stop.

"Did you find them? Whoever left those?" I asked.

"Nah," Lou said, his black hair pulled into a ponytail. "But I'm not worried."

But I was.

**

Without having much else to do and being in disagreement over when we should continue to my parents' house, Amelia and I accepted an offer from Lou the following week to visit the construction site where the pods were being built. It was roughly fifteen miles away, he explained, at the base of the Minnewaska Mountains.

On a chill morning, bundled in clothes taken from the town's sporting goods shop, Amelia and I clambered into a rusting golf cart that spewed gas fumes, leaving Pepper and Piper behind at the hostel. A small metal trailer was attached to the back of the cart, piled high with sleeping bags, canned goods, and various camping gear and construction tools that Lou had managed to collect around town.

"Why not just live in New Paltz?" Amelia asked Lou over the rattle of the trailer as we trundled along the road, avoiding stalled cars and now-quiet traffic accidents.

"That was the original plan until the college caught fire over the summer, leading to a few gas explosions. Lucky for us, the building is located a ways out, or it would have burned the whole town down. Since then, there have been smaller fires, but without a working fire truck, there's really no other option but just to let it burn."

"Surely there was a fire department here with trucks?" asked Amelia skeptically.

"Three were destroyed in the initial chaos of the virus, and the engine won't turn over in the last one that's left. No one has the faintest clue about engines. Well, maybe Heath, but he's only worked on smaller two-stroke engines, like for dirt bikes, and what have you."

"What's to stop these pods from catching fire?" I asked.

"Well, there's no gas lines or combustibles, and if a pod does happen to catch, they're built far enough apart not to be a danger to the whole lot. For heat, we're foregoing open fireplaces for enclosed wood stoves. And to be honest, the fire at the college was suspicious. Could be there's a firebug roaming locally. We chose this location for the pods because it's hidden from the main road, less likely to be set upon and destroyed."

"Have you encountered anyone unsavory like that at the welcome stand?" Amelia asked.

"A few," Lou admitted. "You can immediately tell when there's something not right. In the way their expressions are, the things they say. Never ones to stick around for too long, so we haven't had much of a problem yet."

We drove past empty homes and stores, rounding a bend where a small bridge came into view.

"Oh!" Amelia gasped, hands bracing against the dash of the golf cart. Sandwiched between myself and Lou, she stood suddenly. I grabbed the back of her coat, fearing she would leap.

"Stop, stop, stop!" I shouted, but it was too late, the tires hitting the hollow-sounding concrete of the bridge, and over we went. Lou jammed the brakes, bringing us to a stop once we crossed the bridge.

"Is everything okay?" Lou asked. "I didn't mean to frighten you."

"No, it's alright. I'm alright." Amelia assured him. "Just not doing okay with bridges or heights lately."

He nodded, putting the cart back into drive and setting out. "We'll do that slower on our way back," he promised.

Amelia groped for my hand and held it tightly, the pulse in her wrist thrumming with adrenaline. I rubbed my thumb soothingly on the back of her hand, afraid she still might dart from the moving golf cart and disappear into the overgrown farmland that bordered the road.

"What did you do before the Panic, Lou?" Amelia asked after a long, awkward silence. She wriggled her fingers loose from mine, braver now.

"I was a manager at the Wadchu Hotel." He kept his eyes on the road, hands at ten and two on the wheel.

"What's that?" asked Amelia.

But I knew it. It was a Victorian castle-like structure perched above a lake. My parents had stayed there on occasion as a romantic place to dine on holidays like Valentine's Day, the sweeping views and rustic style appealing to them.

"It's a hotel on the mountain over," Lou explained. "We tried to quarantine ourselves, but the fever got in somehow. I think people were smuggling in their loved ones. Then it seemed like everyone was suddenly sick. We set up a makeshift hospital in the ballroom, but it was of little use. I walked out of there alone on the fifteenth day, but we had lasted longer than most."

Onward we went, leaving behind the flat farmland for winding mountain roads where the forest was on fire with fall leaves. When our faces were properly cold, and I had to keep snuffing back snot, we turned into a parking lot, but instead of stopping, Lou drove towards a small trail off to the side. The tires skidded on the dirt path, the trailer behind us bouncing wildly over dried ruts and exposed tree roots. White birch trees grew close together, their thin trunks spotted with mushrooms.

We heard music faintly at first, then louder as we drew closer to the encampment. I imagined a utopia of chic cabins set against the mountains, with cows grazing in an open field, clean sheets, and blue jeans blowing on clotheslines, what I had seen through Instagram filters and posed settings.

As much as we all loved to believe the curated, camp lens of social media was real, we knew it wasn't yet still allowed ourselves to feel inadequate as we scrolled. To be thinner, to be stronger, to be richer, to be more in love. If only we bought that or changed this, we too would be able to post serene beaches or soulless Scandinavian neutral garb that clung to our sculpted, macerated bodies.

Here, there was much more mud and no livestock. People were busily moving to and fro, tasks mid-finished. A few drifted over to start unloading the trailer, Lou providing cursory introductions.

"This is incredible," Amelia said. "It's like a bustling village."

I gazed around quizzically, trying to see what she was seeing. There couldn't have been more than two dozen people. It was like we stumbled upon a sixties-era commune, complete with a white woman with bleached locs.

"Anyone new turn up?" Lou asked a man who'd introduced himself as Heath.

"Just one, half-starved and with a fever. Found him out on the road. We put him in the far pod to quarantine."

"Has Nancy taken a look at him?"

"Yeah, she gave him some Tylenol and prescribed food and rest. Nothing more she can do since she's laid up with a fever as well. We think she caught it from the newcomer."

"No one, and I mean this sincerely, is to have physical contact with either of them until they recover."

Lou took us on a tour of the construction site, explaining that the pods could each sleep up to four people comfortably and came equipped with a rain catchment, chemical toilet, and stove. Each pod was designed to be self-sustaining. A few even had small solar panels affixed to their roofs, enough to charge a small light or device. Individual pantries were kept stocked in addition to a community kitchen that anyone was welcome to use.

"Is this somewhere you could see yourself wintering?" Lou asked.

"The leaves are just changing," said Amelia. "Don't you think it's too early to start thinking about winter? My god, the summer heat has been brutal."

"I've got a feeling that it's going to turn up with a wallop," he said. "We dug our own graves with this climate crisis."

"We got all of what, a few inches of snow the past couple of years?" I asked. "Why should this year be different?"

"Isn't it already different?" Lou asked.

Goosebumps rose along my arms in response as I considered his question, a palpitation deep within my core at the truth of it.

In the end, we agreed to help Lou and Pepper pack up the last of the supplies at the hostel in exchange for a golf cart ride some miles in the direction of my parents' home. We'd be given fresh packs filled with food and camping gear with the promise of a pod should we want to return.

I still hoped we'd find my parents alive. They had always been industrious, having eked out a small vegetable garden from their rocky, wind-blow property. Never having much money, my dad had learned to fix things around the house, the boiler, minor plumbing, and even the odd electrical issue. They were used to making something from nothing. They'd done it all their lives.

If they had isolated, ignored the government's directives, and waited it out, we'd find them well. My mother would put the kettle on to brew chamomile tea, and my dad would bustle nervously around the small house, waiting to be released so he could attend to one of the multitudes of tasks he kept busy with.

Amelia and I would sleep on my childhood bed that squeaked with every innocent movement. We'd stack wood for the coming winter and pickle the summer's last cucumbers. I had to swallow the immediate urge to set out right then, so powerful was my atypical longing for them.

Lou took it slower this time when driving back over the bridge. Amelia squeezed her eyes shut but was otherwise okay. Once we got back to the hotel, I helped Lou pack up boxes of supplies, water bottles, towels, blankets, canned goods, and socks, but it still didn't seem like enough for a group as large as theirs to make it through the next few months on this alone. Lou explained that they planned on doing weekly gathering runs for whatever they still needed.

Amelia took the baby from Pepper and played with her on the floor in the front room, reading her children's books and creating little sensory games that made Piper laugh with delight. It surprised me to see Amelia this engaged. Until now, her typical day revolved around getting drunk and floating in the pool, wallowing in what had been lost.

"How's your head feeling?" Lou asked me over a dinner of gluey boxed potatoes and beans later that night.

I wiped my mouth with my napkin. "Hasn't been giving me any problems."

We sat out on the back patio, enjoying the cool evening, Piper in her highchair giggling at Amelia as she fed her. The citronella candle kept the worst of the black flies away.

"That's great. Head wounds can be really finicky. How'd you say you got it again?"

"Fell from my bike coming across the pedestrian walkway in the dark."

"Grown and all falling from a bike," Pepper laughed, but not unkindly.

I'd gotten to understand Pepper better since we arrived at the hotel. She was resilient and friendly, quick to say what was on her mind in a plain-spoken way. She'd been living with a foster parent after her mother kicked her out of the house for getting pregnant at 16. After the Panic, she'd been pushing Piper in a stroller down Main Street looking for food when she'd stumbled upon Lou sitting out front of the hostel.

"It's stupid, I know," I smiled.

"These days, even a small accident like that can kill you," Lou added. "I never understood the perfunctory nature of life until I lost my wife. When I think of her, it's of her profile as she sips coffee. It was her favorite time of day, wrapped in a robe, with our dog at her feet. Her mom was Onondaga, so she had the most exquisite cheekbones. I dream of her." Lou's words trailed off into silence, and he closed his eyes as if absorbing his pain, metastasizing it.

"She called Lou while he was working to tell him not to come home. She was already bleeding," Pepper said quietly.

I grasped for Amelia's hand beneath the table, squeezing it to reassure myself that she was still here, that I could still see her in profile as she drank coffee on a quiet morning.

"If we lose those who define us, are we still ourselves?" Amelia asked. "When all the pieces have been carved from us, what substance remains?"

"I suppose you build yourself anew," Lou said. "If you can."

"Who's going to help us?"

"Ain't no one but yourself," Pepper said.

A key jangled in the front door, and Lou was on his feet instantly, striding inside with purpose.

"It's just us!" a voice called out, the door slamming shut. Charlie and Mabel, the two painters we'd met on the road, followed Lou out onto the patio. Charlie was wiry and compact, full of buzzing, uncontained energy. They had large, expressive eyes and a quick smile. Mabel was affable, quick to remember Amelia and I, and asked after our well-being.

Charlie set their pack down on the patio and pulled their sweatshirt off, using it to wipe the sweat that dripped from their temples.

"Is that a tiger's eye stone?" Amelia asked Charlie, gazing at a red-brown stone that hung on a long golden chain around their neck.

"Oh, yes! It's a protective stone. I attribute my survival to it."

"Thanks for helping us," I said.

"You two look a hell of a lot better than before. I'm glad you've settled in. Will you be staying the winter with us?" Charlie asked.

"We're considering it," Amelia said. "Perhaps we'll finish our intended trip and then make our way back."

"Where're you headed?" Mabel asked.

Amelia gestured to me. "To see if his parents are alive."

"Ah, now, why put yourself through that?" Charlie asked.

"Not everyone hates their parents, Charlie," Mabel said gently.

"Won't be easy to get there. Can't just get in a car and drive anymore, not with all the traffic jams and trees down," Pepper said. "Four-wheeler maybe, if you can find one."

"Did that tornado come through here too?" Amelia asked. "It flattened our house and almost killed us."

"We saw it from a distance, but it didn't touch down here," Charlie said. "Lucky thing too, because we've been staying in a yurt down by the river. It was part of an artist enclave before the fever."

"It's been cold at night," Mabel said. "These past few mornings we've been able to see our breath before the sun warms things up."

"Is the mural complete?" Lou asked.

"Our message is clear enough, I think," Mabel said but paused. "It's safer here."

"These past few days have felt ominous," Charlie said. "It's stupid what I'm going to say, but if we can't be honest in a world like this, what do we have left?"

"Go on, then," Pepper said, bouncing a sleepy Piper in her arms. "Can't be any stupider than the shit my momma used to say after leaving the social services office."

Charlie chuckled at that before beginning. "I used to play in my driveway as a kid, riding bikes and things like that, and I'd sometimes get this feeling that an ice cream truck was trundling towards me, hidden round the bend, driven by a man with a shark's smile.

"I'd forgotten all about this childhood fear until just a few days ago when I thought I heard a car. We were up on the billboard platform, so I grabbed the binoculars and searched but didn't see anything at all. I've heard it many times since then, and I can't get the image of an ice cream truck out of my head."

"Not to mention that we ran out of paint," Mabel said, rubbing Charlie's arm reassuringly.

I glanced at Amelia, and she shook her head almost imperceptibly, the memory of the walkway crackling between us. If they thought we led some evil enemy here, they might throw us out to fend for ourselves. Did we? Was it real?

"Our packs were left at the welcome stand," Amelia said. "Was that you?"

"No," Mabel said. "Nor have we seen anyone pass since you two."

"It's easy to detach from reality in times like these, but we've got to keep our heads on straight, or we're never going to make it through," Lou said, breaking the forbidding silence that descended over us.

"How did you misplace your packs?" Charlie asked, sniffing us out.

"Atticus was in a bike accident coming over the pedestrian walkway. We crossed it too late and, in the darkness, crashed. We got turned around and separated and spent a night hurtling around the woods trying to find each other, let alone our packs."

"That means there's another person, or persons, wandering about. If we come across them, great, but I don't think we should actively search. I don't have a good feeling," Charlie said.

"I'm going to put Piper down to sleep," Pepper said, excusing herself.

We drank wine in flickering candlelight and listened to the soft white noise emanating from Piper's baby monitor. Mabel retrieved a sketchbook from her pack and drew Amelia in charcoal, capturing her perfectly, down to the sadness that lingered around her eyes.

It was alien to be part of a group dynamic again after months of just Amelia and I, alone. I felt caught between being comforted that people still existed and mistrusting who these strangers were.

Later in bed, Amelia sleeping next to me, I thought of the story Charlie had told, examining it from all possible angles. It felt so similar, so familiar to what happened to us.

A terror, acute, yet undetermined in its physical form. Could it be a traumatic stress response from the Panic? A looming, disguised fear of impending doom that will snuff the life from us? In an empty world, would fresh horrors spread anew? Or was it simply the echoes of the dead?

NOW

Roman's body floated away serenely in the marsh's current. Flies alighted on his back, and vultures circled above, eyeing their decomposing feast. I watched his progress from the muddy bank, concussed from being clobbered by rocks and fists. To staunch the bleeding, I packed moss into my head wound and kept pressure on it. Horse flies stung relentlessly, their hum enough to drive you mad. I pulled a tick from my arm where it had started to gorge.

Water lapped at the overturned canoe, wedged on a bend farther down the channel. My vision went black when I tried to stand, and I came to sometime later, the blood drying to stiff flakes on my face.

The whistles started blowing around sundown, disguised as birdsong but becoming shriller the longer they searched for me. The cacophony of peepers in the marsh drowned out my cries.

The temperature fell rapidly after the sun set behind the mountains. I shivered uncontrollably in my wet clothes. The ground was squishy and permeable, with not a dry spot to be found.

I rolled onto my back and gazed at the night sky, beautifully illuminated by an expanse of stars. If this was it, I could accept my fate. With Roman dead, the group would be safe. With one less mouth to feed they'd have better luck making it through another winter. It would be okay to let go.

The fuck it would, Matilda spit, mad as an adder. *If you can't walk, crawl.*

Crawl where? We're in the middle of a marsh.

West, through the cordgrass.

I'll get lost in there, and no one will ever find my body, I said. *I want Amelia to have closure.*

You'll die having never attempted to find your parents. Their home is no more than a two-day hike from here. Why haven't you gone yet?

Because they're dead like everyone else.

And if they're not?

My parents, part of the Gen X generation, who were given the keys to the kingdom of modern society but squandered their privilege and opportunity by getting sucked into the vortex of capitalist propaganda. There was something to be said about that generation's forced ignorance and platitudes. They were the middle child between the shining, wasteful boomers, and horrified hopeless millennials. Gen Alpha was supposed to be our savior but, alas, the babes were all dead. Even sweet Piper, who Amelia said had tried to force herself back into existence.

My parents, maybe acknowledging their generations' failings to a certain extent, lived quiet, solitary lives. I knew of no other friendships they cultivated outside of a woman named Rosemary whom my mother spoke to on the phone a few times a year, especially around the holidays, but never extended an invitation to our home.

They ate meat only once a week and deep cleaned the recyclables, removing any labels and lids that would jeopardize their reincarnation into more useless junk. They believed that they were the cause of the climate crisis through their consumption of plastic packaging. It never occurred to them that this narrative was insidiously planted in their minds by the plastic-producing companies.

When I moved to the city, they came to visit me exactly once on a frigid winter day. I took them to Flushing for soup dumplings, and I realized my mistake the moment we got onto the subway. My mother's hand, so known to me the way all children know their mother's hand, was gripped so tightly to the pole that her knuckles were white. My dad kept touching his pants pocket where his wallet lay.

Flushing only furthered their disorientation and alarm at the sheer amount of people flowing around them, the restaurant's menu, and the noise permeating every facet of city life.

If they didn't get sick with the virus, I found it implausible that they'd search for help. It'd just be them, alone, like they always had been. What if only one of them got sick and died, leaving the other traumatized and isolated? To think of them not as a pair both saddened and startled me, like discovering a prized saltshaker sans pepper.

In muck up to my elbows, I pulled myself through the marsh. Matilda urged me onward, her eyes shining with purpose. The skin on my stomach was scraped raw, and I lost my shoes to the sucking mud. Dehydrated and exhausted, I couldn't be sure how much time had passed. Matilda jump-started me like a battery each time I drifted off.

I'll tell you of a dream I had, she said as I crawled. *I dreamt of a swamp and a great beast that prowled through the muck. You rode upon it with your knees held tight to its mangy coat. Amelia walked behind you, stepping into the watery footprints of the monster. She was a queen and wore a crown of bones upon her head. In your wake, the animals fled or bashed their heads into the ground, birds drowned themselves, and raccoons gnawed on their own paws. You were a blight on this earth, reanimating the destruction of the human race.*

Did you know that swamps absorb the impacts of hurricanes? But for a century we've been backfilling them with parking lots and amusement parks.

Why is that your response to what I said? Matilda bristled. *You never hear me.*

I rested on a dry mound of grass, out of breath. *I didn't know you slept.*

You've never asked me about myself.

A jab of fear so small, like a fiberglass sliver under a fingernail, pierced my heart. *You're a ghoul I manifested in a time of emotional upheaval. What's there to know?* I asked. *You are me and I am you.*

She grinned. *If you say so.*

A shrill whistle startled me. Flashlight beams crisscrossed in the darkness.

"Here!" I called out in a raspy voice.

"I think I heard him!" Heath yelled, followed by the sound of footsteps crashing and splashing through the marsh.

A bright beam of light fell upon me. "I found Atticus!" Heath called out triumphantly. "Over here, he's hurt."

"Are you able to sit up, Att?" he asked. "Where are you injured?"

"Head," I croaked.

Amelia stumbled through the cordgrass, followed by Mabel and Lily. They all wore headlamps and were caked with mud from the waist down.

"Oh god," Amelia cried, throwing her arms around me. She pulled me onto her lap and cradled my head, wiping away the muck from my eyes and ears. "He's cold. We've got to get him back to the tree house."

"Is he hurt?" Mabel asked, kneeling by my side. "Is that a head wound?"

She tentatively touched the moss bandage. "How did this happen?"

"Did Roman do this to you?" Amelia asked.

I thought of being a liar, well, I was a liar, but maybe it wouldn't do any good to keep it from her. "Yes."

"Is he dead?"

I remembered him thrashing beneath the water, then going quiet and still. "Yes."

"Fucking Christ," she cried.

"We can all feel bad about it once we're home," Lily interjected. "Let's focus on getting ourselves out of this stinking swamp before the coyotes find us."

Hoisted between Amelia and Heath, we made our way step by step out of the marsh. To Matilda's credit I'd only been about a hundred yards from the nearest trail.

"Lily, can you run ahead and get the fire started for the bath?" Heath asked. "Take the coals from the fireplace in the tree house to get it going quicker. We've got to get this mud off him to see if he's injured anywhere else. The shower will be too cold."

When you live without electricity, there isn't a whole lot you can do about a warm bath. We had a shower rigged near the stream because magic would have been easier to perform when it came to figuring out indoor plumbing.

Heath realized we desperately needed a better solution for the stench coming off our bodies. He hemmed and hawed until finally devising an ingenious way to have a heated bath.

Using a metal trough, Heath set it on a small wooden platform near the edge of the stream. From there, a pulley system of buckets scooped water that then filled the trough. Metal piping led into a large copper pot that sat atop a stone fire pit. When the fire was roaring and the water boiling, you slid a piece of metal out from the piping, letting hot water flow into the trough, mixing with cold water from the stream.

By the time we arrived home, the fire was roaring with gusto. Amelia rummaged through a small metal lockbox near the tub, searching through the soaps packaged in cheesecloth. Lily and Mabel had made these, boiling down wild roses and then dumping the mixture into a large vat of animal fat. They had let it dry and cut it up, making countless bars.

After throwing soap into the tub, Amelia released the hot water. Steam rose in lovely curlicues, the scent of roses filling the air.

Lily nudged Mabel. "Let's go inside and find the first aid kit. That wound needs to be dressed after it's cleaned."

Heath helped me undress. The drying mud made the clothes stiff as cardboard, and they cracked and crumbled as Heath peeled them off. I winced as cuts and scrapes were exposed to the cold air.

I stepped into the tub and immediately sighed with relief. The water was pleasantly warm, and all the tension left my body, easing the aches in my muscles.

Wreathed in bubbles, I floated with my nose just above the water. I found the soap along the bottom of the tub and started lathering my hair, taking special care with the scalp wound. Amelia helped me pull the moss bandage away, sodden with blood.

"I'll be right back with a towel," Heath said.

The tub water had taken on the color of a dirty puddle. The bubbles were starting to dissipate, and a cold breeze rippled the water.

"What are you holding in your hand?" Amelia asked. She leaned over the tub, working my fingers open gently. A fishhook sat in my palm.

"My hook," I whispered. My physical being seemed caught in suspension, and my heart silenced for half a beat before resuming its rhythmic journey.

It was the very same hook that had helped entangle the fishing line around Roman's neck. I knew it was the same because it was the only blue lure that was in the tackle box. The others were rubber worms and mismatched sinkers and metal hooks. Amelia plucked it from my hand and set it aside.

I struggled to remember the crawl through the marsh. There's no way I could have held onto it that entire time and not noticed.

A large mass floated down the stream, a bloated body indistinguishable from a distance. It bobbed in the current, bouncing lightly off rocks and dipping into deeper hollows. The matted fur, I realized, was what was left of Peaches' skin.

Roman rushed past, his face grotesque where fish had eaten his lips and the cartilage from his nose. His neck had expanded over his shirt collar, giving the impression of a fat man in a too-tiny suit. As he spun in the current, I saw his one remaining eye swivel towards me and wink.

In an instant, he was gone, cascading over the waterfall. I pressed my hand to my heart, where it beat wildly, fear obscuring the world.

I found it impossible to imagine a way for Roman's body to make it out of the marsh. There were just too many obstacles and animals that would have dined on him until there was nothing but bones, and those bones buried in silt.

"What's wrong?" Amelia asked, alarmed. "Do you see something?"

"I...can't be sure," I said.

"Ready?" Heath asked, back with a towel. He helped pull me to my feet and dry me off, wrapping a shabby robe around my shoulders.

"I can carry you," he offered. "If you don't think you can walk."

I shook my head and stepped out of the tub, holding his arm for support.

"Want to rest in my bed? Your hammock might be too difficult to get into right now," Amelia said.

"Thanks," I said, "but I'll be okay."

"Put him in my room, Heath. I don't care what he says. He's hurt."

Back inside, Heath held onto my arm as we climbed the stairs, round, and round until we reached Amelia's bedroom. A threadbare quilt covered the mattress, the stitched pattern worn with age and overuse. Various baskets of yarn and fabric cluttered the tiny space.

Amelia worked on getting me under the blanket, fluffing the pillow, and tending to the gash on my head. It felt like these were my last days, Amelia as the hospice nurse leading me gently into death.

If we had a therapist here, one who had their office on the top floor of the tree house and prescribed things like rest or milk thistle, they would tell me that I was simply impressing my morbidity upon the world. I chuckled at the thought.

Heath swabbed my head wound with alcohol and held me steady as Amelia, with careful precision, stitched it back together.

Amelia brewed an earthy-smelling tea that slipped me beneath consciousness.

Darkness greeted me again when I woke. I must have slept through the entire day. My head pounded, and I shivered with a fever.

The door handle turned quietly, and I bolted upright. The door swung inwards with a squeak, and a dark figure slipped inside, shutting the door.

"Atticus? Are you awake?" Amelia asked quietly.

"Yes," I said, relieved.

"How're you feeling?"

"Cold, like I have a fever."

"Hang on. I'll be right back with Tylenol."

She reappeared a few minutes later with a glass of water and two pills. "I hope the cut on your head isn't infected."

I swallowed the pills with a gulp of water and laid back down, drawing the blankets up to my chin. "It wouldn't be the first time."

"I thought it'd be your body that we'd find. I couldn't imagine anything but death would keep you from coming home. I've never felt so helpless before."

She wrapped her arms around herself and doubled over, tears dripping from the end of her nose. Her body was wracked with shuddering sobs that shook the bed.

"I did this to you. I did it because I was hurting, but in the end, I hurt you instead. My mother was right about me. She could always sense there was something rotten, not quite right. That's why I'm still here, to be punished and made small.

"I have betrayed everyone I ever cared for and loved. Bridget, who I loved deeply, but instead, dated every loser that came into my orbit because I was afraid if I let her in, I'd infect her with my self-hatred. And Pepper, who I shot and let her baby freeze to death because I was too self-absorbed with my own misery.

"And you, Atticus. I've probed your love for every crack imaginable, trying to drive wedges into the weak spots to prove to myself that I was unlovable, that I deserve the kind of hate I have for myself, a well of vitriol that I bucket up."

With exquisite pain radiating from my head, I reached for her hand, tugging her towards me. She acquiesced and laid beside me. I drew her close, holding her tightly until we fell asleep.

Morning sunlight shone through the porthole window, warming the bed pleasantly. The day was bright and cloudless, the sky beyond the tree branches an endless blue.

Amelia lay with her back to me, the sheets rising and falling as she slept. I remembered somewhere someone had said the hourglass shape of a woman was intrinsically beautiful.

I crept from bed to use the chemical toilet, checking out Amelia's stitch work in the mirror while I took the longest piss of my life. The wound was still tender and throbbing, but it hurt less and didn't seem to be getting any worse.

Something in the reflection caught my attention, and I stood there, trying to figure out what it was. Something seemed off about my eyes, haunted-like. I suppose the act of taking a life changes you, your soul, maybe, or your humanity.

I gripped the sink and leaned close to the mirror, studying myself. There, in the pupils, another set of eyes looked out. Then as quickly as I recognized it, it was gone, a trick of the mind.

You'll not find anything you don't already know, Matilda said, her black hair floating loosely around her head.

What do I know? I asked.

She grinned sardonically but said nothing. I was reminded of how unsettled she'd made me feel during the crawl through the marsh.

Suddenly, vertigo washed over me, and I lowered myself to the floor, holding my head between my knees. Roman's face, twisted with rage, flashed before me, and I squeezed my eyes tight against the vision.

A knock on the door startled me. "Att, are you okay?" Amelia asked, pushing the door open a crack. "Why are you on the floor? Did you fall?" She peered at me with one eye through the opening.

"Vertigo," I said. "Just like I had when I was out in the marsh."

"It's because you probably have a concussion." She pushed the door open and grabbed both of my elbows to lift me to my feet. "Let's get you back in bed."

She led me back to her room. We climbed into bed and faced each other, our noses nearly touching.

"Forgive me," she whispered. "For everything." Her eyes, magnified by tears, were bloodshot and vivid.

"There's nothing to forgive. I will love you through it all."

"Don't give up on me," she whispered. The hair on the back of my neck prickled, and I shivered as the feeling traveled through my body.

She tipped my face up to meet hers, kissing me lightly. It was as if my heart was made of molten gold, spilling forth through my veins, rushing through my spinal cord, flushing all the hurt, loss, and disappointment from the memories of my muscles. I was filled with a light that crackled upon my skin.

Amelia pulled her lips away, laying her head back against the pillow. Gazing into my eyes, she took off her nightgown and gently slid the blanket down her body, stopping just above her hips.

My breath caught at her beauty. Delicate blue veins were visible beneath the skin on her freckled breasts, her nipples a soft pink color.

Tentatively, I trailed my fingers along the hollow at the base of her neck, the dips and juts of her collarbones, and between her breasts where her heart thudded.

I had longed to know these contours. Would she slip away again? Would I have to dream about this moment for the rest of my life? My fingers traveled the ridges of her rib cage to the tautness of her stomach, beneath the blanket, and into the soft folds of her.

Moving to sit atop me, she leaned in to kiss me, her strawberry hair encapsulating us in a private moment of bliss. She shifted her hips forward, bracing herself on the bed frame so that she seemed to float above me. I gazed upward in adoration as my mouth found her.

"Atticus," she gasped softly.

I held onto her breasts as she rode me, sashaying her hips in measured movements so that my tongue could find those secret, lovely crevices. Her moan reverberated my chest when I slipped my finger into her, fervently discovering the points of pleasure that arched her back in orgasm. It was not like the drunk, fumbling love from the early days of the Panic.

She rummaged through the side table drawer, finding a condom, and handing it to me.

"You don't owe me anything, Amelia."

"I don't want to feel used anymore. I don't want sex to be transactional. I just want to feel loved."

"I loved you from the first time we held hands and ran for our lives. I remember your fingers, how they fit perfectly in mine and how your name sounded leaving your lips."

"So you still want me despite everything I've done?"

"There's nothing you can do to make me stop loving you." I rolled the condom onto myself, the rubber feeling foreign and compressed. Amelia kissed me deeply, her tongue down my throat. She guided me inside her, wet and swollen with want.

After, we lay together, arms and legs tangled in comfort. We snacked on last night's leftovers of wilted chicory salad and foraged chicken of the woods mushrooms. Bird song drifted pleasantly through the open window.

It took courage to ask it, but I felt compelled. "Why the sudden change of heart about our relationship?"

"I've lost everything but you. The anguish I felt when you were missing was akin to madness. I never want to feel that again. And to find out that Roman was the one to hurt you, well, that makes it my fault."

"No, we all let him stay. We couldn't have known what he was capable of."

She laughed derisively. "You don't know the half of it."

I lifted myself onto my elbows so I could look at her. "What do you mean?"

"With Roman, the act of sex was dispassionate and austere. He'd climb on top of me, and if I wasn't ready yet to take him, he'd spit into his hand to wet me. Then, as he thrust, he'd stare straight ahead, jaws clenched and eyes distant. Sometimes the only sounds we made were the rhythmic thumping of the bed or, if we were outside, the leaves crunching beneath me. It was an bestial act in its simplistic brevity.

"I soon realized that he was trying to get me pregnant with clinical precision. He'd always slip the condom off before he came. I protested the first time it happened, but he slapped me, and that was the end of ever saying no to him. It was the most degrading thing anyone has ever done to me, and I nearly enjoyed it because I thought that's what I deserved.

"Each time we had sex, I'd attempt to capture that softness Roman had with me when we first met. I'd try tricking myself into believing that he cared for me, but it takes a monster to know one. When Roman was fucking me, I could see the cruelty in his heart as clearly as if he had translucent skin. As embarrassing and gross as it is to admit, I hoped he'd strangle me so I'd go out like a sex-trafficked teenager, my mother's worst fear. I was just so tired of struggling for survival."

"If I had known this was happening, I would have thrown him from the tree house."

"I hid it because he fed me an endless supply of painkillers. It was understood that if I stopped fucking him, the pills would stop being popped into my mouth. They made me feel weightless and unbothered. Who cares if your lover hits you these days? Where are the judges, district attorneys, and police officers? Dead, all dead."

"I could have stopped it. I was always there to help you."

She smiled sadly. "You were, but not with a pocketful of pills and enough hate to make me feel worthless."

"I'm sorry."

She shook her head, "don't be. What was it like with Mabel?"

"Tender, but sad. We both wished the other to be the person that we love. When I was with her, I'd think of that terrible song about loving the one you're with and not the one you love. You can find comfort and stability that way, and I respect that, but she'd always be waiting for Charlie. And I, for you."

"Does Mabel really believe Charlie will come back?"

I shrugged. "If it were me, I'd never stop searching either."

Amelia was silent for a long time, breathing quietly, eyes locked onto some distant point in her mind. "I'll tell her what happened to Charlie. She deserves to know."

NOW

The following morning, Amelia herded everyone into the kitchen before they could dissipate into their various tasks of the day. She perched on a stool and compulsively picked at her nails as we shifted uncomfortably from foot to foot in the crowded space, like impatient children.

"What I have to say is for Mabel, but I owe everyone here honesty..." The words died in her throat.

"Well, what is it?" Lily asked after a beat of silence.

Taking a deep, nervous breath, Amelia began. "I thought it was a kindness to keep it from you, Mabel, but I see now that it was a cruelty. Charlie isn't ever coming back, I'm sorry. They're dead." Amelia's bottom lip quivered, but she held steady, chin high and jaw set tight, awaiting Mabel's judgment.

"What are you saying?" Mabel asked. "We never found their body. How could you know they're dead?"

From her pocket, Amelia pulled out a long necklace. A brownish-gold gemstone hung from it, the same one that Charlie had worn. A Tiger's Eye. Mabel reached for it with quivering fingers.

It was as if the evolution of two people was unfolding right before our eyes. Amelia, brave and honest, laid bare in her faults and reborn. Mabel, collapsing under the weight of grief, her joists of hope finally rotting through, tumbling the reality of Charlie's death upon her.

"Oh, Mabel, I don't want to hurt you. If you need to know, I understand." Tears splashed down Amelia's face, and she brushed them away forcefully with the heel of her hand.

"Tell me," Mabel whispered.

"It was after we found Piper dead and realized you were missing. I found Charlie in the snow beyond the birch grove. They'd been mutilated."

"No, that can't be right," Mabel cried.

"I went back later that night to gather what was left of their body. I burned them on the same pyre as Pepper and Piper. We didn't find you until the following day, and you were so distraught that I thought it would kill you if I told you. And then, I figured, what did it hurt to give you a little hope? I was wrong, and I can now see the purgatory of suffering you've been living in ever since.

"I thought because you had hope, it made what you were feeling less than what I was feeling, which was a mainline of grief over everyone I had lost. I hated your hope, even though I knew it was predicated on a lie. I don't deserve your forgiveness."

Mabel sagged forward onto the floor, her knees connecting with the wood in a painful thump. Amelia rushed to catch her.

An inhuman sound of agony tore through Mabel, the heartbreaking sound of someone who will never again be the same. A rending of a before and an after.

***

We dressed in all black and descended the mountain. The girls wore lace veils and velvet capes that dragged behind them as chapel trains. The velvet was meant to be used as drapes, but Amelia repurposed them on her Singer.

As we walked, Mabel plucked wildflowers from the ground, filling a basket with daffodils, tulips, trilliums, and bluebells. Tears ran freely down her face that she didn't bother to wipe away.

The Lark Ascending swelled elegantly from Lily's violin, hauntingly sad, yet filled with hope. The woodland birds quieted as we passed, listening curiously to the white-haired creature emanating such divine sound.

Health carried a small toolbox with stone carving chisels, his expression stoic and distant, lost in his thoughts. Amelia held my hand and hummed a mournful melody.

The clearing where we had once lived and lost was quiet and bright when we arrived, warming in the morning sun. Mabel made simple bouquets from the flowers she collected, giving each person one to hold. We stood in a loose semi-circle around where the pyres had burned.

Heath cleared his throat. "I don't think I'll ever understand why we were spared when so many were not. Why have we been forgotten and discarded, left to remember a world that no longer exists?

"I held my father as he hemorrhaged his life away, and I could do nothing to stop it. It was only when his body became stiff in my arms did I let him go. This man who had shown only kindness and love was gone. "We are alone, abandoned, and cast out as freaks from the reckoning of our species. We were chosen to feel the searing loneliness that comes with being the last of your kind. A judgment and sentence from endlings and the mother herself." He laid his flowers down and stepped back.

"Before the Panic, I lived a hard life," Lily said. "I was always hungry and never had enough of anything. Just my ma and I surviving as best we could. Then her shitty alcoholic boyfriend cracked her head open like a cantaloupe one night after she refused to give him her bartending tips."

Her face collapsed into an anguished, silent wail as if there wasn't enough pain in this world to express herself.

"I needed my ma, and she was gone. He took her from me when I was just 17, and nobody gave a fuck about me. I sometimes fantasize about finding my way back to that town just to see if he's alive so I can crush him the way he crushed her. I will find ecstasy in the sound of his bones cracking, so when I think of my mother's death, it's his death I will see and not hers anymore."

"Jesus, Lily. You saw him kill your mom?" Amelia asked. "Count me the fuck in whenever you're ready to find him."

Lily nodded, accepting her offer. "Humanity's last act was to lock me in a strip club. I'd be dead if Heath hadn't found me. This might sound callous, but the last couple of months have been some of the most stable in my life, with certain instances notwithstanding."

Amelia stepped forward and laid her flowers down. "I want the yoke of sorrow lifted from around my neck. I want to love myself. I want to forgive myself and to be forgiven." Tears leaked from her eyes. "Please, it hurts."

Mabel laid Charlie's necklace down amongst the flowers. "Growing up with vitiligo was difficult enough without throwing in identity confusion. I was adopted at birth by a well-meaning white couple who were told they'd never be able to conceive. When I was a kid, I remember feeling cherished even if they didn't quite know how to do my hair or integrate my culture into their lives.

"Then, when I was seven, my mom got pregnant and had twins. They called it miraculous, a gift from god, a blessing given to them for their selfless act of adoption. To this day, I still don't know if it was internalized sibling jealousy or if I truly was regulated to a second-tier kid. It sure felt that way. When I left for college, they could finally be the nuclear family they always wanted to be with blonde ringlets and community functions. What's the saying? There's no hate like Christian love.

"You know what's awful? I've rarely thought of my brother and sister since the Panic. I've always assumed that this new world wouldn't allow such perfect specimens of everything wrong with the old one to survive.

"It wasn't until I met Charlie that I started to accept myself, to lessen the furnace of self-hate and doubt I kept within myself at all times. I learned to love myself through Charlie's love. If they found me worthy, I must be worthy. I stopped straightening my hair and covering my vitiligo patches with makeup.

"When Charlie disappeared, I held out hope they'd find their way back. I knew they'd never abandon me like my family did. I'm angry that you kept it from me, Amelia, but I understand why you did. I don't think I would have made it through last winter without a purpose."

What will you have to say for yourself, Atticus? Matilda sneered. *Bare the soul that murdered your rival, that has forgotten his parents in pursuit of a woman who doesn't love him?*

I laid my flowers on the ground. "I've brought instability, jealousy, and bitterness into our home that we have all strived to build anew. I've cleaved the community everyone else has worked so hard to foster. For that, I'm sorry. I've been in a singular mindset of survival, and it's time to put that aside."

Using a hammer and chisel, Heath carved WE REMEMBER into a small boulder near the old pyre.

Back at the tree house, the setting sun cast deep red shadows onto the walls. The windows were open, a warm breeze blowing through the kitchen as Lily and Heath made a dinner of rabbit stew. Amelia garnished our cocktails with foraged dandelions that lent a honey-like taste to the bourbon.

Mabel oscillated between crying jags and tearful reminiscences of Charlie. "After graduation, we were going to move to Palm Springs, live in a mid-century house with a butterfly roof, and make it big as artists," Mabel said. "We'd hang out at North Beach and sell weed. Like George and Tuna, except we'd be in love. We'd thrive in golden sunshine and subsist off soup kitchen specials."

"I thought all those mid-century homes got bought up by investors and flipped as short-term rentals?" Lily asked.

"Housing crisis aside, that was our dream."

We'd never, as a group, discussed our previous aspirations and career goals. That mentality had collapsed almost a year ago, and how silly we'd all been! To be so dedicated, so committed to a job! A job where you worked for years yet still lived paycheck to paycheck. They told us that raising the federal minimum wage would increase prices for food and bare necessities, so we believed them and acquiesced, but they raised prices, nonetheless, blaming inflation and calling us lazy. And by lazy, they meant powerless.

The American dream was sold to us as a lottery ticket. Only the sociopathic ruthless with family money hit the jackpot, and don't try to fool yourself that it was any other way. We were the stepping stone in the mud with their boot prints on our backs.

And it wasn't just in the corporate world, it was everywhere, from accountants to contractors. It made me sick to contemplate it, that cheerful façade of miserly misery. No, we'd not go back, and we'd not think of it again. We'd not suffer that existence.

"We should go to Palm Springs," Amelia said. "We can drive around in a convertible, never worrying about winters. It'll be a revival!"

"There's a whole country between Palm Springs and us," Lily said. "I can't imagine we'd be able to get there safely."

After we ate, Mabel suggested a shot of bourbon as a toast to Charlie's life. From there, we left all pretenses of garnished cocktails behind and drank doubles, the bourbon smoky and smooth. We shifted to the living room, draping limbs over couches and chairs.

"Lily, I wanted to tell you how brave you were today to share what happened to your mother," Mabel said, eyes bloodshot and watery.

Lily shifted uncomfortably, "I thought I should finally name my pain to you all."

Heath nodded gently, encouraging her. Lily squeezed his hand. "My ma was a bartender at the only tavern in town. She got to know all the bar-flies and, I guess, became one herself. Most of the men were harmless, but there were a few who got possessive. One guy in particular thought he could control her. My ma and he were sleeping together even though he had a wife. He was always down and out, never a dollar to his name, so he was always begging off my ma even though we hardly had anything either.

"One night, when she pulled into the driveway, another car pulled in right after. I heard her yelling, so I ran to the front door to see what was happening, and she came flying through and slammed it behind her. You know, in movies, how they get to the latch or lock just in time before whatever is chasing them catches up? She fumbled it, and he burst through the door with such force that my ma was flung backward and caught the base of her skull on the corner of the kitchen counter.

"He just stood there heaving over her before rifling through her purse and taking all the cash. I didn't call 911 until the blood seeping from her head touched my bare toes. I knew she was dead. What were they going to do about it?"

"What happened to the guy?" Mabel asked.

"Nothing. His wife alibied him. I think the cops didn't want a murder case, so they just concluded that she was drunk coming home from the bar and fell. That was the worst part of it, that they blamed her."

"I need to get some air," Amelia said. "I think I'm going to be sick." She disappeared down the front entrance with wobbly caution.

"You better follow her, Att," Heath said. "It's not safe to be out after dark."

Amelia took off down the twisting dirt path running wildly. Moonlight dappled the wildflowers in silver. I followed her to the waterfall, where she stood on the precipice, dress swirling around her feet in the cold water.

I slipped my arms around her waist, sliding my lips across the neckline of her dress. Her skin glistened with sweat in the moonlight. We gazed out onto the dark land that was both mighty and mediocre.

"At first, I wondered why I was spared, why I didn't die along with everyone else, and then I thought, since I didn't die with these first million, I'll surely die with the next millions as they starved and stole in through windows, beating each other to death over canned food. But I'm still here, blinking, breathing, and thinking," Amelia said, her words barely audible over the rush of the water. "The very thought of endless rest sounds so sweet, to lie still under dirt with thirsty tree roots snaking through my eye sockets."

A dark shadow crawled hand over hand up the waterfall, sure-footed on the slippery rocks. I thought for an insane moment Roman had crawled out of the abyss to pull me back down with him. But there was nothing there, only a trick of the shifting light filtered through the tree canopy.

"You're being morose," I said, discreetly shaking the vision from my head. "You were spared because of some DNA quark or early childhood sickness that left you immune. To think more of it is to consider yourself above the laws of nature."

She looked as if I said something outlandish, her face stricken. Standing on tiptoes, she leaned in close and whispered hatred into the ear Matilda had once slipped down, her syllables tickling the fine hairs making me want to squirm away.

"I'd bind your hands, hang you from a ceiling fan set to low. You'd revolve ever so slowly, an animal on display. Women would parade in to see the art exhibit, sighing in their breasts that it was one less dick they'd have to worry about getting forcibly shoved down their daughter's throats. I'd carve the flesh from your bones until you screamed, yet in your screams, you'd still say, 'Amelia, Amelia,' and I'd cringe at your unwavering, sick love."

"Amelia, what's happening to you?" I asked quietly. I felt a profound sadness for this creature that could not cope in the new world, a place of loss.

"My head is a helium balloon rushing towards the sun," she murmured.

"Come back home," I said. "We shouldn't be out here like this." I pulled on her hand gently, leading her back to the tree house. "And you're drunk."

In the time we'd been gone, the party had dispersed. Glasses and dishes were left out unwashed, stale smoke hanging around the lights from rolled cigarettes.

"Do you think Mabel forgives me?" Amelia asked, her eyes glittering and unfocused.

"I think she knows you did it to protect her."

She took a glass from the cabinet and poured herself another shot of bourbon.

As she walked up the stairs, the hem of her dress left a slick trail of water where it was still wet from the stream. "Come," was all she said.

Fumbling in the dark of her bedroom, she guided me inside her, and I felt like a seal getting devoured by a great white shark, resigned to destiny, the world as it should be.

With her hands on my chest, she moved against me, and I held her hips. Her face was that of a jackal, thick matted hair and tall pointed ears, teeth bared in pleasure.

"No," I whispered.

I stood in the corner of Amelia's bedroom after, blowing smoke out of the open window. The cigarette was stale, and it made me nauseous, but I didn't care.

Matilda, what happens when you get everything you've ever wanted?

Misery, she sighed.

"What's wrong?" Amelia asked, tangled in the blankets on the bed. Smoke from a cigarette curled past her fingertips.

I searched the catalog of various stressors for something to say. "Lily's crops. I'm worried another late frost will kill what's left."

Amelia sighed. "I mean, did we really think a plot of land tilled on the side of a mountain would work? We should have gone over to the Black Dirt Region if we wanted to be farmers, but then you open yourself up to all kinds of danger from roaming idiots stealing your food and your lives. The forest will feed us. We've got smoked fish, venison and berries, and edible plants. But that's not really what you're worried about, is it?" She didn't blow the smoke but talked with a mouthful of it like a sleeping dragon.

Wearied, I crawled back into bed and wrapped my arms around her, drawing her close so I could breathe in the smell of her. Her feet were cold despite the mild night.

"I just wonder about my parents. Pepper and Piper lived through the Panic, which makes me think it's genetic. Or maybe not at all. It seems more like pairs of people made it out together. You and I, Pepper and Piper, Mabel and Charlie, Heath and Lily."

"Heath and Lily don't count. They found each other after." She stubbed out the cigarette right on her side table, already pockmarked with similar circular burns. "Att, we don't know, and until scientists drive up this mountain and liberate us, we can only guess. You should go, see if you find your parents before winter makes it impossible."

"Would you come with me?"

"I can, but only if you want me to. I don't think it's the best idea, do you? My track record of chaos is telling. Anyway, it'll only take you a few days. It can't be that far away. Check out the park map. It'll tell you which trails to take to avoid the road."

She didn't look at me when she said this, her face purposely benign. We both knew she was reneging on her original promise she made all that time ago.

Later that night, I woke to a whisper. At first, I mistook it for a branch scratching against a window, and then I thought it must be a conversation carried from Heath and Lily's room. The more I listened, the surer I was that it was a one-sided monologue. Amelia slept deeply next to me, her mouth parted slightly.

I got out of bed and opened the door, standing stock-still. It was fainter out here, just the creaking of the wood as the big oak tree shifted its weight in the wind.

I went back to bed but lay awake for a long time, listening as the whispering gave way to a faint scratching sound. Like an unstoppable movie reel, I imagined it was Roman, having crawled out from whatever stagnant body of water he now rotted, to drag himself back to the tree house to scratch at the door downstairs until it drove us all to madness.

***

Sharp splinters of wood crunched beneath my boots as I walked across the second floor landing the next afternoon, coming home after tramping through the trails, checking traps.

Amelia had still been in bed when I left that morning, looking cherubic still in her drunken stupor from the night before. I had kissed her lightly on the temple, whispering that I'd be back soon.

Her bedroom door hung crookedly from its frame, the top hinge wrenched awkwardly. The wood itself had been hacked to pieces with fervor, the metal door handle battered and chipped in the madness.

Amelia sat on the floor amid the wreckage of her belongings, an ax sunk deep into the floor next to her. Her bed was overturned, revealing a ghastly underbelly. Carved a thousand times was Amelia's name. Some signatures looked hewn in anger, others were whittled in an elegant script.

Matilda, you've been busy...

I lingered in her doorway, attempting to correlate the scene before me to the one I remembered from earlier this morning.

Amelia looked at me expectantly. "Atticus, what is this?" She gestured to the carved bed frame.

I crouched beside her and followed one of the names with my finger, admiring the dedication and compulsion Matilda had corralled for her project.

What have you done, Matilda?

She snickered, that decomposing skeleton that lived in my head.

"What is this?" Amelia asked again, her voice going pinched with bubbling hysteria. "There was a noise beneath the bed. I got down to look, and there was a shadow where there should not have been one. It looked like an urchin stuck to the underside of a boat. And it said my name."

Matilda laughed again, slapping her knee in merriment. She did a little dance and bowed.

"It doesn't live under the bridge anymore, Atticus. It lives under my bed." She rose, wrenching the ax from the wood.

I lunged, grabbing her ankle, and spinning her onto the floor. She landed with a heavy thump, rattling the windowpane. Screaming, she rolled across the floor, rising to her feet with a snarl. I snatched the ax away, holding it behind my back.

Did you do this, Matilda? Why?

Matilda threw her head back, positively howling with jollity. Her teeth, I noticed, were sharpened to points.

I did it for the laughs! Oh, it's been such fun.

A shiver traveled up my spine, and the coldness of pure terror spread through my body. Matilda wasn't real, and when you're not real, you cannot manifest in the physical world.

I could barely hear anything over Matilda's laughter, so loud and hysterical that it drowned out all else.

"Shut the fuck up, Matilda!" I screamed, clutching my head.

"Matilda? Who's Matilda?" Lily asked, coming to a stop on the landing, both hands flying to her mouth as she surveyed the damage to Amelia's room.

"I have to go," I said.

"Stop," Amelia said, grabbing my arm. "Go where?"

"Who did this?" Lily asked.

I pushed past Amelia and Lily and went into my bedroom, finding my pack and stuffing random articles of clothing into it. Amelia followed me and tried yanking the pack from my hands. "Atticus, what the fuck is going on? I don't understand."

"Someone needs to answer me right now," Lily said. "Are we in danger?"

Matilda roared with laughter, becoming so vast in my mind that I could keep the focus on only a single purpose—run. Before I could take the first step, I was enclosed in a set of arms that constricted my movements. I struggled weakly before collapsing into Heath's embrace, and like a mute button had been pushed, Matilda's screeching laughter was cut short into dizzying silence.

I rooted around the inside of my mind, searching for her, but the space she had occupied was indeed empty. A raw place, like the state you would find an ear canal after extracting a malignant, oversized bug.

THEN

Pepper locked the front door to the hostel with finality, hiding the key beneath the welcome mat. Piper babbled happily from Amelia's hip as we took one last long look at what had become a place of comfort and safety for us.

The golf cart was loaded to capacity, sitting low on its wheels. We'd scoured and collected anything useful, amassing a dragon's hoard of supplies. We were magpies when we should have been bears.

Lou had already brought Charlie and Mabel to the pods the day prior, knowing there'd be little room left to fit us all. We squeezed in together, and off we went, leaving behind the empty little town, empty little welcome stand, empty, empty, empty. Who left to fill it?

When we arrived at the pods, I was heartened to see how much progress had been made. I could almost see their utopic vision if I squinted. More buildings had gone up, and it seemed Charlie and Mabel had begun painting each of them, making it look homier and less like we were kids out in the forest waiting for our mom's whistle for lunch.

Lou walked around, asking questions, and sharing laughs until our feet ached from standing on the cold ground, and Amelia chewed her lip impatiently.

Finally, we were shown to one of the pods, names exchanged with our neighbors but promptly forgotten. I kept waiting for someone to recite a long list of rules or spout post-apocalyptic indoctrination so that I could grab Amelia's hand and sprint away, all the while feeling the phantom pain of a bullet or spinning knife in our backs. But it never came, and people were quite lovely, if not a bit aloof.

For all Lou's espousing, the pod was nothing more than a hastily constructed one-room shack. A bunk bed took up the wall directly to the right of the door, weak sunlight coming from a window situated between the top and bottom mattresses. A small stove sat in the far corner, flat black with no fire burning.

To the left, a sink stood. Amelia crossed the room and tried the taps, but no water came through, just the squeak of the handles as she pushed them back and forth. Shelves lined the remaining wall where various canned goods were stacked. But the type of canned goods you'd find in a food drive, store brand SpaghettiOs and sliced beets and Lima beans.

The ceiling consisted of exposed two-by-fours, markings in pencil clearly visible. The wind tickled the back of my neck with a cold draft. I pulled my coat up around my ears.

"How do we cook anything?" Amelia asked.

I looked around stupidly, searching for an oven. "I suppose if we found a pot, we could put it on the wood stove. Not sure how hot it'd get."

She gave me an annoyed look like I promised to provide an oven but had shown up empty-handed.

"Can we at least get a fire going? I'm freezing," she said, shivering.

"There's no installation. What are they thinking?" I marveled, peering through a crack in the wall that looked directly outside. "We can't stay here for the winter, Amelia. They're not prepared at all."

"And what are we prepared with, Att? Huh? The only possessions I have right now are my pack and a useless air rifle. What can we do that's better than this?"

"My parents' house. It's a nice place tucked away down a dirt road with two cords of firewood."

"And what if they're not there? You could stand it there all winter?" She sat on the lower bunk, testing the durability and comfort by bouncing slightly.

And I know what she meant to say was what if they're dead and we have to bury the corpses and live in a house where they rotted for the past four months? I didn't answer, leaving to collect split wood from the woodpile.

I came back twenty minutes later, finding Amelia laying down with her knees drawn up, looking small and cold, her nose running. She didn't sit up but watched me stoke the fire, eyes boring into the back of my head. I had never actually used a wood stove, but the kindling took, and I slowly added larger pieces of wood until the little room warmed. There was a draft still, a coldness that crept along the floor and whistled in particularly big gusts of wind.

I sat next to Amelia on the bed, and she tugged the back of my jacket to lie down. The mattress was thin, like what you'd find during a grippy sock vacation or a $40 hotel room. The window showed daylight fading, getting beaten out by dark clouds that gathered across the sky.

We fell asleep soon after, our clothes and shoes still on. I dreamt of bone-chilling cold, of slogging through waist-deep snow. Amelia walked on top of the snow with light feet, annoyed that I was taking too long to get anywhere. She threatened to leave, and then she did. I watched her figure get smaller and smaller until I was alone in the swirling snow.

I woke suddenly, my heart beating fast. Amelia still slept by my side, curled into me for warmth. And it was cold. There was a blanket on one of the shelves, a thin cotton one with rips and holes. I brought it to my face, smelling mildew. I cast it aside in disgust but thought better of it, afraid the fire would die down again, and we'd freeze. I laid next to Amelia, pulling the blanket over us, but I could not get comfortable, smelling the faint scent of mildew. I kicked it off grumpily, like a child who's just been told no.

The next morning there was a rapping on the door. Amelia opened it cautiously, her clothes rumpled from sleeping in them. In walked a man, his arms loaded with blankets, towels, and toilet paper. A girl followed him, her hair white.

"Hi," she said breathlessly, "I'm Lily, and this is Heath. I'm sorry we didn't get a chance to stop by sooner. Were you cold last night?"

Amelia smiled, taking the supplies from Heath. "Honestly, we're a bit disoriented. And yeah, it was frigid."

"Not supposed to wear shoes to sleep," Heath commented. "Cuts off the circulation."

Amelia nodded thoughtfully.

"There's a toilet around the back of your place. It's chemical so just remember to turn the handle when you're done," said Lily. "Are you hungry? Poor things, you're all bones. Come, there's a stew cooking over in the shared kitchen."

***

"Lou is missing," Lily said.

"No," Pepper corrected, "Lou left. I know what it feels like to have someone abandon you, and this surely is it."

"The question becomes: do we search for him? Could be that the golf cart broke down, or he got into an accident," Heath said.

It was a few nights later and we were crowded into Pepper's pod, having been woken up by frantic knocking on our door. We yawned and stamped the cold from our feet.

"Has he seemed off to you, Pepper?" Lily asked. "I know you two were close."

"No, if anything, he's been happier to be here instead of sitting by himself all day down at the welcome stand."

Amelia took Piper from Pepper's arms and blew soft raspberries into her neck, making her laugh.

"Where would he go?" asked the woman with bleached locs.

"Since the golf cart is gone, it's likely he's traveling by road. I say we send two search parties out, one to go back into town and another to follow the road in the opposite direction," Heath said with authority.

Pepper shook her head sadly. "The more I think about it, the more convinced I am that he's gone back to be with his missus."

"Didn't she die in the first wave of infection, though?" Amelia asked. "He mentioned it when we were staying at the hostel."

"My fears exactly," Pepper said.

"At daybreak, let's put together a small crew and walk a mile in either direction. We don't have the time or resources to be out searching for someone who's left on their own accord," Charlie said. Mabel clung to their arm and nodded in agreement.

The search party returned with grim news. They had found the golf cart in a ditch with a broken axle and a flooded engine that would not start no matter what was tried. Dried blood was found on the steering wheel but no trace of Lou. There were no discernible tracks other than what looked like a single bare footprint that led off into the woods.

Pepper cried heartily at the news, and then Piper, sensing something terrible was amiss but too young to understand. All this careful planning, this gathering of survivors and supplies, was for naught as it seemed the wheels were coming off the wagon. A radical element of instability had entered the picture, and things felt uneasy, if not unsafe.

"I think we'd bring suspicion on ourselves if we leave tomorrow," Amelia said, poking the fire in the stove with a stick.

"You don't have to come with me," I said reassuringly. "I promise if I find my parents safe, I'll bring them back here. I won't be gone longer than a week at most."

"Don't be foolish," she snapped. "If we split up, that's it. There's no way I'd be able to find you again if I was forced to flee the pods.

"I know what I promised you, and I fully intend to keep my promise, but I can't leave Pepper alone with Lou gone now. She's a teenager with a baby."

"What do I do then, Amelia?" I asked, exasperated.

"I'll figure it out. Just give me time to think of a plan."

***

But it grew cold, a latticework of ice coating the windows each morning. And Amelia grew cold, complaining of hidden aches within her body. She began to have a wild, gamey look about her, something that lingered in her gaze, a look of desperation, like a muskrat with its paw caught in a steel trap.

The heat she loved, stoking the fire in the little stove so frequently that I felt I could not keep up with splitting wood.

Snow came before the fall leaves had time to drift to the forest floor. Trees fell, and limbs broke under the extra weight of it all, sounding like shotgun blasts that shook everything not nailed down.

Snow settled heavy on the pod's roof, piling in drifts against the door and windows so that it was perpetually dark, like we were sealed within a tomb. I worried the roof would collapse on us, burying us in cheap plywood and ice.

The snow muffled all sounds so that it felt like we were underwater, a feeling of complete aloneness.

Gone were the reassuring clanking of pans from Lily and Heath's pod, the distant cooing of Piper, the stereo pumping out music on battery juice from our neighbors. The bitter cold kept us all inside, separate.

It was claustrophobic, being shut up that way, with nothing to do. Amelia took to reading the only book, *Henderson's Field Guide to Wild Plants*, immersed as only someone flirting with lunacy. I took to carving, studying the arrows that had come with the bow Heath had given me, mimicking the fiberglass straightness on bows of Douglas fir taken from the surrounding forest. With the birds I shot with Amelia's air rifle, I'd try gluing feathers to the shafts, testing them for accuracy on days when there'd be a break in snowfall.

At first, it had been fun, like an apocalypse within an apocalypse. Everyone had that nervous excitement, speculating on the ferocity of the storm and the depth of the snow. There had been a few parties in various pods, Lily gathering everyone and passing around a canteen of powdered chocolate mix, tipping in rum whenever the mud-like liquid ran low. She knew how to play the fiddle, and we crammed in together, smelling like the sweet-juice smell of unwashed clothes. It was the first time I had felt glad in a long while.

I had expected Amelia to sing, to find happiness in the bluegrass melody of the fiddle, but she sulked instead, always choosing to sit off by herself, sometimes taking Piper from Pepper and bouncing her while Pepper danced and laughed. I had asked her what was wrong, but she ignored me, eyes hard and distant.

After, we'd tramp back home, the blowing snow sticking to our clothes and hair. To open the front door, we'd have to dig to avoid a small avalanche spilling onto the floor and melting in great big puddles. Amelia would stoke the fire, turning her back to the stove once it got going and pulling off soaked clothes until she was down to a pair of leggings and a tank top.

She would shiver until she eventually gave up and crawled into bed. She slept in the top bunk, the air near the ceiling warmer. The bed creaked each time Amelia tossed above me, whispering plant names like conium maculatum, daucus carota...

Soon enough, the snowstorms lost their appeal and once colds began getting passed around, no one wanted to fraternize anymore, tacking sheets and towels over their windows to discourage visitors and to keep whatever heat they generated inside.

Just like when we were staying at her parents' house, Amelia was happiest in the water. I found a large metal washtub that I dragged to our door. I dared not use the hose stuck into the stream to fill it. The water no longer had a refreshingly cool quality, but rather a dark hint of pneumonia in the bitter cold temperatures.

So, every few days, I'd heat pot after pot over the stove, dumping the steaming water into the tub. Sometimes people would watch, going so far as to trail their fingers through the delightfully warm water until Amelia waved them away, sliding in naked with the field guide clutched closely in her hands.

Amelia started rising at noon to use the chemical toilet before creeping back under the covers. She asked me once if I had read the Little House on the Prairie series, and I had said no, but she giggled to herself anyway. The batteries for the electric lantern ran low, flickering feebly for a few days before calling it quits altogether. The only light came weakly from the stove.

From there, a strange flu-like illness descended upon our mountainside community. People I had spoken a few conversations with in passing or at those early pod parties stopped coming outside, maybe to scoop snow from their stoop for water, but that was all. Even those we knew better, like Heath, Lily, and Pepper, kept to themselves. I had a sneaking suspicion about the illness, but I ignored it, thinking I was becoming paranoid.

***

Things started slipping once Charlie disappeared. A particularly violent storm moved in, seemingly stuck in place, with endless dark days of snow and days of silence from Amelia.

We stood outside, the snow falling in hard granules that collected swiftly in the folds of jackets and hats. Heath blew into his hands to keep them warm.

"What happened?" he asked Mabel.

"They've been feverish the past few days. We went to bed early last night to try to get some rest, and I woke up from the cold. The door was swinging open, and Charlie was gone." She wiped away tears with mittened hands.

The sun had not yet risen, stuck somewhere in the earliest dawn hours. Mabel had woken us just minutes ago, frantically knocking on doors and screaming for help.

We set off across the snow, walking in step with our arms linked together. We knew to do it from cop shows where detectives would find little girls' bodies dumped in swamps and suitcases.

"There!" Mabel shouted. "Footsteps!"

Snow had already weakened their dimensions, threatening to cover them completely lest we move any slower. Onward we marched on our ominous task, calling out for Charlie. Through the forest, down to the parking lot, where their footsteps ended mid-step as if snatched from above. Somehow, we knew this was different from Lou leaving us on his own accord. Screams from Mabel, her tears frozen on her lashes like melancholy crystals.

"Mabel, we have to call it off until this snowstorm passes," Heath called out over the howling wind. "It's impossible to see more than a few feet ahead of us."

"We can't give up. Charlie needs us!" Mabel cried.

Amelia shivered next to me, and I knew she thought of a monster with hooved feet who liked to devour the lost.

"I'm going to keep looking," Mabel said with force, dropping Lily's hand and trudging forward through the snow.

"Mabel!" Lily called. "Come back!"

Frozen and disoriented, we made it back to our pod, stoking the fire to warm the small space. Amelia hung a lantern from the eaves of our front door, hopeful that it would help Mabel's search.

A weak pounding at the door woke us later that night. I untacked the towel, looking out of the window, hoping it was Mabel with good news.

"Who is it?" Amelia mumbled.

I wiped the condensation from the glass and squinted. A face in extreme anguish peered back at me, and I gasped. Pepper gripped the windowsill, barefoot with only a thin nightgown on, the hem heavy with snow and ice.

"Oh my god," Amelia said, rushing out of bed and to the door.

"Don't open it," I yelled, positioning my body in front of the knob.

"We've got to open it! She'll freeze to death. And where is Piper?" Amelia threw her weight into me, and we wrestled for control of the door.

"She's sick!" I cried, now certain of what that wandering man had spread to our community.

"How do you know?" she asked, violently pulling my arm in an effort to throw me off balance. I shook her off.

"She's got typhus."

Pepper pounded, pounded, pounded on the window.

"And how the fuck do you know?"

"There's a rash covering her body, Amelia, except for her face and hands. It must be typhus, caused by infected lice. If you let her in here, we'll catch it too, if we haven't already."

"It's just a rash, so what?"

"Besides the gas chambers and bullets, it's what killed the most during the holocaust. The Allies found mass graves of people who died of typhus when they liberated the camps."

Amelia pulled the air rifle down from its hook, pumping it furiously. "If you don't move, I'll shoot you. I swear I will."

"If you must," I said softly.

Her brows unknotted, and she gave the air rifle one last pump.

"What reason would there be to lie?" I asked.

Pepper's pounding grew weaker, fingertips black with frostbite.

"She'll die?" Amelia asked, chin crumpling in sadness.

"Yes, she would have needed a round of antibiotics early on. I don't know which kind, and I doubt there's a cache of antibiotics available."

Amelia raised the rifle, clicking off the safety with finality. The barrel swung wide, and with a pop, Amelia put a bullet between Pepper's eyes. The low caliber caused a second delay in her death, her cyanotic features rearranging in shock and then nothing as she slipped forward, knocking her forehead against the window as she fell, a streak of bright red blood left behind.

The wind whistled through the tiny hole in the window, a hairline crack snaking upwards. Amelia walked towards the sound, placing her finger over the opening before collapsing.

And what awaited us was life-altering grief. With rags covering our noses from the stench, we found Piper and other quiet pods filled with the dead. Heath, always perceptive, wrestled the gun just in time from Amelia's mouth as we set them on fire, anguish stamped across our hearts forever.

I reviewed the map once again, rotating it so I could read the legend. I marked a red star where the tree house was located and then where my parents' home was, amongst the many wave-like topographic lines. Roughly thirty miles lay in between. In my estimation, I could walk there and back in less than a few days, two days if I really pushed it.

We lived in a state park, but I had never quite realized how huge a place it was until now. It was marked on the map as an enormous green swath amid municipalities that soon would become green too with no one left to pull the weeds. Trails and paths were notated on the map with minute icons.

Shandelee Trail snaked through the Catskills Mountains, twisting through the Shawangunk Ridge and Sam's Point Preserve, once a lodestone for local twentysomethings that returned to hike the same trail over and over, posting identical images of swinging legs over a precipice because they could not fathom that there was anything more to the world beyond their county lines.

Sam's Point Preserve would put me near Ellenville and Rt. 209, a two-lane highway that wound gently to my hometown. There had been a derelict gas station my father had frequented for lotto tickets, and I still remembered the sun-bleached cigarette ads in the window featuring women with 90s-style shoulder pads and lip liner.

I envisioned my hometown as a sleepy town made sleepier, perhaps more wildflowers and scrub weed than was usual but not much else different. The Catskills had been emptied of its vacationers half a century ago, nostalgia for what used to be still suffocating us all.

The Catskills had succumbed to population loss a lot sooner than the rest of the state. Once the cost of airline tickets became affordable in the 1960s and more exotic locals attracted the middle incomers of New York City, they abandoned their Borscht Belt playground, leaving it to rot. Only black and white pictures remained of the swing bands, the comedians, and the women with coiffed hair in high-waisted bikinis.

Before the Panic, there had been just a hint of a heartbeat felt in places like Bethel, Livingston Manor, and Narrowsburg. Yuppies from the city realized that homes here were dirt cheap and the metropolis of New York less than two hours away. A no-brainer for the weekend warrior. They planted clover yards for the bees and rented it out during off seasons to country-living cosplayers.

I left the tree house just before dawn, in that eerie quasi-night where it feels revolting to be awake. I hiked through the meadow, leaving behind the sleeping inhabitants.

I promised Amelia I'd return, promised I'd look for a replacement for the field guide on my parents' bookshelves. She shrugged at this, shrugged at everything I said until I wanted to shake her. It was the first decision I had made since we met that didn't include her, and it grated and frayed.

Forking left at the trailhead, I opted to climb the rockier pass, my muscles jumping to expend energy. In the dawn light, the forest was an indescribable collage of vivid green. The beauty of the mountain range was breathtaking, with sharp peaks and deep valleys awash in color, each tree individualistic in its majesty to create the collective.

I looked about with wonder and felt that hint of warmth deep in my chest that speaks of unbridled joy. I imagined finding my parents, a little worse for the wear, but alive. It was the feeling of buying a lottery ticket and dreaming of what could be.

My pack was heavier than usual with an extra water canteen and containers of dried berries and nuts, boiled crayfish, and packaged jerky. I could try to forage what I came across, but nothing was guaranteed.

I hiked beyond our local trails, the paths becoming wilder with overgrown brambles and downed trees. I soon switched off the headlamp I wore as the sun rose high, packing it away and wiping the sweat that beaded across my forehead.

The day grew hot, and the trails hopelessly unnavigable. I searched for the trailhead with the map clutched in my hand, becoming more discouraged by the moment. Frustration coiled in my belly, and I felt confused and helpless as I careened lost through the underbrush.

I finally sat, sipping water, and eating a piece of jerky. It was eerily quiet. I couldn't pinpoint why it was so. It came to me suddenly, the reason behind this hush.

Matilda, where have you gone?

Why had she fled? Was it her that had carved Amelia's name over and over into the underside of the bed? I was utterly confused, and quite devastated.

After hearing Matilda's name spoken aloud last night, the other tree house occupants had pressed relentlessly to know who she was. I tried explaining as best I could until Amelia finally understood. "Piper whispered to me too while I was pregnant," she said. "Is it like that?" All I could do was shake my head, helpless and devoid of answers.

Wiping away the snot from my nose, and embarrassingly enough, tears from my cheeks, I got back on the trail, embracing the quietness that enveloped me. But I kept returning to Matilda's lair, poking it like one would a hole left by a pulled tooth.

The trail marker turned up shortly, undisguised as a round piece of plastic tacked to a tree. I began seeing more and more after discovering the first one, little colored beacons disappearing into the forest. I was grateful we'd only pulled off the markers near the tree house and hadn't branched out farther. I'd never be able to find my way.

I blew out my cheeks and rolled my neck, my feet following the winding, untended trail. It should have been so obvious. There, affixed to a tree, was a campy wooden sign announcing the trek with a warning to stay on the trail with a phone number to call the rangers should you get lost. Would anyone pick up if I found a working phone?

A cackle cut the air, and the sweat that had been so hot and moist froze to my skin. I whirled around, nearly losing my footing. There was no one.

I listened intently, remembering how hideously Roman had surprised me in the swamp and the shadow that followed me in the pine forest. Fitting an arrow to my bow, I waited.

"I killed you once, Roman!" I shouted to nobody, at nothing.

I came across a bear carcass. A ten-foot radius of coarse black hair surrounded it. The skin had decomposed around its snout, like a permanent snarl. There was no way it could be a wild bear. It must have escaped from someone's backyard petting zoo.

I approached cautiously, crouching when I got near enough. The bones weren't pulled apart and scattered had coyotes or wolves taken it down. Starvation or sickness then?

I itched to pry its nails from knuckle joints but was hesitant, not wanting to disturb the body. I had heard of animals eating poison berries from ornamental shrubs and dying, but I couldn't see where it would have found many of those types of plants flourishing. They tended to need copious amounts of water and be burlapped in the winter to ward against frost.

Perhaps radiation poisoning? Is the Poughkeepsie nuclear plant finally melting down? It had been over a year. How long did their backup systems last? It didn't matter because we wouldn't know how to fix it even if we tried. More than likely, a cloud of radiation would blow our way sooner or later from some abandoned corner of the country. We needed a Geiger counter so that it could tell us in ticks how fucked we were. I left the bear to molder alone, suspicious of what had befallen it.

The sun waned, and I made camp at the base of a craggy cliff, about a hundred feet off the trail to avoid any nocturnal animals in search of a snack. With my back to the rock, I made a small fire and uncurled my sleeping bag, brushing away bracken and pebbly rocks that would wreak havoc on my back.

I drank water and ate an expired package of mixed nuts, watching twilight fall into impenetrable blackness, the light of the fire blinding me to all else. I'd brought a book on electrical engineering, knowing that there'd be these long periods with nothing to do on this trip. The thought of unpacking it exhausted me, so instead, I poked the fire with a stick, shifting the hot coals around.

Sitting there in patched clothes and cured fur, it felt archaic. We had fallen a great distance as a species and as a society. After the Paris Climate Agreement was pulled apart, it was only a matter of time before things started crumbling. How could they not when our main medium of communication was social media, and dictatorship our leaders' main motivation? Their methods were elementarily simple, just a regurgitation of past evils from leaders who wielded power by spewing lies and sowing distrust, legislating away our freedoms with incremental laws.

Americans had learned to mistrust hyperbole in the media. Who would have believed such a thing was even possible in our days of antibacterial soap and pharmaceutical giants? If the Panic had not ravaged us, an ecological disaster or nuclear war would have rubber-stamped us anyway.

I considered what had become of Matilda. She'd been a crutch for so long, someone to spill my guts out to, someone to confirm suspicions, warn of danger.

"Matilda?" I shouted, but only the chorus of crickets answered me.

I slept a dreamless sleep that night, away from the rabid glow of Amelia or the weight of Matilda. Feeling refreshed the next morning, I lingered at my makeshift camp, making tea and eating breakfast. It was the first day of summer vacation with not a soul around to tell me what to do.

The forest seemed friendlier, lit with warm sunlight and a cacophony of birdsong. Hiking to the town limits, I crouched in high grass, taking a sip from my canteen, and waited. It resembled New Paltz in its abandonment, with looted storefronts and cars crushed against each other accordion-like. It was depressing in its sameness, and I wondered if future scientists would study these towns like they once scrutinized endangered species. I imagined a questionnaire: were there mating pairs? What was the life expectancy? Were there only sociopaths left? The results would be conclusive.

Seeing no danger, I set off down Route 209, detouring for an ice cream stand that I remembered licking cones in a dripping bathing suit with my friends, coming from the hidden waterhole just south. I found an unopened bag of sprinkles and delightfully stuffed it into my pack. The hardware store next door had snow blowers and behemoth grills but nothing of use, at least not that I could carry.

I walked along the sidewalk until it dwindled into nothing but shoulder. There were slight indications that someone or something had passed through recently. A leaf would be flipped to its wet, fish-belly side, dirt brushed from the yellow centerline, betraying their journey by its unnatural brightness.

Resting from the afternoon sun, I laid on the shaded front porch of a house I used to trick-or-treat at when younger. It had been a favorite because of the consistent full-sized candy bars the woman would hand out, exclaiming over our clever costumes. My parents always checked the contents of my bucket at the end of the night, looking for poisoned needle holes and razor blades, something the newscaster had told them over and over to be wary and vigilant about.

I rose and began the final trek upwards, onwards, following switchback roads that led me home. The lightness of the morning was seeping from me, the thought of finding corpses or emptiness haunting. I longed for Amelia's steadfastness, to follow her.

My parents' house stood just as I remembered it, down a long straight driveway with a detached garage off to the right. It was a raised ranch, pieced together in the early 90s. Many of the kids I went to school with lived in these same houses, featuring identical layouts. You never had to ask where the bathroom was when visiting.

There were broken tree branches and leaves littering the driveway. The yard was overgrown with flowers and native grasses. The storm door had blown off its hinges, lying mangled in the yard below. There was no sound other than the crunching of leaves as I walked up the driveway and the occasional whisper of wind in the stumpy mountain trees.

I peered through the garage window, rubbing a circle into the dust. The cars were missing, leaving behind nothing but an oil stain on the concrete.

There was a flicker, and I spun, hand on my bow. It was only a robin, cocking its head in curiosity, bouncing on a branch.

My heart grew heavier and beat slower. My parents weren't here.

The sheer size of the house seemed enormous after living in a tree. With black windows, it looked impenetrable and malicious. I realized at that moment that I missed my real home, with cheerful smoke puffing from the chimney, the constant babble of voices, and rough-hewn timbers that would splinter into your finger should you touch it the wrong way.

A bird's nest was built into the rafters beneath the front porch, white droppings coating the wood. I climbed the front steps, looking between them to see if there were any chicks. It was empty.

The door's bright green paint was dulled by dirt, standing slightly ajar. I pushed it open, holding my breath in anticipation of the stench of rot and fever death. My head swam, and I finally let it out, breathing in the simple smell of a home not lived in.

I waited for my eyes to adjust to the darkness, blinking stupidly. A single set of footprints led off into the house, turning left down the hall and out of sight. I crouched to examine them, my stomach swooping uncomfortably with dread.

There were toe imprints, and there, the nails, uncommonly long. I traced it with my finger, wondering what made them. Not bear, there was no width to it and not coyote either, the stride was too far apart.

They could only be human, someone who wore no shoes. There was a squeak in the basement. I shot upright, listening intently but couldn't hear anything besides my own whooshing blood in an adrenaline-heavy frenzy.

Was it my parents living discreetly? The cars were probably dumped somewhere, hidden under bows of pine. Was there a garden deep in the woods with golden corn and fat pumpkins? Of course, there was, of course, of course, of course...

Matilda, I need you.

Following the footprints, I passed through the living room. The kitchen was dark. The cabinets were thrown open and empty. A few plates had been smashed on the linoleum floor, not out of maliciousness, it seemed, but out of hurry. The pantry was nearly empty, save for a sleeve of muffin cups and a stack of paper plates.

The footprints abruptly disappeared down the basement steps. I stood at the top of the stairs, the basement's thick green carpet made greener by moss and mold. The landing below was dark and empty. A mildewed smell emanated from its depth. Perhaps it had flooded, the cement walls oozing rain and slime.

If I ventured down there, there'd be a monster with yellow eyes and Roman's face, but grotesque like his insides. I shut the door quietly, not quite ready to venture down into that darkness.

Continuing down the hallway, I gazed at my childhood pictures. The glass was shattered in one frame, cracking outward from my face where I sat with my parents as a preschooler. I was surprised to find that I had forgotten their faces until now. Unhooking it from its nail, I pried apart the ruined frame and let it drop, folding the picture and slipping it into my pocket.

The first bedroom on the left was mine. It had been kept the same as always, with a twin bed on a squeaking frame and childhood artifacts stowed on nightstands and bookcases. One corner had become a dumping ground for the unwanted things that were possibly still of use, an old vacuum, a printer with no ink, a busted laundry basket...

I stood looking out my window, taking in the familiarity. My dad had never been one for landscaping, choosing the perennial peonies and coneflowers that came back year after year.

My breath caught. Something was moving along the road, the thick vegetation only allowing for quick glimpses of motion. I wanted to run, but the awkwardness of the movement held me. It could be a hurt animal the way it bucked and wobbled. It came ever closer to the mouth of the driveway, yet still I stood there. And then I knew, the moment before she rounded onto the driveway.

Matilda.

Something warm and wet trickled along the inside of my brain, something broken. Her masticated foot stepped onto the blacktop. She wore no pants, just like when I had first found her murdered in the library bathroom. Her knees were decayed, and she walked with a painful-looking lurch.

Matilda came to a stop at the bottom step of the porch. Glass eyes were set into her head, marbles that held galaxies. A horrid stench filled the air. Matilda curled her skeletal fingers around the railing, pulling herself up the stairs.

I retreated slowly, thinking such an apparition could not possibly be real. But there she was, just as I imagined her. I also knew instinctively that she was here to kill me. To what gain, I knew not.

How had she gotten free? Perhaps she was a parasite, grown strong enough to leave its host, then feed upon it, like those wasps that lay their eggs within caterpillars. Parasitoid wasp, my brain suggested helpfully. "Yes," I whispered. "That's it."

I ran, feet pounding down the hallway, kicking up dust. I avoided the front and back doors, hoping to escape out the window in my parents' room. There was a BILCO door that led up from the basement just below the window, close enough to jump down onto. The tree line was just a few short bounds away from there, where I maybe had a chance of losing her. It didn't seem like she'd be able to travel very fast through thick rhododendron and blueberry bush undergrowth. Not in her current state, at least.

Throwing open my parents' door, I froze, coming to an abrupt stop. There, amongst their things, was a nest. Made of sticks and fabric and a weird grayish cohesive, it took up an entire corner. Frantically, I tried to convince myself that it could be an eagle's nest or a beaver's dam. But that was stupid because hanging over the side was Peaches' skin, with her tell-tale black and white patches. It was scorched in places as if it had been in a fire. I feared to look inside the nest, at what I would find. A father's work boot, a mother's hair clip, burped up by a horror.

It was the nest Amelia had imagined for her monster, the one that lived beneath the walkway. What it was doing here, I could not fathom. I knew that my coming here could not have been an accident, that I was not meant to leave this place.

I opened the window and squeezed out, Matilda's footsteps dragging down the hallway echoed in my ears. I landed on the BILCO door with a bang and ran, screaming and screaming with terror. I chanced a look behind me and saw Matilda climbing out the window after me.

The sharp pain in my legs surely meant shin splints. If I dared turn around, she was always coming, always on the horizon. I tried driving, as alien as it felt, but the engines wouldn't turn over. Either the batteries were dead, or the gas was stale. And then she'd be almost on top of me again, searching with those horrible glass eyes.

I arrived at the trailhead just as the sun was setting and plunged headlong into the forest. It soon became too dark to discern the trail markers. Doubling back, I was terrified of encountering Matilda, so by the second or third time I got turned around, I shimmied up a tall oak, hoping she wouldn't be able to climb.

I crammed myself in the crook of the highest possible limb that would hold my weight and waited, listening for Matilda's methodical steps. Trees had saved me before when a man had wanted to murder us on the train tracks going north all that time ago. I hoped they would save me again.

I drank what was left in my water canteen, my throat burning with thirst and strain. Needing to rest, I closed my eyes, but a vision blossomed before me like an unfurling dream in a corny movie. It was of Matilda, patiently waiting at the foot of the tree, gazing upwards as I died of exposure and eventually falling into her widened jaws.

The crickets began their chorus, and it was impossible to hear the crunch of leaves, the snapping of twigs of Matilda's tireless march. I peeked beneath my branch every so often, afraid of giving myself away but more afraid of not knowing if she was indeed below. I spent the time thinking about how this had happened but could find no credible answer. Frustrated, I focused on how to escape. If I could make it back to the tree house, we could pull up the ladder and shoot her from the window. Would she die?

With no warm campfire, the cold crept into my body through the tips of my toes, my fingers, and my nose until I shook with it. I slept fitfully, dreaming of Matilda, balancing precariously on the end of my tree branch. She pursed her lips in what I thought was a kiss until a fat, obscenely enlarged tongue protruded and waggled in my direction, searching, it seemed, like a blind snake.

"Matilda, your tongue is lolling," I said.

She grinned and slurped it back in like spaghetti, and I got the distinct impression that she meant to strangle me with it.

I awoke groggily the following morning, at first disoriented when realizing I was secured with my belt up a tree. My clothes were damp with dew, and I flicked away a dicey-looking spider that had found a new burrow in my pants pocket.

In the dawn light, it all seemed so unreal, but still, I waited, patiently analyzing each sound and movement in the surrounding woods. Out of habit, I kept wanting to ask Matilda what she thought, and always it would lead me back to her newly emptied lair, that sore spot. I had birthed her.

I craned my neck cautiously, expecting her to be waiting patiently at the foot of the tree, insatiably hungry. There was no sign of her, just a quiet, serene forest. Could it all have been a hallucination?

Then the whistle started blowing.

I climbed to the ground, my legs numb and tingly, trying to shake my head clear. I ran until I had no breath, moving on pure adrenalin. When I felt myself faltering, I ran harder, a machine with a sole focus. Every stream I came across, I'd fall into, sucking water into my heaving body before moving on again.

I threw all unnecessary items I carried, leaving a breadcrumb trail of canteens, books, and ice cream sprinkles for my dear Matilda, who surely still came for me or worse, was waiting for me at the tree house.

I sprinted the final distance into the dense copse. Chairs were overturned, and shards of plates littered the ground. The stone fireplace had been pushed over, ash coating everything in a greasy blackness.

Amid the wreckage, Mabel lay, her eyes open to the sky. She was covered in blood, and her leg was a mangled, ruined thing. My metal whistle was still clutched in her hand.

NOW

I thought I once knew what guilt felt like, the acid that ate away at your core. Gazing upon Mabel's body, I understood that anything similar I had felt up to this moment was a shadow of the crackling, molten shame and remorse that now flooded me, threatening to split me in half.

I knelt by her side, taking her hand in mine. She turned her head ever so slightly, "Atticus?"

I gasped, "Mabel, you're alive!" I threw my arms around her and sobbed, knowing I didn't deserve such grace.

Touching her leg gingerly, I peeled back the torn fabric of her leggings. Bite marks, those of a human, covered her upper thigh. Some were just teeth indentations, others terrible enough to have torn the flesh. One wound pumped blood ominously with each heartbeat.

"Who did this?" I asked, keeping my voice as level as possible, panic and fury competing for headspace. I pressed my hands down on her leg, trying to staunch the loss of blood.

"Roman came for Amelia at dawn. But he was transformed, not a man," she managed. "We woke up to a whistle in the forest, going on and on. We thought for sure you were in trouble. But it was Roman, waiting in the meadow. He's grown horns, Atticus."

"What happened? Mabel, god, what happened?"

Again, I had misstepped, thinking that by going to find my parents, I'd settle those heavy feelings of abandonment and return a better person for it. Roman knew it, Matilda knew it, and they laid in wait for a fuck up and fuck up I did, leaving the tree house vulnerable on a fool's errand. I gained nothing and lost everything. Who is coming to collect my gambler's debt?

"Roman took Amelia. There was a fight, and Heath was hurt. When we tried to follow him, a monster, like a corpse, came lurching from the forest."

"What was it?" I asked, though I knew the answer.

Mabel was surprisingly stoic, holding back tears with her chin lifted in defiance. "I thought I was dreaming until it grabbed me around the throat and dragged me down. It bit and tore, eating me alive.

"Lily pulled it off me. Then it advanced on her, so she and Heath fled into the forest to draw it away."

I spun on the spot, peering through the trees. A faint smattering of blood speckled the trail that skirted the meadow in the direction of the pine forest.

"She couldn't have gotten far."

"She? How do you know it's a she?" Mabel asked, suddenly wary.

"She...that's Matilda," I confessed.

"Matilda?"

"I shared my every thought with her, and she betrayed me. I don't know what's happening, how it happened."

"Will I be okay?" Mabel asked, her eyelids fluttering with the effort of keeping them open.

"I'll be right back," I assured her, already sprinting to the tree house. Inside, I yanked open the pantry door and grabbed the first aid kit and a blanket. I covered her, rubbing her arms to warm her. She was in shock.

I slathered antibiotic ointment onto her wounds and then wrapped them tightly in gauze, thinking that if the infection wasn't prevented, Mabel was guaranteed to lose that leg. What kind of bacteria lived in the mouth of a horror?

Blood quickly blossomed through the gauze, and we looked on helplessly. "You might need stitches if the bleeding doesn't stop," I said.

"Amelia can do it. She's good with a needle and thread."

Good old Mabel. Sowing the seeds of hope. I could have cried with gratitude.

"I know. I've got to find her. Can you use the leg at all? If I can get you up into the tree house, I think you'll be alright if you pull the ladder inside. Matilda can't climb."

I coaxed her into getting onto my back and holding me tight around the neck. Slowly we climbed into the tree house, my hands slick on the ladder rungs from Mabel's blood. I laid her gently onto the couch and elevated her leg, wrapping her again in a blanket. I tied a tourniquet around her leg with a rubber hose I found beneath the sink.

"After Amelia told me how she found Charlie, I imagined their death over and over. How terrible their last moments must have been. When I felt my flesh grind in Matilda's molars, I knew in my heart that this was Charlie's death.

"But it wasn't Matilda, was it? It was Charlie's childhood fiend from the ice cream truck. Do you remember them telling that story at the hostel?"

I gave Mabel a Tylenol and filled a canteen with water. "I do remember."

"I think it's the same," Mabel said.

I crept, hidden within the forest on practiced silent feet. Fog drifted between trees and lay in deep hollows. Following a grisly trail of blood droplets, splashed onto the leaves of bushes, the ground, and trunks of trees, I searched for them. I wept at the pain I had caused, the destruction. At a fork in the path, I could discern clear drag marks one way and blood the other. A choice then.

The trail I followed used to be crushed gravel but was matted now with new vegetation. Horses used to walk this, lifting their tails to leave steaming piles of shit that hikers skirted around with mild indignation. I pretended they were there now, so I wouldn't feel so terribly alone.

Matilda...

Brighter the light shined until I reached the apex, the trail depositing me into a circular stone courtyard. Abutting a sheer cliff face, a glittering lake far below, sat an ancient wooden cabana. In the sweeping views behind it, the Wadchu Hotel lay opposite, a smoldering ruin now.

Amelia leaned against one of the cabana's beams. Fishing line was looped around her neck dozens of times, holding her tight to the beam. Crimson blood welled where it had begun to slice into her skin.

She still wore her pajamas, now caked with mud and ripped at the knees. Tears stuck to her eyelashes, clumping them together.

I approached cautiously, hand on my bow, remembering how Roman seemed to materialize out of nowhere when we first met him on the bridge.

"It's a trap, silly," she whispered.

"Where is he?" I asked.

"Close."

I unsheathed my knife and cut through the line, freeing her. She rubbed her neck, dark bruises blossoming on her wrists where he hurt her.

"Remember the bakery?" she asked.

I did, that confectionery prison where we had first huddled together against a dying city, where I had first loved her.

"We should have died there." She took my hand and squeezed, just like I remembered then. "Because what happens when your fears open their eyes on the world?"

"We'll leave then. I'll find a plane, and we can fly down to Florida, eat crocodile fritters and frog legs in the swamp, wear wizard capes, just like you always wanted to."

She smiled wanly, and I pulled her hand, leading her away from the cabana. I felt immensely free. We'd wander the world together and forget about our nightmares. We could fly to LA in the winter and Juno in the summer. We could leave all this behind. We could forget.

"Can everyone come?" she asked.

"It wouldn't be the same without them."

She laughed, relief spread wide across her face. And then she screamed. Matilda, in all her rotten glory, took an exaggerated step out from behind a tree, the ligaments in her leg stretching like old leather. Her grin was pronounced, her glass eyes rolling in their sockets.

Balancing on tiptoes, Matilda came closer, the stench of her filling my nostrils with noxious death. I grabbed for an arrow, my hands shaking so badly that I struggled to fit it to the bow, my fingers slick with sweat.

"Finally," Matilda said, bowing at Amelia. Her voice was dry and scratching like words scraped on sandpaper.

"Have I lost my mind?" Amelia whispered her hand over her mouth. She kept averting her eyes at the perversity before us.

"You're a traitor, Matilda," I said, sending the arrow thunking hard into her chest. She screamed, but backward, sucking air through windpipes unused to human chatter. Then she pounced on me, this creation of mine.

With a searing pain that drove all thought from my head, Matilda bit my shoulder. I writhed in agony, not having the strength to scream. Instead, I gasped, my fingers fumbling and jerking with shotgun mechanisms. I could feel each tooth as they punctured and cracked muscle and bone. Her fingers interlocked around my other shoulder, holding us together in an intimate embrace as she ate me. And they were cold and slimed, like an amphibian.

My knees buckled, and I felt like an antelope does beneath a lion, jaws of crushing death upon me. I stumbled towards the cabana, not wanting to be dragged into the depths of the forest and feasted upon. In a desperate bid for survival, for Amelia's, I used the last of my energy to vault us from the ledge to the lake far below.

The water wasn't deep enough. Matilda took the brunt of the fall, her body slamming against the rocks so stealthily hidden in the murky shallows. The air was forced from my lungs in a comic bubble, and I felt my ribs crack.

Matilda's hold weakened, and I floundered, prying apart her jaws, drowning. She loosened in a cloud of blood, and as I kicked to the surface, she floated with me, always the constant companion, my dear Matilda.

Her body was crushed, the back of her skull caved in by the impact. I feared she would wake again, even in her jellied state. I reached the surface in a shock of light and air, screaming in fear and rage.

I pulled myself onto the narrow rocky shore and lay broken, coughing up blood. My left arm, from shoulder to fingertips, was numb. I tentatively explored the wound, my hands coming away covered in gore.

"Atticus!" Amelia cried, her tears falling around me, peppering the stones as she peered cautiously over the edge on her hands and knees.

I looked at her, thinking perhaps it would be the last time, but what I saw instead was a horror come into focus, like gazing into a stereogram until the monster shocks you in its obviousness.

Roman towered behind her, impossibly huge. Short antler-like horns protruded from his skull. A surge of recognition flooded me as I remembered a fever dream in an SUV outside New Paltz after the disastrous Walkway over the Hudson crossing. He had come for us, for her, from beneath that bridge in Poughkeepsie. Disguised as a lover and a friend, his trickery had been acute and devastating.

One of his eyes, the one I had stabbed with the fishing pole, was gone. All that was left was a black hole like it had been scooped out and eaten as a delicacy. The remaining one found mine and winked.

Amelia, unaware of his presence, bleated my name like a lamb, waiting for me to say I was alive, going to live. He grabbed her lovely strawberry hair and yanked her backward, away from the edge.

She shrieked a shrill cry of pure terror. The forest groaned at the sound, concerned that its queen was in deathly danger. But it did not care to help, such was the way of things. Humans, these flighty creatures, loved with intensity and mourned placidly and forgetfully.

I began the grueling climb up the rock face. I would not quit. I would not die. Leaving a slug's trail of blood, I pulled myself up, finding footholds in jutting roots and rocks. The rope ladder at the tree house had been my practice and had given me the strength to ascend.

From above came the sound of Amelia whistling. It reverberated and echoed off the expansive lake, a plea for help, a call to arms. Then it was cut short, and the sounds of a violent scuffle of colossal force ensued.

Heaving myself over the lip of the ledge, I lay panting. Roman kneeled on goats' feet, hooves sprouting from beneath the cuffs of his leather pants. Amelia stood before him, palms outward as if to say timeout.

One of Roman's horns was splintered, but I could see no other injury inflicted. His mouth moved but with no spoken word. Amelia swayed slightly to it like a charmed cobra.

Her nose was wrong somehow, bent at an odd angle. No attempt, it seemed, had been made to staunch the blood flow, which ran in slasher film fashion down her neck and soaked her shirt.

"From you, a legion of beings will spring forth, bearing my power to begin an era on earth never before seen."

"Fuck you," Amelia snarled, mouth dripping venom. "Not me."

"You are hollow inside. What do you care?" he asked. "You are livestock."

She laughed derisively. "Says the beast with hooves for feet."

Heath did not slink. Heath did not fear. Heath approached that malignancy with Amelia's air rifle raised. From the same pebble path as I had come, he walked with slow purpose, surveying the scene

before him. He nodded his head just slightly to acknowledge that I had seen him.

"Roman," I called, struggling to my feet. With
a tick-tick-tick like a mechanical wind-up toy, he
turned to face me.

"Swamp didn't do it for you?" I taunted, keeping subtle tabs on Heath's movements. I spit blood
to the ground, clearing my throat. "Stinks like your
ass must stink in those ridiculous leather pants. No
wonder you crawled out of there. Can't blame you."
At that, my legs gave way, and I slumped against the
cabana.

Roman rose, pawing at the dirt with his great
hooves, leaving gouges in the earth. He opened his
mouth to speak, his block teeth huge and yellow.
Without the hesitation Hollywood gives the villain
to make a last grandiose speech, Heath fired, the
bullet missing its mark.

Mouth set tight, shoulders squared, Heath
pumped the air rifle, the clack of it filling the air.
Roman laughed, that same laugh he had used on our
very first encounter on the bridge as we slid down
the embankment together. I had mistaken that initial laugh for madness, but it wasn't. It was mocking
the very thought that we could possibly hurt him.

Roman stood to his full height, head oscillating
with a horse's habit. "I'll trample you to death until
you're unrecognizable, just another casualty," he
said, his voice still oddly humanoid.

Heath nodded, accepting what was either a lie or truth, and raised the gun again, quick like a western sheriff, and pulled the trigger. Roman's head snapped back, and an arc of blood rose high. He fell like the ancient mammoths would have fallen, the earth quivering in anticipation of the weight of it all. But he did not stay down, he did not follow the rules of nature with two ruined eyes. He did not die. Thrashing, Roman gurgled incoherently, flecks of dark blood dampening the ground, his leather pants slick with viscous bodily fluids.

From the forest, Lily strode. Held in her hand was an iron garden spike. The point of it still trailed delicate roots ripped from the soil of her garden. White hair loose and wild, she was unicorn-like. On her cheeks were salt tracks from tears, but now, she showed no emotion other than focused, deadly rage. She was the pale horse of the apocalypse, she was Victory, she was Conquest.

With courage I could not fathom, she descended onto the monster, raising the stake high before plunging it into the cavity of one of his missing eyes. With a great sigh, Roman was still at last. Heath advanced, pumping the gun before nestling the muzzle into Roman's ear canal and delivering the insurance shot.

There's a permanence about a dead body, a complete lack of regard for anything other than itself and the business of decay. It will not shake itself off and rise again to go about its day. It doesn't care if you need it, care for it, cherish it. Was once what moved it trapped inside, destined to rot as well? Or has it been loosened upon the world?

My vision blackened at the edges, and I struggled to stay conscious. Nuclear plant alarms wailed in my head at the sheer pain of it all.

"Atticus?" Heath called, "you alive?"

"I'm here," I said.

"Is what's down there dead?"

With a horrifying effort, I turned my neck to study Matilda's broken, water-logged body below. The small lapping waves pulled and pushed at her gently, face scraping against the rocks, rank hair floating blissfully, a mermaid killed by an outboard motor.

My chin crumpled in sadness for my friend, my parasitic friend. They say that sailors mistook the manatees for mermaids but had there been mermaids, we would have systematically slaughtered them too, saving the last of the species to be gawked at in tanks.

A warm, sticky hand rested on mine, and I turned to Amelia, crouched low and close. White bone shone through the cartilage of her nose. I touched it tenderly, and she winced.

"I love you," she said.

ACKNOWLEDGMENTS

I'd like to thank my husband, Daniel, for his unwavering support of my dream to become an author. Without his constant reassurances, this novel would have languished in a forgotten Google Docs folder until the end of times.

I am forever grateful for my family, best friends, and beta readers, Erica Hanger, Jocelyn Justiniano, Christine Schneider, Kristin Buchholz, Jo-Ann Buchholz, Alysia Kovitch, Mary Ryan, and Jess Condor, who suffered through endless drafts and concepts yet still believed in this story. Thank you for championing me to the finish line.

ABOUT THE AUTHOR

Michele Friedman was born in the Catskill Mountains of New York. At 18, she moved to New York City to earn her degree in advertising and public relations. She currently lives in Virginia with her family and an expansive garden for their bees. Gadarene is her debut novel.

www.ingramcontent.com/pod-product-compliance
Lightning Source LLC
Chambersburg PA
CBHW020519260626
47156CB00006B/2054